I0540927

THE DRAGONS OF THE BLACK CASTLE

BY

JANINE SUMMERS

Janine Summers

Dragons of the Black Castle

ISBN: 13-978-0988142329

Janine Summers

ACKNOWLEDGEMENTS

There are so many people involved in helping me with this project and I would like to say thank you. But the most important people are my family. My mother who always took the time to read my manuscripts, my sister who finds all those errors I missed. I love you all.

To my husband, none of this would be possible if not for the belief you have in me and my writing. Thank you for everything you do for us, and know that I love you.

Janine Summers

Dragons of the Black Castle

Janine Summers

THE DRAGONS OF THE BLACK CASTLE

BY

JANINE SUMMERS

CHAPTER 1

JENNY'S LIFE

Nothing exciting ever happens in Morgansville, Alberta. A sleepy little town where five thousand people share their daily lives and live in harmony—everyone but the occupants of a small house situated on a quiet crescent, surrounded by tall trees and lush green grass. In this house no colorful flowers bloom in the barren gardens. Here, the feeling of pride and love is lost.

In this small, brick house, a lonely girl lived every day in fear of an aging and sinister aunt. Jenny Saunders sat alone studying in a small kitchen. A dark braid hung down her back, while green eyes surveyed her book. Her concentration on her schoolwork was evident.

"Dinner's almost ready! Clear the table!" Nora Bartlett, a middle-aged woman with short hair, screeched at her ward. Her large, intimidating form hovered over Jenny until the child moved to do her aunt's bidding. There was nothing maternal or gentle about this woman. If Jenny could use one word to describe this woman who'd taken her in it would be nasty.

"Yes, Aunt Nora." Jenny piled her books and placed them on the chair next to her seat. She stood, went to the cupboard, and returned to set the table for the evening meal the way she did every single day. No excitement or adventure lived in this house. On the contrary, if she didn't abide by the routine set out by Nora, punishment usually followed. That's just the way things were in this house, and Jenny tried her best to conform to the rules and regulations set out by her aunt.

Jenny looked at her aunt, but caution gave her pause and she felt this wasn't the best time to ask for anything. The silence that descended over the small, pristine, eat-in kitchen overwhelmed her. And even though she'd lived in this house for the past six years, Jenny felt the hatred flow from her aunt with the same intensity as she did on the day she first came to live in Morgansville with Nora.

A few minutes later they sat around the table, and as always they ate in silence. Jenny was used to the silence that fell over the room and the house whenever she was close to her aunt. Nora barely looked in her direction unless she wanted her charge to perform some chore for her. Jenny played with the food on her plate, her mind on a sensitive topic she needed to discuss with her aunt, but feared her reaction.

At dinner's end, Nora glared at Jenny. "Clean the table and wash the dishes." As an afterthought, she turned toward her niece. "As soon as you're done, go to your room. I'd rather not have to look at you." The scowl upon her large face told Jenny more than her words.

"Yes, Aunt Nora." Jenny hung her head in defeat. She sensed this wasn't the best time to ask for a favor, but she was out of time. She'd waited until the last possible moment to approach Nora. Steeling herself, Jenny squared her shoulders. "Oh, before I forget, can you sign this form?" She asked, trying for a nonchalant lilt in her voice. She feared this moment more than she feared walking into school and facing her teacher.

"What's it for?" Nora barely glanced at the paper.

"A school trip."

"Where are *they* going?" Nora's hand rested on her large hip.

"To the Royal Alberta Museum in Edmonton." Jenny crossed her fingers at her side for luck.

"Do you need money?"

Jenny knew this wouldn't be easy. It never was. "Yes, we need money to get into the museum, and for lunch. Please, Aunt Nora, just this once?" No matter what kind of trip her class planned, Jenny was always the one left behind. She wished that once, only once, Nora would say yes. It would surprise her more than anything ever had in her entire life.

Nora slowly passed a hand through her hair. She stared long and hard at Jenny. She deliberately turned and walked away from her and stood by the sink. She waited. Finally, after what seemed like forever, Nora spoke. "No. I think you should stay at school." A smile of pure enjoyment crossed her thin lips as she left the room.

Jenny followed her in a futile attempt to change her mind. "But Beth is going. Please, Aunt Nora," Jenny implored, "just this one time? I won't ever ask for anything again. Please!"

"No! Now stop whining and do the dishes," Nora said with booming finality.

Tears burned her green eyes and streamed down Jenny's cheeks as she ran from the kitchen and up the stairs. She ran into her room and fell onto her small bed. The tears flowed freely as she cried and cried. Even though deep down inside she knew Nora wouldn't sign her form, Jenny held on to the smallest measure of hope that one day Nora's heart would soften toward her and she would surprise her with a yes. But true to form, Nora did the same thing she did any time Jenny asked for something.

She left the bed and walked over to her dresser. She gazed at her reflection. Large green eyes stared back her. They shone with unshed tears and glistened like emeralds.

"This isn't fair." Jenny turned away from the mirror and lay down on her bed. Thoughts of the fun she would miss twirled inside her mind. There was nothing she wanted more than to join Beth and her classmates on this trip. She could only imagine what the other kids in her class would say when she turned up without a signed permission slip. Every time this happened, Jenny became

11

the brunt of every snide comment and pathetic joke in her classroom. Why should anyone have to be the subject of such abuse? There was no fairness or reprieve in Mrs. Parker's classroom. Jenny wondered why people in this town felt as though this kind of treatment was what she deserved. Even in the midst of their behavior, a small ray of hope lived deep within her heart. She always tried to help her aunt around the house and outside, but it just wasn't enough. She turned and put her face into the pillow and cried herself to sleep.

* * * *

Another morning came to taunt Jenny awake and force her to face yet another day at school. Dejected, she dressed for her lonely day at school. At least she didn't have to worry about what she'd wear. It wasn't like she had a large choice when it came to her wardrobe. She owned two pairs of jeans and a couple of tops. She had one sweater and this she wore almost every day. She looked in her closet and chose her outfit... the other pair of jeans and her other T-shirt. No use trying to make herself look presentable. She had nowhere to go today. There was no use feeling sorry for herself — she had to accept what life had given her; otherwise, she'd always be unhappy and that was something only she could control.

What distressed her most wasn't the lack of apparel. Oh no, Jenny didn't care about that. What bothered her most was that in the past she'd been forced to attend another grade where, according to Mrs. Parker, Jenny had need of supervision. The last time she'd been left behind, she'd been placed in the fourth grade for the day. She could still hear the taunts and offensive remarks hurled at her by the other students.

She checked her reflection and was as disappointed as she was every day before school.

"Oh well, it doesn't get any better." She went downstairs and sat down at the table. She put some cereal into a bowl and added milk.

"That's enough milk." Nora grunted under her breath and stuck her fork into the mound of eggs and bacon on her plate. She bit into her toast and glared at Jenny who cowered beneath the venom she saw in her aunt's brown gaze. From time to time, she'd look up and try to understand the hatred behind her aunt's glare. What had she ever done to merit this hatred? She always tried to do everything Nora asked of her, but for some reason it wasn't enough. Nothing was ever enough.

"I'm sorry, Aunt Nora." Jenny lowered her head and at her cereal. Her thoughts traveled away from this house to a place where she could find happiness and be loved like a daughter should be loved.

If only her parents were still alive. At least she'd know what having a family was really like. She wished she remembered what it felt like to be loved by a parent, but she didn't remember her life before Nora at all. At night, Jenny dreamt of her father coming to the house and taking her away from Nora and Morgansville, where they could live in another town where no one knew her. Jenny could start all over again without being painted as a virtual pariah. She dreamt of being taken to another town where no one knew her. She wished that one day she'd wake up and she and her parents were a family again. Jenny sighed knowing thoughts like these depressed her further. She was an orphan and she should be grateful that Nora took her in when no one else wanted her.

After breakfast, she decided to give it another try. "Aunt Nora, please sign my form. I'll do extra chores around the house to earn the money."

Nora laughed. Not a happy laugh, but one built on years of anger and cynicism. "No. Now leave me alone." Nora's tone bore a finality Jenny recognized.

"Why do you hate me?" Jenny wanted to know the truth as her eyes welled up with tears.

Nora stopped walking. She turned toward Jenny, who cowered at the venom spewing from her eyes. "Because you're just like your mother. Now go!"

Defeated, she left the small kitchen and readied herself for school. Risking one last glance in her aunt's direction, Jenny understood her defeat. She left behind the house and any chance

13

of joining her classmates on this trip. She'd just stepped onto the sidewalk when she heard someone call to her. Elizabeth Brown, Beth to all her friends, ran down the street.

"Hey, Jen, wait up!" Beth's blonde hair floated in the wind, her bright blue eyes shone with merriment. "Hi!"

"I love your new outfit," Jenny said and looked down at her own clothes, feeling uncomfortable in her worn attire. Absently, she smoothed out her wrinkled T-shirt.

"Thanks. My mom bought it for this trip." Beth turned this way and that way to show off her low-rise jeans and her blue and white empire style blouse. Faint makeup gave her a soft sheen.

"Your mom's great. You're really lucky." Jenny tugged her sweater in a futile attempt to soften the look of her secondhand shirt. Once a year Nora went to the Goodwill store and purchased a few T-shirts and a new pair of pants. She'd never had anything new or pretty. Even when she wanted to put her hair up, she had to use old rubber bands she found in the kitchen after Nora pulled them off the vegetables.

"Did you get your aunt's signature?" Beth asked, hope alive in her eyes.

"No, she refused to give me any money or sign my permission slip. Guess I'm stuck at school… again." Jenny tucked a loose hair behind her ear. She hated having to tell her best friend that, once again, she couldn't go with her. For Jenny, this had become the norm, and although she wouldn't lie and say it didn't matter, it did matter to her. She didn't know what to do to make her aunt like her, and as long as she took out her hatred for her mother on Jenny, she'd never win.

"Sorry, Jen."

"It's okay. I'm used to it." Jenny sighed.

"I can't believe her. I wish my mom could've signed your form. At least you'd be able to go with us." Beth's voice rose in anger, as it usually did whenever she was upset about something Nora said or did.

Jenny looked at her friend and smiled. Beth's temper rose and colored her pale cheeks. "So do me. Still, I wonder what Mrs. Parker will have to say about this. You know how she loves to humiliate me."

"Yeah. It depends on what your aunt tells her about you. It's too bad Mrs. Parker and Nora are such good friends. It doesn't help your situation. It makes it much harder for you."

"Tell me about it. Mrs. Parker tells Aunt Nora everything I do in class." She made a face at her friend.

"Yeah, and that really sucks!" Beth giggled.

"Oh well. I'll never change Aunt Nora. She'll never accept me, and she'll never allow anyone else to accept me either." Jenny wished she knew what happened to her parents. She knew deep in heart that this kind of existence wasn't normal. If her parents were alive she'd be happy instead of feeling so lonely and undeserving. She wanted to believe her parents were alive, but couldn't fathom they'd left her here with Nora. That was too much to bear. Then again, she didn't want to believe they were dead. She had to believe that they were alive, and for some strange reason they simply couldn't get to her. Yes, Jenny wanted to hold on to that thought. It was better than thinking she'd been abandoned.

"Then I'll stay at school with you."

"No, Beth. You go to the museum and have fun, but you have to tell me all about your trip." Jenny smiled bravely at Beth. It was difficult, but she put on a happy face, especially when she so desperately wanted to go. She'd never been to a museum before. This would've been the most excitement she'd ever had. Jenny's eyes took on a faraway look as she dreamed of a life filled with adventure. She wanted life to take her away from Nora, but that would never happen. Jenny sighed. She had to accept the inevitable and shook herself back to the present.

"That's a promise."

The school loomed before them. The seventh and eighth graders went inside, while the younger children stayed outside to play until the last possible moment. At their lockers, Jenny removed her books and brought them with her. She knew Mrs. Parker would assign enough work to keep her busy for the entire day. This was a common occurrence whenever she was left behind during school outings, and since Jenny wasn't allowed to participate in any of the school activities, this part of her life became an unwanted ritual.

When the bell rang, Mrs. Parker, a tall, and thin woman with more salt than pepper in her short hair, sat behind her desk and surveyed her class.

"Good morning, students. Did everyone bring their signed consent forms?" Her eyes immediately locked with Jenny's. "Place your forms on my desk." She perched her small square glasses on the edge of her abnormally long nose.

Mrs. Parker sifted through the signed forms. A smile tugged her thin lips when she noticed which document was missing. "Well, now, Miss Saunders, where is your form?" She took advantage of even the smallest opportunity to humiliate the young girl.

"Right here."

"Bring it to me." Mrs. Parker eyed her suspiciously.

Jenny stood and kept her head down, as she slowly made her way to the teacher's desk.

"Loser!" someone called out, causing laughter.

"Look at her clothes," Bridgette told Leah. They were two of the most popular girls in school and loved to make fun of anyone who wasn't part of their clique. They were the "in crowd."

Jenny reached the front of the class amid sneers and snide remarks, and she handed the teacher her form and took her seat. She refused to make eye contact with anyone but Beth.

"Miss Saunders, this isn't signed."

Jenny sat quietly by, and allowed her teacher to have her say. She would no matter what. This was the norm and although you never got used to the humiliation, you learned to toe rate and then ignore it.

"Oh my, I guess you must remain in school today." She smiled and looked around the classroom. The students laughed again.

Beth looked at her friend and tried to reassure her with a smile.

Jenny dropped in her seat, eyes downcast. She had to remember that it didn't matter what others thought about her. All she cared about was her friendship with Beth. She was the sister Jenny never had, and she thanked her lucky stars that Beth was here. If not for their friendship, Jenny didn't know if she'd survive.

"I'd like everyone to wait for me in front of the school. Anyone not there when I come out will remain in class with Jenny," Mrs. Parker said. She waited until the classroom emptied and then she turned toward the lone student still in her seat. Mrs. Parker approached her and placed a manila folder on the desk with a nasty grin. "Your aunt informs me you have far too much time on your hands. This should keep you busy here and at home."

"She would," Jenny mumbled.

"Don't be insolent."

"Why not?" Defiance shone in her eyes.

"Ungrateful! That's what your aunt called you and she was quite correct!" Mrs. Parker's voice rose inappropriately.

Jenny sat still, refusing to shed a tear, refusing to show the hurt. "So, which class are you sending me to?" Her hands were securely clasped in her lap in a weak attempt to stop them from trembling.

"You'll stay here. No one wants you in their classroom. Not that I blame them."

Jenny didn't even bother to respond to this particular insult. "May I go to the library and work there?"

Mrs. Parker thought for a moment and finally nodded. "Just behave."

"Yes, ma'am." She watched her teacher leave the room.

Smiling, Jenny took her books and the folder, and left the classroom. She went down the stairs and walked slowly, but with purpose. She entered the library and chose a table at the far end of the room. She sat down, opened the folder, and looked over the assignments written within. A smile crossed her full lips. Most of these assignments were complete. Homework was all she had to do when she was alone in her small bedroom. And to keep her busy tonight, Mrs. Parker assigned an essay. At least this would be an easy day for her.

* * * *

During her lunch break Jenny took a walk, even though she knew this was against school policy. She spotted the principal

17

heading her way and ran down the stairs. She stopped and listened for the sound of footsteps. She wondered if she'd given the principal the slip. Up above, she heard the door open and close. She was forced to run through the basement until she reached the other end where she hoped another door would lead her back to the stairwell.

She looked back to see if anyone followed her, but to her delight, Jenny was alone. She breathed a sigh of relief. The consequences of capture would entail detention and a severe grounding from Aunt Nora. When she turned to run, a door appeared with such abruptness that Jenny's heart skipped a beat. Still, without hesitation or thought, Jenny opened the door and went through. The door closed with a thud, startling her. She looked around, but only darkness greeted her.

"I don't think this is the way back to the library," she said out loud, trying to see through the darkness. She wondered if she should go back, but at the same time she was intrigued by this new discovery. She tried to suppress her fear with the sound of her own voice, but it didn't help. She was still cautious.

A torch sprang to life. Her heart skipped a beat. She wondered who else lurked in the darkness. "Hello! Is anyone there?" She tried to see beyond the light of the lone torch, but only silence and darkness hung in the stale air. This was too creepy for her. She tugged on the handle, but the door refused to open. Jenny's hands trembled as she continued to tug the handle.

"Please open," she said, wondering what she'd gotten herself into. She tried to open the door again. She tugged and tugged at the door, but it refused to open. "Why won't you open?" Tears started at the corners of her eyes as the fear of being trapped down here overwhelmed her.

"No! There has to be a way out!" Steeling herself, Jenny took charge of her emotions. This was ridiculous. After all, this was still part of her school, so this corridor had to come out somewhere. She turned away from the door and looked around. A maze of corridors fanned out in every direction. Should she explore them? Her eyes searched the area, and almost instantly she felt an odd familiarity tug at distant memories. Had she been here before? She walked a little further and was assaulted by the stench of decay. Removing the torch from the wall sconce, she took a few more steps into the catacombs, but was stopped by more corridors. She took the passageway to her right. A few steps further into the tunnel and another set of corridors materialized.

"Where did that come from?" She knew that being down here alone wasn't a smart move. She went back the way she came, and to her surprise the door opened effortlessly. She stepped through the opening and found herself back in the basement. A sigh of relief escaped her. She leaned against the door just as the school bell sounded. How long had she been in there? What seemed like minutes to her had suddenly turned into hours.

The other students hadn't returned, so Jenny made her way home alone, but the memory of her secret find lingered long after she left the catacombs.

CHAPTER 2

THE DREAM

That night as Jenny slept, darkness surrounded her and held her prisoner. She looked around, and much to her surprise she was back in the catacombs trapped behind a wooden door. The darkness and the stone walls seemed to close in on her. Frightened, she tried to outrun the dark and damp walls moving closer and closer to her. She stopped when she heard a strange voice bounce off the walls and touch her. The voice called out to her in a familiar, yet strange, tone.

"Athelina, it is time." The haunting voice floated around her with a chill that crawled over her flesh and through to her bones.

Jenny rolled over and pulled the blanket closer to her as she tried to warm herself.

"Find us before it's too late. Our time has come." Sharp teeth and the devil's own roar startled Jenny awake.

She sat up as fear clung to her. She tried to steady her breathing.

"Wow! That was freaky!" she said, thankful it was only a dream. She convinced herself the dream held no meaning, just a child's imagination gone wild. After being trapped in the catacombs, her mind was playing tricks on her, but when she fell back asleep, her steady breathing produced similar dreams.

Jenny tossed and turned. "Help us! Find us!" The intensity of the voice increased.

"Who are you?" Jenny asked in the darkness. She wanted to see the face of the person calling for aid. She wanted to discover the owner of the hauntingly soft voice. Where was the unknown hiding? Why was she entering her dreams and asking for help? How could anyone enter the dream world and communicate with someone fast asleep?

"Help us! Find us!" The voice slowly faded, as Jenny fell into a deep and dreamless slumber.

* * * *

"Jen! Wait up!" Beth called out as she caught up with her friend the following morning.

The sun shone brightly. Another warm day greeted the residents of the small town. Jenny loved the sunshine. She inhaled the sweet smell of the many flowers growing in the gardens along the houses they passed. Large trees shaded the sidewalks as she walked next to her friend.

"Hey, Beth. How'd it go yesterday?"

"Great. We had an awesome time, but I missed you. It's not the same without you."

"Thanks."

Beth went silent. "So how was your day?"

"Weird." Jenny remembered everything that happened yesterday in the catacombs and the weird dreams that haunted her sleep. She didn't know if she should tell Beth all that had happened to her in such a short time. Maybe it would be best if Beth experienced some of what happened to Jenny firsthand.

"Why? What happened?"

"I have to show you something I found." Jenny hoped Beth would be open to new adventures. She wanted to search the catacombs, but feared doing it alone. With Beth at her side, she'd be able to discover all the deep and dark secrets a place like that held.

"Intrigue. I like it. So, what did you find?" The look on Jenny's face piqued Beth's curiosity.

"I can't explain it. I'll have to show you." Jenny gnawed her thumbnail, a habit she developed shortly after coming to live with Nora six years earlier. Every time she'd have problems with her guardian, or if Nora decided to scream at her, Jenny would gnaw her thumbnail. Now she couldn't seem to stop doing it.

"Okay, you've got my attention."

"Good. I'll show you at lunchtime." A smile tugged at her lips when she thought about exploring the catacombs with her best friend. How exciting to share this new adventure with Beth!

Jenny spent the morning watching the clock. On two separate occasions, Mrs. Parker noticed her lack of interest for the subjects at hand, and shrieked, "Miss Saunders, is there a problem?"

"No."

"Then I'd appreciate it if you paid attention in my class, or would you prefer I call your aunt?" She stood at the front of the class, hands on hip as she screeched at the young girl who turned a lovely shade of pink.

"I'm sorry." Jenny lowered her eyes in defeat. The last thing she wanted was for Mrs. Parker to call Aunt Nora who would punish her for this behavior. She tried to hold her head up high, but it was difficult when she heard laughter followed by some nasty name calling from her classmates.

"You certainly are sorry… a sorry excuse," Mrs. Parker stated. The students laughed even more.

Jenny tried to hide the tears that threatened to spill over. She kept her thoughts fixated on the pending exploration of the catacombs with Beth. Strange, but she felt there was something special waiting for her, and nothing else mattered. She wanted to find out why she sensed something familiar waited for her within the dank walls of the catacombs.

The slow hand of time mocked her excitement until it finally struck twelve. Everyone filed out of the classroom and headed for the cafeteria. Jenny walked next to Beth and tried to convince her to skip lunch so she could show her the special find.

"But I'm hungry," Beth said at the thought of finishing her day without lunch.

"I've got a sandwich in my locker. We can share it." Jenny watched her friend with renewed hope.

"Okay, but this secret you keep talking about had better be something really awesome." Beth took the half sandwich offered. "Thanks." She bit into the bread as the friends walked side by side.

Something waited. Something pulled her into the catacombs. Something called to her.

"Where are we going?" Beth asked between bites.

"We have to get to the basement." Jenny smiled.

"Wait." She stopped her friend from walking any further. "Did you say the basement?"

"Yes, I did."

"What's in the basement?" Beth followed.

"You'll see."

"This is getting too weird."

There were some things that people did on faith, but there had to be more to this so-called secret find.

"Trust me, Beth."

"You know I do. I just don't understand what you're up to. I'd feel a whole lot better if you told me what's going on."

"You'll see." Jenny was even more excited now that they were on their way to the catacombs. She didn't know what they'd find, but she was certain they'd find something cool. There had to be more to the catacombs than what she'd witnessed on her previous visit.

An open door gave them easy access to the basement. Small lights twinkled like a million stars in the night sky. Boxes lined the walls and a large boiler sat at one end of the vast room. The area was immense and mostly empty, especially once they'd passed by the boiler. Jenny put a finger to her lips before Beth uttered a word. She pointed toward the office where the janitor sat behind his desk eating his lunch and watching a program on his small TV screen.

"Come on," Jenny whispered and crouched down so as not to be discovered.

Beth followed and together they passed by, unseen. "Jen, I don't like this. I'm a little scared."

"Just let me show you what I found, and then we'll go back."

"I don't know." Even though Beth was skeptical, she was curious enough to give in to the temptation of a new discovery.

"It's only a little farther." She wanted Beth at her side when she explored the dark catacombs. The thought of entering the catacombs alone was daunting, but she would if she had to. On the other hand, if Beth was with her, she'd be able to enter the catacombs and explore its contents without any of the fear she'd felt while she was alone. For some strange reason, she knew she was meant to come down here and discover something that was hidden from her. And more than anything, she wanted to see who was trapped within the darkness of the catacombs.

"Okay, okay. Let's get this over with." Beth stood with her friend, but her blue eyes darted back and forth hoping to see one of the faculty members.

"There… there's the door." Jenny's excitement grew at the sight of it.

"This is what you wanted to show me?"

"Partly."

"Jen, I've seen doors before."

"Beth, do you really think I'd bring you down here to look at a door? I'd like to think I'm a bit more creative than that." Jenny continued toward the door.

A sound behind them alerted the girls to an unexpected visitor. They stopped moving and listened. They had to discover the identity of the intruders. The sound of approaching footsteps caused panic within the girls. They looked at each other in wonder that quickly turned into panic. A few seconds passed and they assumed the danger had also passed with the ticking of time, until another sound gave them cause for alarm.

"What's that?" Suddenly, Beth wanted to be anywhere but here.

"I don't know, but we'll be in serious trouble if we're caught down here."

"So what do we do?"

"I'll show you."

Voices raised in heated conversation reached the frightened girls.

"Who is it?" The fear of getting caught was clearly visible in Beth's eyes.

Jenny didn't have to see the people in order to recognize their identity. "My guess is Mrs. Parker and Mr. Bailey, the caretaker."

A measure of fear crawled into her. She knew what Mrs. Parker would do if she caught her down here, but she feared what

Aunt Nora would do to her when Mrs. Parker divulged Jenny's exploration. No, she had to hide before they were caught.

"If they find us down here, we'll be in detention for the rest of the year. I'll miss graduation." Beth was panic-stricken.

Jenny giggled. "That won't happen, but if Nora finds out, I don't even want to think what she'll do to me." Jenny used a lighthearted lilt in her voice to quell Beth's fears, but deep down inside, Jenny was just as scared as her friend, and perhaps even more. Beth's mother would never allow Mrs. Parker to treat her daughter in a ghastly way, but Nora would relish the punishment Mrs. Parker would inflict upon her. Of this, Jenny was certain.

"You do have a point. So why aren't we hiding?"

"You're right." Jenny pulled the door open and pushed her friend through. The door slammed shut with a loud thud.

CHAPTER 3

THE DOORWAY

Footsteps closed in and halted before the door. Jenny leaned in closer wondering if they would get caught. Muffled voices filtered through. Jenny and Beth jumped back, terrified. The girls stood still behind the safety of the wooden door in the hope that Mrs. Parker wouldn't attempt to open it.

Jenny glanced at Beth, who trembled with fear.

Mrs. Parker bellowed. "I saw this door close." She tugged on the handle without success.

"You're dreaming," the old caretaker stated. "This door's never been opened." He scratched his head in contemplation. "Don't think it does."

Mrs. Parker tried the door once more. "Look, I saw that girl come down here. Now help me find her."

"I'm gonna go eat," the caretaker said.

"Oh no you're not. You're going to help me. Now do it!"

The frightened girls heard some grumbling from the caretaker. Quietly, they waited for the footsteps to move away before uttering a word. If they heard Mrs. Parker and the caretaker talking, then it was a certainty that they'd hear them talk.

Jenny pulled her friend away from the door, still wanting to explore the catacombs. "I wonder why the door wouldn't open for Mrs. Parker."

"I don't know. Does it lock?"

"I don't think so. I opened it on the first try." Jenny thought it best not to reveal yesterday's experience when she couldn't open the door either. But then again, she couldn't open it only after she'd been trapped within the catacombs. She was able to enter the catacombs without effort.

"That's weird. Maybe this isn't such a good idea." She moved closer to the door with the intention of opening it and leaving the catacombs.

"We can't go out there right now. Mrs. Parker could be lurking around the corner. I think we should go on," Jenny said, grateful to Mrs. Parker for giving her the chance to explore the catacombs.

Beth looked around and noticed a lone torch sitting in a wall sconce. The flame illuminated their immediate surroundings. "Where are we? And what is that smell?" She covered her nose with her sleeve.

"The catacombs." Jenny watched her friend closely. She wouldn't give up her one chance to walk through the catacombs. After seeing Beth's reaction to this adventure, Jenny was certain Beth wouldn't return with her. She had to do what she came here for. Something told her she had to be here in order to discover the reason behind the weird dreams.

"What are you talking about? Since when do we have catacombs?" Beth kept her nose covered as the scent of stale air and decayed water assaulted her. Nothing down here made Beth eager to travel within the darkened passageways.

"I guess they've always been here, we just never knew they existed. Isn't this exciting?" Jenny removed the torch and made her way toward the first corridor.

"Not really. This place stinks, and it gives me the creeps." Beth put her hand on Jenny's arm. "What's that?" Beth strained to see down the passageway.

"It's probably a mouse."

"Oh Yuk! That's not helping." Beth's eyes moved over the slimy walls to the stone floor where condensation pooled. The last thing she wanted was to run into a mouse or a rat, or something bigger and creepier.

"I was here yesterday and I'm fine." Jenny didn't think this was the right time to divulge yesterday's experience within the corridors. And after seeing Beth's reaction, she wasn't sure she should share the odd dreams that held her prisoner last night.

"I still don't like the idea of walking around these catacombs. We should go back and face Mrs. Parker."

Maybe she should tell her friend the reason why she needed to explore the corridors. Would Beth think she was losing her mind, or would her friend believe and understand her need to fulfill this prophecy? She wanted to believe in her best friend. She had to. Beth was all she had.

"Beth, there's something else."

Jenny decided to share her nightmare with her friend. She told her all about her dream and then she waited for Beth to say something. But to her dismay, her friend just stood quietly by. Jenny decided to say something to cut through the silence. "I don't know why the dream I had felt so real, but I think the answers I seek are down here. So, no, Beth, I can't go back. Not just yet." Jenny turned to face her friend. "Please." She gnawed her thumbnail as she waited for Beth's answer.

"I can't believe there's anything down here."

"I don't expect you to understand what's happening to me, but I need to find out why it's happening. I know it sounds surreal, but all this began after my visit to these catacombs. There must be a reason for that." If she had to, she'd explore the catacombs by herself, but she really didn't want to do that. She felt safer having Beth at her side.

"You were down here alone and you were probably scared. Your experience gave you nightmares. It didn't mean anything."

"I wish I could explain it to you, but I can't. I'm asking you to help me… to trust me."

"Jen, I'll help, but I think you're confusing a dream with reality."

"Maybe I am, but I think my dream is somehow intertwined with this reality. That's why I'm here. I need to figure out if everything that happened was nothing more than a dream. If there was some reality blended in with my dream, then I need to know what that reality is. Does that make sense?"

Beth thought for a moment. "Not really, but if it'll make you feel better, I'll stay by your side." She relented and made the decision to stay by Jenny's side.

"Thanks." Jenny wondered if she'd ever convince Beth that what she felt wasn't a dream. Jenny knew that whoever had tried to get in touch with her did it through the dream world. In the back of her mind, she believed there was another reason for what was happening to her. Either way, she felt this was her destiny, and she had to see it through.

"Jenny, did you ever consider that we could get seriously lost down here?"

"Yeah, I did. Here you go." Jenny gave Beth a handful of small paper balls. "I made these last night. I thought to use them to help mark our trail. Toss them on the floor as we walk deeper into the catacombs."

"Sure, why not?" Beth threw down the first ball of paper. "I still think this is a bad idea."

"Why?" Jenny hoped Beth hadn't changed her mind about helping her.

"We don't know where we're going or where we'll end up. The last thing I want is to get trapped in this stinky place."

"I know. That's the exciting part." Jenny smiled. "Come on, let's keep going." She didn't wait for Beth to answer her; she simply kept walking.

"No, I don't think so," Beth said.

"Why?" Jenny feared her friend's next words.

"We have to get back to class." To make her point, Beth showed Jenny her watch. "It's almost one o'clock, and Mrs. Parker will freak out if we're late."

"You mean if I'm late."

"That too."

"Can't we go a little farther?"

"Why does this mean so much to you?"

Jenny didn't know if she should tell her friend the truth about this so-called dream. Maybe if she told her everything, Beth would be willing to continue.

"I didn't want to tell you this, but in my dream I heard a familiar voice."

"What are you talking about?"

"That's what I'm hoping to find out. I heard voices telling me to find them." Jenny couldn't turn back. "I need to know."

A few minutes ticked by. "Okay. But you do know that we'll be in detention for the next month."

"Yeah, but if we find something cool, it'll be worth facing Mrs. Parker and Aunt Nora."

"And if we don't, we'll just be in deep, deep trouble. You more than me."

Jenny laughed. "So what else is new?" Even though Jenny made light of the situation, she secretly feared Mrs. Parker and Nora's sinister punishments. "They'll probably make my punishment a team effort." Deep down inside, she wanted to experience the adventure at hand, and she was willing to face the consequences in order to seize the moment.

"That's true."

"And I'm willing to take that chance."

"But I don't know if I am."

"Beth, I need to do this." Jenny's panic-stricken face implored her friend to yield and face the exploration by her side.

"What do you expect to find?"

"I… I don't know." Jenny kept her feelings a secret. Some things were better left unsaid.

"Do you think you'll open a door and find a new place to live?"

Tears glistened in Jenny's eyes. She pushed a lock of dark hair away from her face and glanced at Beth. "I don't know."

"Oh, Jenny, I'm so sorry. I didn't mean to make you cry."

"I don't know what I'll find, but I have to keep hope alive." Ever since her parents disappeared, Jenny wanted to find them, or find out what really happened to them. She always imagined she would find out the truth about her parents, and for some strange reason she hoped the catacombs held some, or all, of the answers she so desperately needed. She felt this was her one and only chance to find the truth, and she refused to waste it.

"I know your life isn't easy, but I don't think going any farther is the answer."

"Whether it is or not, I have to see it through. If I don't find anything, then at least I'll have my answer, but what if I do find something or someone? Either way, Beth, I have to see this through." Jenny refused to give up. She needed answers to the questions burning inside, and this was the path to those answers.

Beth let out a deep breath. "Okay, okay. I give up. If you want to go on—" She paused for another breath, "then I'm with you."

"Thanks." She hugged her friend.

A corridor loomed ahead of them. Jenny held the torch higher hoping to see beyond their immediate area. Slowly, they walked down the stone passage. Dark walls closed in on the girls as they walked its length. Damp stones were murky with condensation that dripped to form puddles on the ancient stone floor. Together, they crept toward the unknown.

Beth stayed close to Jenny who didn't seem to fear the darkness closing in on them. "I don't think there's anyone down here, Jen."

"We haven't gone that far."

A cluster of passageways appeared, startling the girls. Lights flickered in the distance, but the girls couldn't see what lay ahead of them. The passageways branched out in all directions and caused the girls' steps to falter.

"Where did that come from?" Something didn't feel right, but then again it didn't feel wrong either. Strange feelings ran through her, and Beth feared what they'd discover.

"I don't know." Jenny had to admit this whole scenario was kind of creepy.

As they made their way down the first corridor, torches sprang to life. Jenny and Beth jumped in fear, hearts thumping in their chests like a drummer beating on a drum. What kind of dangers lurked within these corridors? Were they safe? Was danger around the corner? No, she didn't want to believe that anything down here would cause them harm. She couldn't.

She kept walking. The weirdest thing about this entire situation was that Jenny felt quite calm within these dark and murky surroundings. She felt a little adventurous, and, truth be known, she didn't want this feeling to end. For the first time in her life she felt alive and in control of her life. She enjoyed the feeling.

"We have to get out of here!" Beth cried out, fearing the unknown. She wasn't adventurous. No, Beth liked security. She enjoyed knowing what is what. This wasn't something she wanted to get involved with.

"Not yet. I need to know who or what's down there." Jenny's bravery did nothing to calm Beth's fears.

"Do you think there's someone at the end of that tunnel?"

"I don't know, but I intend to stay here and find out."

31

"I don't think you'll find your parents."

Those few words stopped Jenny cold. Tears flooded her eyes and rolled down her cheeks. She looked at Beth wondering why she was being so mean to her. She'd spent years trying to remember her family, without success, and Beth knew how much it meant to her to find out what happened to them. She'd wanted to find something that would tell her something about her parents.

"I'm sorry. I had no right to say that to you."

"No, Beth, you didn't." Jenny's voice was barely a whisper. "I don't know what I'm looking for, but I have to go on. There's someone calling for help, and I need to find out who it is and why they're calling me."

"I know. I'm really sorry." With a smile and a renewed sense of courage, Beth squeezed her friend's hand. "Let's find the owner of that voice."

"Thanks, Beth." Jenny wiped the tears from her cheeks and walked down the corridor. The soft trickle of water fell gently down the sides of the walls. Puddles formed on the stone floor and emitted a musty scent.

The two girls moved slowly down the passageway hoping to discover the reason for this journey. They approached another corridor when a soft voice called out to them. Not a word was uttered as Jenny looked at Beth. She didn't want to turn back, and so she walked toward the owner of the hauntingly soft voice coming through the walls. Its gentle tone floated on the stale air.

"You heard that, right?" Jenny finally asked, making her way toward the eerie sounds.

"Help us," the voice called out.

A shiver passed over the girls.

"Okay. That one I heard," Beth said.

"Come on. We have to find out who's down here."

"Why should we?"

"Maybe someone's in trouble. If they are, we have to help them."

"Sure. Why not?" Beth laughed nervously. "But in case you're wondering, I really don't want to find the owner of that mysterious voice. I can survive without knowing the identity of the person dumb enough to get trapped in a place like this."

Jenny sensed Beth's fear, but she was excited at the prospect of finding the person invading her mind and her dreams. The trail seemed endless and dank, and only a few torches gave them light, but for Jenny this was now a mission of discovery. A mission she was determined to fulfill.

"I still think we're alone down here. There's no one here."

"Beth, the voice we heard is the voice from my dreams. There has to be a connection."

"Maybe, but I still don't like this."

"I know. And you may be right, but I can't give up, not now. Besides, the only way to know for sure is to find the trail's end."

"Yeah, but that's only if there really is an end."

Jenny stopped and looked at her friend. "You think we came all this way for nothing?"

"I do. I'm sorry, Jen, but I think the only thing we'll find down here is this dirty, moldy water."

"No. That can't be all there is. You heard the voice. There is someone down here." Jenny turned away from Beth and nearly collided with the sudden appearance of a large, mysterious door.

"Ah! Where did that come from?" Beth cried out in fear.

"I don't know. It wasn't there a moment ago." Jenny had to admit there was a sense of panic deep inside her. She pushed the feelings down and tried to show her brave side.

"I think it's time to leave," Beth said pleading.

"Not yet."

"You're not planning on doing something stupid, like opening that door, are you?"

"What?" Jenny's mind was already a million miles away. Another door. Would this one reveal some secrets, or would they find more passageways? She had to know what was hiding behind that door.

"The door." Beth's shaky hand pointed toward the mysterious door. "You're not thinking about opening it. Are you?"

"Well, yeah. Don't you want to know where it leads?" Her excitement piqued.

"Not really."

"Beth, I have to know what's on the other side." Jenny faced her friend. "Look, I'll make you a deal. I'll open the door and then we'll leave, okay?"

"Okay, okay. Go ahead," Beth said. "Even though I think this is a big mistake." Emotions flitted across Beth's face; she nodded toward Jenny.

Jenny extended her hand toward the brass handle. A pale light ran through the door. She pulled her hand back in fear. The light was extinguished.

"Cool," Beth said. "Let me try."

"Sure."

Beth's hand reached for the handle, but the light failed to appear. She looked at Jenny and tried again. Nothing.

Jenny approached and the light flowed brightly through the wood like a river running through a canyon. The door came to life at Jenny's approach. She wondered why this happened to her and not her friend.

"I don't understand. Why won't the light shine for me?"

"I don't know. Well, here goes nothing." Jenny grabbed the handle and watched the brass spring to life. All around the door a light shone brightly and ran through every vein in the wood, illuminating the surrounding catacombs. "Wow!" She pushed the handle down and unlocked it with a click. She looked at Beth and smiled. "Are you ready for this?"

"Nope."

Jenny pulled it open. "Beth, look at that."

They stared at a beautiful meadow. A blue sky played host to a large sun. As far as the eye could see, a multitude of colorful flowers grew wild throughout the meadow.

"Come on." Jenny pulled Beth through the doorway.

They'd just stepped over the threshold, when to their horror the door slammed shut and locked. Desperately, they pushed on the door in an attempt to open it, but without success. No matter what they tried to do, or how much pressure they applied, the door refused to open.

"What do we do now?" Beth cried out.

Jenny looked around trying to figure out where they were. "I...I don't know."

"Where are we?"

34

"I'm not sure. Maybe we're on the other side of the school grounds?" Jenny scratched her head and surveyed the meadow trying not to panic, at least not just yet. The sun shone brightly and warmed the meadow, and touched her skin with tenderness. She raised her head toward the rays and breathed in deeply the fragrances permeating the summer air.

"No, we're not. I don't recognize this place." Beth's eyes grew large at the prospect of being led far away from school.

"We didn't walk all that far into the catacombs. We should still be somewhere near the school." Jenny's eyes scanned the area and searched for some form of familiarity. Secretly, she hoped she wouldn't find any. What an awesome adventure for them to partake in!

"I know. It's weird."

"I'm sure we haven't strayed too far."

"Jenny, look at that!" Beth pointed to the sight behind them.

Jenny turned around and stared at the door. Her eyes widened at the sight before them. Slowly, the girls walked around the door. It stood sentry in the midst of the field. There was nothing in front of it and nothing behind it. The only item out of place in this meadow was the lone door.

How could this be? Jenny had never seen anything like this before. There was a solitary door, which only moments before guarded the catacombs, but now it stood on its own power. It wasn't possible, and yet there it was. A tall, wooden door guarding secrets they'd barely uncovered.

"What's going on?" Beth demanded.

Before they could react, the door vanished.

"Where did it go?" Jenny looked all around. Her eyes scanned the entire area as she tried to make sense of what was going on here, but nothing came to her. She didn't understand what had happened or how it could have happened. She had no explanation to offer. Jenny knew something wasn't right, and she wanted answers to the onslaught of questions forming in her mind.

"Jenny, what's happening?" Beth cried out in utter fear.

"I don't know."

"I want to go home," Beth whined.

Jenny thought for a moment. "Let's try to find someone who can help us."

"How do we do that?"

"We'll start walking."

"You want to walk? In which direction do you want to go? I don't recognize anything!"

"Let's go this way." Jenny wondered what really happened to them.

"Why this way?" A slight trembling passed through her small form.

"I'm not sure, but something tells me we should go this way."

With a shaky smile, Beth conceded. "Well, at least we can say we're in the midst of a small adventure."

"See, now you're talking." Jenny's smile brightened her face. She only hoped they could find their way home. At this moment, she wasn't so sure. She didn't want to frighten her friend, but something bizarre had indeed happened to them, and for some strange reason Jenny believed this had all happened once before.

"Do you have any idea what Mrs. Parker will say when we're not in class when the bell rings?" Beth smiled a sly smile.

"I can only imagine. What scares me most is what Aunt Nora will do to me when Mrs. Parker calls her to let her know I missed the second half of the day." Jenny rolled her eyes as thoughts of detention and grounding raced across her mind. She hoped this adventure was worth the punishment she'd suffer when they finally found their way back home.

"You won't see the sun for a month."

"At least a month." She thought about her aunt, and just as quickly she shook the thought from her mind. "Oh well, what's done is done. Let's keep walking. Maybe we'll end up near the school."

"I doubt it. Nothing looks familiar to me, and I know the school grounds real well. This field isn't a part of those grounds, Jenny." Beth looked directly at her friend. "I think we're seriously lost."

CHAPTER 4

SNAKE IN THE GRASS

Jenny and Beth took a couple of steps into the field of flowers where a myriad of colors graced the countryside. For a moment, the beauty of the field relaxed the lost girls. All around them colors bloomed to create a picture-perfect portrait. A dark forest loomed in the distance and created a barrier between the field of color and the unknown dangers hiding within.

The girls looked around, and then at each other. Where were they? Jenny sensed they were no longer in Morgansville. On the contrary, they were somewhere they'd never been before. She admired the beauty before her and wondered why such strange feelings washed over her.

They took one step at a time and noticed that with each step they took, the stems and petals of the colored flowers gently shook as an unusual floral scent assaulted them. From their depths, a soft tune floated on the wind. All around, the song of the sirens grew and filled the air. The lilting tones rose and touched the girls, rendering them far too sedate. Their eyes glazed over as the song took hold of their thoughts and movements. Mechanically, they walked in the direction of the tall grass and the darkened forest, unable to stop.

"Jenny, what's happening? I'm losing control. I feel... helpless." Beth's tone was lethargic.

"Me too."

In the distance, blades of grass fell over as something large made its presence known to them. Although the sound they heard was frightening, they couldn't stop themselves from walking into its deadly wake. Something strange pulled and prodded them along. Unable to control their motions, the girls were steered toward certain danger.

A hiss, something they'd never heard before, wafted through the air and touched the girls. With every ounce of resolve she could muster, Jenny managed to turn her head toward the sound she heard in order to better view her surroundings and discover what lay behind the hiss. She struggled to catch a glimpse of whatever lurked beyond her sight, as the heady tune continued to draw them toward the peculiar hissing sound. The power of the sirens' song held over them was frightening. The girls' steps were controlled by some unknown force.

Jenny struggled against the power, but whatever held them in their control was much stronger, and far more dangerous, than she imagined. She tried to break free of this hold, but without success.

Tears flooded their eyes, but their movements remained under the control of the soft tune the flowers emanated. Just as Jenny was ready to give in, thinking there was no way out of this predicament, the voices that guided her through the catacombs broke through the haze of the flowers' song.

"Athelina, concentrate on my voice and only my voice. I will guide you back from the land of the sirens." The soft, yet familiar, voice called to her and forced her to concentrate on the words spoken by an unknown woman. A moment later, Jenny shook herself awake. She looked around amazed by what had transpired. Searching the area, she noticed her friend still walked toward the tall grass in a strange stupor. Without thought for her own safety, she ran to Beth and tried to bring her back to the present.

"Beth! Don't listen to the music. Listen only to my voice!" She spoke as loudly as she could. She had to cut through the song the flowers used to ensnare the young and unsuspecting.

Beth didn't respond. Her steps were still mechanical as they closed the distance with the terror lying in wait. She failed to acknowledge her friend's presence. Jenny smelled the floral scent as it strengthened to capture and renew its hold on this particular prey. Standing strong, she decided to use the same technique as the voice that broke the spell upon her form and returned her to the present. She only hoped it was enough to save her friend. She didn't know if the voice she heard used some sort of hypnosis on her or if it was magic. Whether it was hypnosis or magic, she didn't care. All she knew was that she'd do everything in her power to help save her friend's life. Jenny only hoped it would be enough.

"Come back to me! Beth, please listen to me! You have to fight this feeling! It's the only way you can break the spell! Please, listen to me!" Her voice rose above the din of the flowers' song. She had to reach her friend's mind, and she thought yelling may do the trick.

In the distance, the hissing grew louder. Something lay in wait. Within the tall grass, danger loomed and Beth was on a direct path with this unknown menace. She couldn't allow this to happen to her friend. She had to try as hard as she could to save Beth's life.

Jenny sensed they were in serious trouble. "Beth, listen to my voice! I need you to open your mind to me." Tears of fear glistened in her eyes. She had to stop Beth from entering the tall grass or she'd lose her best friend.

Eyes glazed and transfixed by the soft tune, Beth walked toward danger. All around them, the flowers shook, but Jenny feared the hissing closing in, even more than the Sirens' Song.

"Beth, you have to listen to me! We have to get out of here! It's not safe! You'll get hurt! Please!" Jenny cried out trying to break through the power of the song.

No response.

Exasperated, Jenny grabbed her shoulders and shook her. "Beth! Beth! Come on! Talk to me!" Jenny's voice rose over the song and deadly hiss. She had to try everything in her power to bring her friend back.

Finally, Beth blinked. "Jenny? What happened? Where am I?" Her head moved from side to side. She tried to focus on her surroundings. She couldn't remember what had transpired.

"No time to explain." Jenny looked at her friend hoping she was feeling better, but right now it didn't matter—danger approached them. She looked around and focused on the tall grass when a large head popped out from where it hid only moments before. A long body slithered and cut through the grass like the flow of a river. Gliding toward a fresh meal, the snake approached the meadow where the two frightened girls now stood. They watched in fear and amazement at the reptile. They never encountered anything the likes of this slithering snake.

Jenny stared at the giant snake and hoped it hadn't seen them, but she wasn't foolish enough to stick around and find out. She took Beth's hand and screamed, "Run!"

A scream tore from deep inside when Beth caught sight of the serpent.

Trying to put as much distance between them and the snake as possible, they willed their legs to move faster. Together, the girls ran and ran as their lungs protested the vicious punishment the girls inflicted upon them.

"Is it following us?"

"I don't know! Run for the forest!" Jenny yelled, but worried that there was greater danger waiting for them within the darkness of the woods. What choice did they have? The girls didn't know the area, and, in Jenny's mind, this was the only way to lose the snake.

They entered the forest and halted. A brief glance around led them to believe they'd managed to lose the giant snake. But then a distinctive sound warned Jenny.

"What's that?"

"What? I didn't hear anything." Beth's voice shook with fear, her breath coming in gasps. "Is it the snake?"

"I don't know. Let's just keep moving."

"Jenny, I don't want to keep going. I want to go home."

"We will, but first we have to get away from that!"

A twenty-foot serpent slithered toward the two frightened girls. Bright yellow eyes followed its quarry deeper into the forest. Its forked tongue slid back and forth from a jaw filled with large fangs eager to sink into the girls. The snake never wavered as it slid along the forest floor always trying to track its prey. The scaly reptile raised its head and then continued to follow the retreating girls.

Trees as tall as a building impeded their progress. Thick roots that purposefully jutted out from the ground caught Beth's foot, and caused her to spill over and land with a thump. She grabbed her ankle and tried to rise, without success. She looked around and saw the snake's scaly approach. Desperate, Beth tried to rise once more, but her foot caused her too much pain. "Jenny, my ankle hurts!" She cried out in fear. "I can't run anymore."

"Can you walk?" Jenny asked when she ran back to where Beth now lay.

She tried to stand with Jenny's help, but couldn't make it. "It hurts too much." She sat back down.

Jenny looked for something she could use as a weapon. Using her foot, she moved leaves aside and found a long branch. She picked it up and held it like a club ready to defend her friend. She watched the snake and hoped she'd be strong enough to defend her friend's life.

The large snake approached them. Its yellow eyes shone in the pale light with menace. Its evil gaze centered upon the injured girl. Slowly, it slithered toward Beth, but Jenny held her makeshift weapon firmly in her hand, ready to battle the giant reptile. She swung the club at the snake's head. She struck it with all her might, but she didn't even break the snake's slither. He snapped at Jenny, who jumped back in fear. The snake turned away from her and continued to move toward Beth. Jenny jumped in front of Beth and struck the snake once more. She refused to allow this creature to harm her best friend. Jenny would do whatever she could to protect Beth.

Jenny kept hitting the snake, but all she did was antagonize the creature. She was no match for this giant snake. He could kill her in an instant. She didn't know what else she could do to save them from the giant jaw that snapped at her in an attempt to push her away from the injured girls on the forest floor.

From high above the trees, a shriek brought Jenny to a halt. What else would she have to battle? She couldn't handle anything else coming to attack them. She couldn't even put a dent in this snake's slither. She chanced a glance upwards and saw dark wings that soared to the clouds. The bird flew through the trees and swooped downwards. It was coming straight for her.

Jenny released a scream when she saw large claws on a direct path with her. Giant claws were drawn, as a large eagle broke through the branches and flew toward her. Jenny screamed when she thought it would try to dig its claws into her flesh, but suddenly it changed direction, and for some strange reason, she sensed the eagle wasn't after her; it was directing its attack at the snake.

The giant eagle raked its large claws over the snake's head. Yellow blood spewed from the injury. The snake snapped its jaw at the eagle. The eagle ignored the snake and continued its attack, scraping his head over and over again. It was relentless in its attack. More blood oozed from the cuts on the snake until it had enough.

Jenny watched as the snake turned and slithered out of the forest and hopefully back toward the grass from where it came. She smiled and turned toward the eagle. He landed, and regally stood on a large boulder with his wings tucked into his side. He watched Jenny's approach with interest.

"Thank you," she told the eagle with an axe-filled smile.

A shriek of understanding escaped the eagle's beak. He bowed his head to Jenny. Gracefully, he spread his wings and flew high above the trees. She watched him fly away, and soon they lost sight of him.

"Wow!" Jenny turned to her friend. "Wasn't that awesome!" She shielded her eyes from the rays of sunlight that peeked through the branches of the trees and touched the ground.

"He came to our rescue in the nick of time," Beth said as she rubbed her bruised ankle.

"He sure did." Jenny had trouble digesting all they'd witnessed. "Are you okay, Beth?"

"I'm fine. I can't stop thinking about that eagle. He was amazing!" She was seeing things, she'd only ever seen on TV, or at the movies.

"I know."

"Did you see what he did?" Beth rubbed her ankle. She had to get up and start walking. The last thing anyone wanted was for her to stay on the floor in this forest with giant snakes on the loose.

"What do you mean?"

"I could have sworn he bowed to you."

"I noticed that too. Why would he do that? It doesn't make sense to me."

"Me either. Then again, nothing I've seen so far makes any sense to me. But I do have one question."

"Only one?"

"Well, one I need answered."

"What's that?"

"Jen, where are we?"

"What do you mean?"

"Come on, we don't have snakes like that in Alberta. I've also never seen eagles that size before."

"Neither have I." Jenny's tone wielded the worry she felt inside. She wondered the same things as Beth, but had no answers to give.

"Are you planning on telling me what's going on?"

"I really don't know." Jenny glanced around the woods. "How are you doing?"

"I'll be all right."

"You sure?"

"Yeah. I guess we should get going."

"It'll be dark soon. We should find a place to spend the night." Jenny saw the position of the sun.

"I have an idea."

"What's your idea?" Jenny's skepticism showed.

"Let's go home."

Jenny laughed. "Fine, which way is home?" Jenny arched an eyebrow and helped Beth stand. "Come on."

Beth tried to put some weight on her foot. Pain shot through her ankle and forced her to pause for a moment. "Which way should we go?" Beth asked, trying to keep her mind off the pain she felt.

"This way." Jenny pointed ahead of them. "I hope there's water somewhere around here. I'm thirsty."

"Do you think we'll find a store?" Beth asked, even though it was unlikely.

"No, but there might be a stream running through this forest." The one thing she sensed was that they wouldn't come upon a store or restaurant in this place. Something told her they'd traveled farther than she ever thought possible.

"Okay, I'll try to keep up." She used Jenny for support, and soon the pain in her ankle eased. "I guess it's only twisted."

"Either way, we'll stop in a little while and rest."

"Sounds good to me." Beth hobbled, but kept up with Jenny.

They traveled through the forest always on the lookout for jutting roots that could injure them even more. After some time, the girls stopped to rest. Jenny kept an eye on Beth as she sat down on a fallen log and stretched her legs out.

"Stay here and rest your foot. I'll scout up ahead and check this place out."

"Okay. Just be careful. You don't know where we are or what's waiting for you out there."

"I'll be careful. Don't worry."

Jenny left Beth and walked toward the setting sun. She carefully maneuvered around the roots of trees and tried to stay away from bushes and rocky areas where any kind of creature could hide and pounce on her. The forest was incredible. The trees wore an ancient mantle and gave too much shade to certain areas, but allowed the sun to illuminate the plants that required the sunlight to live.

Here the forest darkened. Jenny trembled from the damp coolness of the woods. She hoped to find the stream that seemed to feed the inhabitants and vegetation within these woods. There had to be some kind of water source close by. Everything she'd ever read in books told her this bit of information.

In the distance, Jenny heard the sound of trickling water. She happily ran back to get Beth.

"I found water."

Jenny helped her stand and offered to be her crutch. Together, they made their way toward the stream. Clear water gently flowed over rocks inviting the girls to drink the cool liquid. They drank greedily wondering if they'd be lucky enough to find water again.

Satiated, they took a moment to rest. Green and yellow grass formed a soft carpet on the forest floor, while flowers and large boulders were dispersed, creating an odd collage. Rays of sunlight filtered through the deep foliage and touched the stream with a gentle caress. If this scenario was not so intimidating, Jenny would have to admit that this forest was outstanding, and the area they were now in was nothing less than beautiful.

"So, have you heard any voices lately?"

"No. I haven't heard anything since the eagle scared the snake away."

"It figures. Those voices you heard brought us here and now they've decided to abandon us. I'm not feeling too good about this," Beth said.

"I know. I feel the same way, but I'm more worried about finding a way back home. Well, that and finding a place to spend the night. I don't want to stay in this forest over night. That would be far too dangerous."

"Do you know where we're supposed to go next?"

"No."

"I'm not sure that's a good thing."

"I know." This troubled Jenny as well.

"I wonder why you haven't heard anything. I mean, the voices took us through the catacombs and then saved us in the meadow, and now that we don't know where to go or what to do and nighttime is coming, the voices are silent. It's just not right."

"I agree. It's really bad timing." Jenny didn't understand why she'd been brought to a distant and unfamiliar land, only to be left alone to fend for herself. Everything about the place scared her, but as long as the voices in her head guided her, she was prepared to try anything. Now she was on her own, and Beth was her responsibility. She was too young and inexperienced to have to carry such a burden.

"I'll look around. Why don't you put your foot in the stream? The cool water should help ease the pain."

"Sure. Just don't go too far. You don't know where you're going, and I need you to come back."

"I'll be fine." Jenny walked away and searched the area, hoping to find someone who could answer some questions for her. Now that she was alone, she had the opportunity to think about everything that happened to therm. She wondered where they were and why they were brought here. Something wasn't right.

Beyond the trees, the edge of a village came into view. A smile played on Jenny's lips as she ran back to tell Beth all about her find.

CHAPTER 5

THE VILLAGE

They followed the stream, and soon Jenny saw the distinct signs of a stone wall surrounding the strange village. But what kind of village was this? They had little choice but to slowly approach the entrance. Two large gates stood open and bid them welcome. They looked up at the gates and stepped through the opening. It felt as though they took a stroll back in time.

Once inside, the girls looked around and tried to get a feel for the unknown town. Jenny led the way, uncertain what she and Beth would find, but hopeful they'd find some help. A long dirt road ran the length of the village. The girls jumped to one side when a wagon pulled by horses passed by. They stared in awe at the sight before them.

"Did you see that?" Beth said.

The girls had seen horses before, after all, they were from Alberta, but at home whenever something was being delivered it was always by truck and not by horse and wagon.

"I did! Come on, let's follow this road. Maybe we'll find someone who can tell us where we are." Jenny pulled Beth along.

Houses in an array of colors created a cheerful ambiance and helped curb their fear. A strange sensation flowed through her. Jenny instantly felt she belonged in this strange place. There was a small amount of recognition nagging at her, but that wasn't possible... or was it? She didn't understand the strange feeling overwhelming her.

A man stood in front of a yellow cottage trimmed with bright orange. His matching robes and colorful hat blended in with the bright colors of his house. The girls laughed at the picture he presented and then moved on. People milled about, chatting in loud tones. They turned and stared at the two young girls.

"Look at how the people are dressed," Beth said. She stared in awe at the villagers' authentic garb. Long colorful robes over tunics and pants seemed to be the dress code in this land. What a strange place this was. It reminded Jenny of *Brigadoon*, the tale of a small town that appeared for one day every hundred years. The people in the story dressed much the same as they did the century before.

"Cool!" Jenny exclaimed.

Beth's excitement showed as she pointed to the people walking around the area. Some wore the brightest colors imaginable, while a few people wore clothes in darker shades. The only commonality was that they wore tunics and pants, or tunic with tights and cloaks to cover their shoulders. Some wore long robes that dusted the roadway with their material.

"This is awesome!" Jenny sighed happily as feelings of coming home overwhelmed her. Something nagged at her, but since she was unable to understand the overwhelming feelings rushing at her, she chose to brush them off and enjoy this moment. "This place is great!"

More and more people stepped out into the yards of the many painted homes on either side of the roadway. They were also dressed in similar, yet vibrant, clothing. The camaraderie with each was nice to see. Everyone knew everyone, and they seemed to get along. This was new to the girls.

Jenny and Beth turned down the only roadway. They hoped it would lead them to a populated area where they could blend in and find out where they were. They walked past more homes where gardens bloomed and dust created the only road leading toward the heart of the village. The girls came to a halt when they saw something was happening ahead of them. Curiosity got the best of them.

"What do you think?" Beth asked when they saw close-knit buildings and colorful rooftops.

"What do we have to lose?"

A short time later they came upon a large outdoor market. Up ahead, small colored roofs stood above the many booths, kiosks, and tables scattered all around the downtown core.

Excitement took over the girls when they saw all the fanfare. They wanted to participate in whatever was happening around them.

"Let's have a look around," Jenny happily said.

Booths and kiosks were set up for the vendors to sell their wares to passing customers. Large tables were filled with cloth, beads, jewelry, and other goods. She couldn't wait to explore the wares. Each booth or kiosk held different wares for sale. No two alike.

Jenny led Beth into the market square. They walked toward the first booth with a tent-like canopy and stopped to stare at a woman with bright orange hair piled high atop her head. She sold garments similar to those she wore. Bright yellow, red, green, blue, purple as well as gold, silver and copper robes hung all around the woman. In an attempt to entice customers to her booth, the girls heard her call out.

"Robes for sale! Buy a new robe and look beautiful!" She continued to say these words when suddenly she quieted. Her gaze never wavered as her eyes locked on the two young girls who stood almost in a nonchalant manner just beyond her booth.

"Do you wish to buy a robe?" she asked Jenny as her brown eyes locked with the young girl's emerald gaze.

"No, thank you." She turned away from the woman's intense stare. "Come on, Beth." Jenny pulled her friend's arm.

"Did you see all those cool robes? I've never seen anything like it before."

"Me neither. Let's see what else they're selling." Jenny's excitement was slightly marred by the woman's strange reaction to her.

"I'm game. Come on." Beth's smile lit her face with enthusiasm.

The next booth in a long row of booths had tops and pants unlike anything they'd ever seen before. Embroidery of the finest quality surrounded the collars, cuffs, and hems on the long, tunic styled tops. Bright colors made customers of all ages stop and admire the lovely wares.

The girls walked through the marketplace unaware of the attention they attracted. Slowly, more and more people stopped what they were doing to stare at the two young girls. They spoke to each other in whispers as they pointed at the oddly dressed girls.

"Jenny, look at all these cool things they're selling."

"I would, but I'm looking at the people staring at us."
Jenny saw that some townspeople wore long and colorful robes,
while others were dressed in pants and tunics with leather boots
touching their knees.

"What? Who's staring at us?" Beth turned around and saw
the crowd gathering behind them. "Why are they looking at us like
that?"

"I don't know. Maybe they figured out we're not from
around here." She saw fingers being pointed at them, and
wondered why they reacted so strangely to their presence in this
quaint little village.

"What do we do now?"

"Let's get out of here."

"Where should we go? It's not like we have a place to
hide."

"I know," Jenny said. Her eyes took in the people milling
around to look them over. "We don't even know who these people
are, or for that matter what kind of people they are. I think we
should make our way through the market and head for the other
side of town."

"Okay. I'm right behind you." Beth motioned for Jenny to
walk ahead of her.

"Gee, thanks a lot." Jenny started to move away from the
booths. They tried to walk away as nonchalantly as possible.
Perhaps the people of this town would soon lose interest in them.
They walked around some booths and came out near kiosks where
something smelled heavenly.

Jenny's stomach rumbled.

"I wish we could buy something to eat," Beth said when
she saw the fresh bread and rolls lining the shelves in the kiosk.
On a stand, off to one side, stood a variety of cakes and pastries
designed to entice buyers into spending their money.

"Everything smells so good. I'm starving," Beth said while
inhaling the fragrant aroma wafting from the kiosk.

"We don't have any money."

"I know, but smelling the food is free." She laughed and
raised her nose into the air for emphasis.

"Would you like to buy something?" A man of unknown years smiled at the girls.

"Oh. No thank you."

The man wore robes decorated with the colors of the rainbow. A white beard covered his jaw, while blue eyes shone from beneath bushy white eyebrows. "No gold coins?"

"Gold coins?" Jenny didn't understand his question. She looked at Beth who shrugged her shoulders. "No. We didn't come prepared to buy anything," Jenny told the man, hoping he wouldn't question her. She wouldn't be able to answer any questions since she had no idea where they were or how they got here.

He looked at the girls. His stare upon Jenny was as intense as the woman with the orange hair. This caused an uncomfortable feeling in her. Why did they look at her that way? Jenny wondered why these strangers were making her feel so ill at ease. She hadn't done anything to attract unwanted attention. All they did was walk around and admire the wares in each booth.

She was just about to leave when the man took something from a tray. "Here you go." He gave each of them a bun topped with chocolate.

"Thank you, sir!" Jenny exclaimed as she accepted the sweet treat. She liked this man who showed her kindness. He smiled at them with gentleness … and what? Understanding? Perhaps he was a kind, old gentleman who figured out they were out of place here. All she knew was that they were hungry and this man took pity on them. Sometimes it was best to not analyze everything and to accept the fact that someone did something out of genuine benevolence.

"You are most welcome. My name is Esther." He bowed to the lost girls.

"Thank you, Esthra."

He smiled at the girls, but found it difficult to take his eyes away from the young girl with the bright green eyes and long black hair.

"Where are you from?" he asked as he continued to place loaves of bread onto shelves. He moved away from the girls and set up his shelves with his baked goods.

"That's kind of difficult to explain. We've been walking for a while," Jenny said, refusing to reveal too much information, even though she didn't know how much information was too much.

"I won't pry, but perhaps you may want to rethink your outfits. They seem to draw far too much attention."

Jenny licked some chocolate from her fingers and looked at Beth. She shook her head. The last thing she wanted was to let Beth say something that could offend this kind man. "As I said, we didn't leave home fully prepared for this."

"Ah." A smile of sympathy rather than understanding crossed Esthra's elderly features.

The girls finished their treat. "Thank you again, Esthra, but we need to get going," Jenny said.

"Then I bid you good day, young ladies. Please stop by and visit me again." His polite smile never faltered.

"We will." They waved and made their way to the next booth.

Jenny noticed that more and more villagers stopped what they were doing to stare at the oddly dressed girls. She thought it had to be their jeans that seemed to attract unwanted attention, but, then again, she could be wrong. She stood rooted to the spot as she tried to make sense of this strange place.

"We should get going." This time Beth had to lead Jenny away.

The girls made their way through a few more rows of booths and continued to walk, still unsure of their destination, but wanting to put some distance between them and the curious villagers. Although they didn't feel as though they were in any immediate danger, Jenny and Beth felt it might be best to stay away from the crowd that gathered and stared at them.

"What do you think?" Jenny asked Beth when they came upon a dirt road. She looked around, but saw little or no choice. This was the only avenue open to them.

"Well, what choice do we have? Let's see where this road takes us."

They walked down the road, but once the market lay behind them, the trees grew tall and flowers abounded. Jenny feared they would ensnare them again and kept vigil. After a while, when nothing out of the ordinary happened, the girls were able to enjoy the beauty of the flowers growing in manicured gardens. There didn't seem to be any sign of sinister flowers trying to feed them to some giant snake. Green grass covered the area beyond the trees and shrubs. At the end of the road, their eyes grew large at the magnificent sight before them.

CHAPTER 6

DEVON

Two menacing gates guarded the most beautiful white castle Jenny and Beth had ever seen. Tall turrets reached for a bright sky, while windows abounded within the stone palace giving natural light to the occupants within.

"Awesome!" Jenny stared beyond the gates to behold the amazing sight. She absorbed all she saw. She even imagined this castle having a moat and drawbridge, the kind you'd see in old movies. A feeling she didn't recognize overwhelmed her. It wasn't exactly recognition, but at the same time she didn't feel as though this were strange to her. Something pulled at her memory just the way it did when she'd first arrived at the gates of the village. She wanted to find out what they meant and why she was experiencing these unusual sentiments.

Intricate gardens decorated the grounds surrounding the castle where a kaleidoscope of flowers turned the gardens into an invitation of exploration. A variety of trees lined the castle grounds, giving shade to the people who wanted to take a stroll on the paths winding their way through the gardens. In the distance, Jenny could have sworn she'd seen some kind of maze carved out of oddly shaped shrubberies. What an exciting find.

"I've never seen anything like this before. It's beautiful!"

"I wonder who lives there."

"Oh, it's probably the royal family."

"Yeah, but who are they?"

"I don't know. Maybe we'll get lucky and see someone come out of the castle. Wouldn't that be great?"

"Before we waste anymore time trying to figure out who lives in the castle, I think we should find a place to spend the night." Beth tugged on her friend's arm, with little success.

"I'd like to stay here another minute, Beth. I want to get a better look at this place." The beauty of the grounds and castle enthralled Jenny. But just like before, she sensed she was forgetting something very important from her past. She wished she knew what that something was and why she had these thoughts and feelings. There had to be a reason behind everything she'd felt the moment she entered this village.

"Jenny, we shouldn't stay here any longer. Someone might think we're up to something. Remember how everyone at the market stared at us? It's not right."

"I guess. It's just that..."

"What?"

"I don't know how to explain it, but for some reason, I'm home."

"Jenny, you're scaring me... again."

"Sorry, Beth. I can't help it. This place feels so familiar to me."

"You've never been here before."

"I know, it's crazy, but I feel as though I have... as if I belong here."

"No, you don't. I think we should leave. This place is having a weird effect on you."

"Yeah, I know it is, but..." Jenny stared through the gates with longing in her eyes. "There's something special about this place." She wanted to understand the feelings that surfaced whenever she gazed at the castle. "Something I should remember but can't." What couldn't she remember? Why should she feel this way if, in fact, she'd never been here before? Something deep inside told her this was home, but her common sense told her to move away and find shelter for the night. She tried to search her memory, but as always she drew a blank.

"Come on, Jenny, we have to go." Beth tugged on her arm.

"I guess you're right." Jenny's feet refused to move. Her eyes took in the sights and allowed them to fill her with a serenity she'd never felt before.

"Jenny, what's wrong with you?" The last time Jenny's behavior turned strange, they'd ended up here... wherever here was. Beth didn't want anything else to happen to them.

"There's nothing wrong," Jenny said with a mechanical tone to her voice, but her eyes were centered on the castle. She wanted to go inside and discover why she felt the castle's pull. What was in there that seemed to want her?

"It's almost dark. We need to find a place to spend the night."

"I know."

"You keep saying that, but you're not moving!"

"I can't seem to leave." Her eyes glazed over with distant thoughts and memories.

"What do you mean?"

"I can't move my feet."

"Well, you'd better find a way to move them. We can't stay here all night."

Jenny turned to look at her friend. "I think there might be a place for us to stay." She turned to face the castle.

"You're not serious." Beth's eyes grew large at Jenny's words.

"I don't know if I am or not, but something's pulling me in there." Her distant stare worried Beth, but Jenny felt perfectly safe standing there. Something was so familiar about the sight before her, and she wanted to find out why she should feel this way. She sensed the castle held answers she desperately needed.

"Jenny, no. We can't."

"How do you know?"

"I don't, but I'm assuming we can't go in there."

Suddenly Jenny blinked and her eyes returned to normal. "I... I know. I don't know what's happening to me."

"You are starting to freak me out."

"Sorry. I guess I was wondering if we'd be allowed to go in there, you know, to take a tour of the castle. What do you think? Should we go inside?" Jenny smiled at Beth, hoping to entice her into a visit.

"I wouldn't suggest that."

At the sound of the soft voice, the girls turned around and came face to face with a young man.

"Who are you?" Jenny asked. He was a couple of years older, with long dark hair and bright blue eyes. He was dressed in similar clothing to the people they'd seen in the marketplace—a deep blue tunic over dark pants, leather boots, and an ominous black cloak. His features were strong and incredibly handsome.

"Who are you?" Jenny asked again, as her eyes traveled from the young man to the castle with longing.

"My name is Devon. And you are?"

Jenny looked at Devon with a questioning gaze. "I'm Jenny Saunders, and this is Beth Brown."

"You are not from around here."

"How can you tell?" Beth asked.

Devon looked at their clothes and then at the blonde girl's hair with a raised eyebrow. "It isn't difficult." He smiled a brilliant, white smile.

"Where are we?" Jenny asked. She had to look up at Devon, who stood a few inches taller.

"What do you mean?" He looked both girls over once more, centering his look on Jenny who bristled beneath the intensity of his blue gaze.

"What's the name of this town?" Jenny asked again, hoping to get a direct answer.

Devon looked at the young girls and smiled. "You're definitely not from here. Perhaps you're from a neighboring town?"

"No, we're not. The problem is, we're kind of lost," Jenny said.

"Where are you from?"

"We're from Morgansville."

"I'm sorry, but I've never heard of such a place," Devon replied wondering at the girls' identity and their reason for being here.

"Oh, great," Beth said. "So now what?"

"I don't know. What's the name of this village?" Jenny asked, worried they may have strayed too far from home.

"This is the Village of Wardell, and you're standing before Wardell Castle."

"Wardell?" Jenny thought for a moment, trying to picture her province. "I've never heard of it."

56

"Well, this is Wardell. I don't know what else I can tell you."

"How far are we from Morgansville?" Beth asked Devon.

"I do not know this Morgansville. I am sorry."

"Beth, I think we're in serious trouble." But Jenny's tone didn't display any sign of upset or anxiety.

"Oh, you think?" Beth shuffled uncomfortably.

"What the devil's going on? How cans something like this happen?" she wondered out loud, but secretly excitement flowed through her. Was this the answer to her dreams?

"Are you asking me, Jenny?" He looked at this strange, but lovely girl. He stood calmly by watching the girls. He waited for something, but Jenny didn't know what to make of this handsome guy who just appeared.

"I'm not sure if I am or not. I really don't even know what to say or what to do. I never thought anything like this could happen."

"There is no need to panic. You obviously went the wrong way. Perhaps if you went back the same way you came, you may find a way to return to your homeland," Devon stated rationally.

"We would, but when we passed through the doorway, it closed and locked behind us. We tried to open the door, but it wouldn't budge. We searched the area and then, as if by magic, the door disappeared. We walked around and ended up here." Jenny spoke the words with haste, hoping they didn't sound as strange to him as she thought they sounded to her.

"Door? What door?" Devon asked.

"When we walked through the catacombs we found a door. When I touched it… well… it glowed." Jenny thought this sounded odd, but when Devon didn't laugh, she continued. "When we stepped through the doorway, it closed and disappeared." Jenny continued to watch his reaction hoping he wouldn't think her crazy.

"I see. Then I'm at a loss as to how I can help you." But there was wonder in his eyes as he looked at Jenny with renewed interest.

"Jenny, I'm scared. I want to go home."

"I know. Don't worry, we'll find our way home. I promise."

"How?"

"You should return to where you first began your journey and attempt to locate this door," Devon said.

"We would, but we really don't know where it is or how to find our way back to the door. So many things happened along the way. I don't think I'd ever be able to find it again."

Jenny looked from Beth to Devon, who shrugged his shoulders. No one knew what to say to calm Beth's fear.

"Do you have a place to spend the night?"

"No, we don't." Jenny chewed her thumbnail, while worry creased her brow. They had no money or gold coins as Esthra pointed out. Where should they go? She didn't relish the idea of sleeping outside in the woods somewhere, especially after the things they'd seen and fought within the forest. What were they going to do?

"Jenny, my mom will freak out when I don't come home tonight." Beth's eyes glazed with unshed tears. She just wanted to go home.

Now that they were here in front of the castle, with Devon, Jenny wanted to see all the secrets the castle held, but when she looked at her friend, her first priority was to find a way to get Beth home before dark. "I know."

"What about Nora? What are you gonna tell her?" she asked.

"Come on, Beth. Do you really think she'd worry about me?" Sadness crept into her eyes and voice.

"Who's Nora?" Devon asked.

"I live with my aunt." Jenny decided to tell him the truth about her situation.

"Won't she care if you don't come home?"

"No. If she didn't have to take care of me anymore, she'd be thrilled."

"I don't understand."

"It's complicated. You see, my aunt... well... she kind of hates me," Jenny told her new friend. Although she wanted to tell Devon the truth about Aunt Nora, she felt awkward telling a stranger this kind of a story, even though she felt relaxed around him. For some strange reason, she felt as if she could tell him anything and he would listen to her every word. What a strange reaction to someone she'd only just met! Usually, she shied away from strangers, but when she looked at Devon, she wanted to spend time with him… to get to know him. She wanted to talk with him, to be with him.

"Why?"

"My parents went missing several years ago, and I was sent to live with Aunt Nora."

"Is she your mother or father's sister?"

"Neither. From what I've been told, Nora was married to my dad's best friend. I called them Uncle Rob and Aunt Nora, but they aren't related to us. Uncle Rob divorced Nora, and I haven't seen him since."

Devon thought for a moment. "How long has it been since he left?"

"He left after my parents disappeared. Why?"

"Did you ever find out what happened to your parents?" Devon's curiosity where Jenny was concerned was more than a little evident.

"No."

"Are they dead?"

"No!" Jenny refused to believe her parents were deceased. "I know one day I'll find them!" Jenny's adamant tone shocked even her. "I will find them," she repeated the words under her breath. "I will."

"And what about your uncle?"

She looked at Devon. "That's the strange part. No one really knows what happened to him. It's like he disappeared with my parents. Isn't that weird?"

"Yes, I suppose it is."

"Devon, maybe we could use your phone. At least we can let Beth's mom and Aunt Nora know what happened to us and where we are. They could come here and get us."

"That's a great idea. Why didn't I think of that?"

"I'm sorry, but what is a phone?" Devon asked, bewildered.

"You're kidding, right?" Jenny wondered if Devon was pulling her leg.

"No, I'm afraid not. I don't know what a phone is."

"A telephone."

"What is a te-le-phone?" His seriousness caused Jenny's stomach to lurch in fear.

"It's a device used to contact people."

"Jenny, Beth, I'm afraid we do not have these devices you call "telephone" in Wardell."

"I think we're in serious trouble, Jenny." Beth didn't know what else to say.

"I know. I'm starting to get scared."

"Starting to get scared?" Beth repeated. "I'm far beyond that. I'm terrified, and on the verge of freaking out. If only we knew where we were, and how to get home, I'd feel a lot better."

"I know how scared you are, but I promise you, I'll find a way home."

Taking a deep breath, Beth tried to relax. "So, what do you think happened to us?"

"Beth, I'm not certain, but I think we've stepped into another world," Jenny told her friend excitedly.

CHAPTER 7

WARDELL CASTLE

"**W**hat?" A shudder passed through her. "You're joking, right? You have to be." Jenny was mistaken. She had to be. As she looked around, her eyes met her friend's and she nodded her head in agreement. Something wasn't right, and maybe they had strayed farther than either one of them ever thought possible.

"No, Beth, I'm not kidding. Look around. Look at how these people are dressed— it's right out of *The Lord of the Rings*. There are no phones, no electricity, and I'll bet there's no running water." Jenny saw the fear in her friend's eyes.

"How do you know?"

"No towers, no wires, and look over there, that's a well," Jenny said.

Devon carefully listened to their exchange. His blue eyes shone in the dying embers of sunlight. He listened, but his features told them he failed to comprehend the meaning of their words. With a raised eyebrow, he stood by in fascination and waited for the conversation to end.

"What are we gonna do?" Beth cried out. She wanted to go home. Traveling here wasn't something she had bargained for.

"I don't know."

"Jenny?"

"I'm sorry, Beth. I never imagined anything like this could happen."

"Well, it isn't all that bad." Devon didn't understand the girls' comments.

Jenny and Beth turned to face their newest friend. Jenny offered him a smile of apology. "We didn't mean to offend you, Devon." She tried to smooth things over. "It's just that this entire situation is quite surreal." She saw the pride in Devon's stance. He was defensive of his home, and she didn't blame him.

"In what way?"

"How would you feel if you took a walk through an open doorway and found yourself in another world?"

"I never thought about it." Devon smiled at the thought.

"But that's what happened to us." If Jenny was anything it was that she was certain of their predicament.

"I understand your dilemma. Is there anything I can do to help?"

"Yeah, you can help us get home," Beth said, her fear making her angrier than she ought to be.

"I'm sorry, but I don't know a way back to your world. If I did, I wouldn't hesitate to help you return."

Jenny saw Devon's sincerity was real, and he seemed genuinely distraught over their situation. She hoped he'd be able to tell them what they could do to find their home. Devon studied them. He smiled at the girls until he saw Berth's reaction.

"Then we're stuck here!" Tears rolled down Beth's cheeks. She wiped them away, but they kept flowing.

Trying to console her friend, Jenny put her arm around Beth's shoulder. "Please don't cry. We found our way here, and we'll find a way back. I promise." Jenny wished she could keep that promise, but she wasn't sure she could.

"No, we won't. We're stuck here, and I'll never see my family again."

"Of course you will. In the meantime, you have to admit, this is quite exciting. I mean, think about it, Beth…another world. This is what dreams are made of, but we've been given the opportunity to explore Wardell. Who else can say they've been to another world?" Jenny's smile helped soothe Beth's fears.

"Jenny, aren't you scared?"

"Not really."

"You seem almost happy to be here." She looked quizzically at her friend.

"Maybe I am. I'll have some time away from Aunt Nora and to me that's worth a lot." She felt free for the first time in her life. She felt as though her life were her own. This feeling made her almost giddy. If it weren't for Beth, she'd jump up and down at the thought of not having to see Aunt Nora.

"I know, but I don't want to be away from my parents. They're good people. I also like my TV, computer, and telephone."

"I know. They are good people, and I love them too. Don't worry, we'll find our way home again." Jenny didn't have any of the amenities Beth described. Her life was far more simple and sparse. She only used computers at school or at Beth's, so this wasn't an active part of her life.

"Jenny, in case you've forgotten, we don't even have a place to stay tonight. What are we supposed to do?"

"I don't know. We don't have any money, either. It won't be easy," she said, "but we'll be all right." She worried her thumbnail.

"Perhaps I can be of service." Devon moved in closer to the girls, now that they'd calmed down.

Jenny smiled. She couldn't help noticing that Devon's presence had a calming effect upon her. "If perhaps you could tell us where we could spend the night, we'd appreciate it."

"Certainly. I'll even take you there myself."

"Thanks. Come on, Beth. Let's try to make the best of this situation."

"Sure. What choice do we have?"

"Good. Follow me." Devon walked through the gates guarding the beautiful castle.

"Devon, we can't go in there," Jenny said, even though she desperately wanted to go inside and explore the interior of the castle, but she feared Devon would put himself in a precarious position that would cause trouble for him. The last thing Jenny wanted to do was to get her new friend into jeopardy.

"Why not?" he asked with a sly smile.

"You told us we couldn't go in there," Beth said with a hand on her hip.

"Yes, but that was before we became friends. Besides, you need a place to stay and you have no money. So, I think you should stay in the castle." He mocked their situation with an honest laugh.

"Oh sure, we'll just knock on the door and ask if we can spend the night in this magnificent castle." Jenny laughed.

"I like the way you laugh."

She blushed.

Devon smiled. "Come on. I'll show you around."

"Thanks, but I still think this is a bad idea."

"Are you anticipating trouble?" Devon raised his eyebrow in mock surprise.

"Of course I am." Secretly, she wished they could visit the castle, but felt they'd be stopped at the gate.

"Don't worry. I know someone who lives here. Once I explain your situation, he'll allow you to stay the night." A sly smile curled his lips.

"Who do you know that lives here?" Beth demanded.

"A friend." He laughed at their mystified expression. "Come on."

The girls followed Devon toward the castle. Along the way, they took notice of the manicured lawns and the lush gardens. A path led them to a large, wooden drawbridge, sitting high above a wide moat, where two armed guards stood on either side of the bridge. Their sole purpose was to defend the entrance to the castle.

Devon looked at the girls and laughed at the fear he saw in their eyes. He stopped when he noticed his friends weren't with him. Laughing all the more, he went back and took their hands in his. Together, they approached the drawbridge. Instantly, the guards came to attention. Devon looked at the girls and laughed at their expression of utter surprise. "I told you I knew someone." Devon wore a mischievous smile.

The walk across the bridge fascinated the two young girls who'd never had the opportunity to approach a real castle and travel across a drawbridge. At the entrance to the castle, two more armed guards protected the castle. The long swords that hung from their hips gave credence to their duty. These guards, like the other ones, stood at attention and allowed Devon to pass through the gates with his guests.

Smiling at the display of honor, Jenny and Beth followed their newest friend into the interior. How exciting to be allowed to enter, and perhaps explore, the very castle Jenny yearned to discover.

Inside, a large marble entrance greeted them. The girls looked around and took notice of a giant crystal chandelier, the size of Aunt Nora's living room, suspended from a painted ceiling. White candles were positioned within and illuminated the entire foyer. All around the room, marbled walls were decorated with ornate gold frames displaying an array of original paintings, and a giant gilt-edged framed mirror. Up ahead, a marble staircase led to different levels within the castle walls. The tour continued down a long hallway to the right of the twin staircase. Slowly, the girls moved taking in the beauty of the rooms.

"Who are these people?" Jenny asked, as she looked at the many paintings of strangers held within golden frames. She wanted to look at each picture and learn their history. She was completely mesmerized by their ancient form and beauty.

"Members of the Royal Family."

"They're incredible! This castle is incredible!" Her excitement threatened to overflow. She'd never felt as excited or happy as she did at this moment.

"Yeah! This place is awesome!" Beth exclaimed, as she looked everywhere at the same time, afraid of missing something she shouldn't miss seeing.

"The castle is quite impressive."

"So, who lives here now?" Jenny wanted to know all the details about the people residing in such a magnificent palace.

"Why, the royal family, of course."

"Gee, I wish we could meet them." Jenny looked up at Devon, who merely smiled.

"One never knows whom you might meet while walking these halls."

Jenny looked at Beth and shrugged. She thought Devon was far too mysterious and didn't know if this was a good thing. Perhaps he was just pulling her leg since she was acting too giddy about being here in Wardell Castle.

"This way."

They turned down another hallway.

"Where are we going, Devon?"

"It is dinner time. I thought you might be hungry."

"Actually, I'm starved." Beth smiled for the first time since their arrival in Wardell.

"Good. Follow me."

"Devon, I don't want you to get into trouble." Jenny was uneasy about their presence in this castle.

"Why would I get into trouble for being in the castle?"

"I don't know. This just doesn't feel right," Jenny said.

"You worry too much." Another hearty laugh escaped the young man. He took their hands and led them past many closed doors. "Here we are."

Two uniformed men stood on either side of the doors. Devon informed the girls that the gold and white uniforms were the colors of the castle's personal guard. They came to attention and opened the doors for Devon, who ushered the girls inside.

The formal dining room was large and displayed many mirrors and paintings on the walls. Seated at a large table were several well-dressed people. A man with dark hair and a thin golden crown sat at the head of the table. He smiled when Devon walked in with two oddly dressed young girls.

"Devon, we'd almost lost hope you'd join us for dinner."

"Hello, Father, Mother. Everyone."

The others mumbled something and bowed their heads. Jenny looked at Beth and turned toward their friend with a questioning gaze.

"I told you I knew someone in the castle." He laughed and removed his cloak, handing it to the servant who suddenly appeared behind them.

"You could've told us," Jenny chastised him.

"Yes, I could have, but it wouldn't have been this much fun." Devon continued to laugh at their expense.

"Are you planning on introducing us to your friends?" the handsome man asked with a wondrous expression that dominated his handsome features, as he looked at the two young girls standing with his son.

"Yes, sir. Jenny, Beth, this is my father, Lord Galfrid and my mother Lady Jemma."

"Hello," the girls said in awe.

"Are you the king and queen?" Jenny asked.

After a moment of uncomfortable silence, Galfrid smiled and proudly addressed the question hanging in the air. "No, I'm the Steward of Wardell and the Keeper of the Crown for the Royal Family."

Jenny noticed the resemblance between father and son. They shared the same dark hair and bright blue eyes. Both men were incredibly attractive. She couldn't believe she stood here in the presence of royalty. Butterflies fluttered in her stomach. Actually, they felt more like pterodactyl than butterflies.

"In the king's absence, my father rules and keeps the lands and people safe. My father is also the guardian of the royal seal." Devon divulged whatever information he could about his family.

"Wow! It's so nice to meet you." Jenny put out her hand, unsure how to greet people of this rank. She'd never expected to meet anyone related to royalty. Shy and a little awkward, Jenny tried her best not to look like a fool.

Galfrid stood and took her hand in his. He kissed it in a very gallant manner. Jenny blushed, but before she could utter a word, Beth quickly followed suit.

Jemma, on the other hand, was lovely with pale hair and skin, her blue eyes were a pale hue next to her son's bright blue, but they nevertheless sparkled with kindness and beauty in the candlelight.

"This young lady is my cousin, Elaria. Seated next to her are Aunt Rowena and Uncle Jerrod. Across the table is Cassandra, also a cousin and her parents." He continued to introduce his other aunts, uncles, and cousins. He then led the girls to the end of the table. Devon opted to sit with his guests.

Galfrid and Jemma smiled at their son's gallantry.

"This is totally wicked," Beth said. "Are all these people royalty?" She looked around, impressed by the people seated at the ornate table.

"Yes, in some way," Devon said, looking around the room.

"Where are the king and queen?" Jenny asked.

The room was silenced by the innocence of her question. All eyes focused on Jenny. She didn't know where to look. "I… I'm sorry if I said something I shouldn't have." She was shocked by the reaction her question had caused. Ill at ease, Jenny fidgeted in her chair. She didn't know why her question would create such a reaction. She'd meant no harm or disrespect. Her cheeks flushed a lovely pink color as she lowered her eyes.

"There's no need to apologize, my dear," Galfrid stated, after a few moments of uncomfortable silence. "They are missing."

"Missing? How long have they been missing?" This piqued Jenny's curiosity.

"They've been missing for about six years now," Galfrid said.

"Funny. Just like my parents," Jenny said matter-of-factly. Everyone at the table, including Devon, turned to Galfrid for answers, but even as he sat and digested the information, he had none to give.

Galfrid looked at Jemma and knew her thoughts wandered in the same direction. A look Jenny didn't miss.

CHAPTER 8

GALFRID

"**P**erhaps you could tell us where you're from?" Galfrid finally broke the heavy silence that descended upon the room and its occupants.

"Well, we're from Morgansville, Alberta."

"That's in Canada," Beth chimed in, wanting to be a part of this conversation.

"Morgansville? The name is unfamiliar to me," Galfrid said.

"And exactly where is this Canada?" Devon's aunt asked.

"It's…" Jenny didn't know how to explain where a large country like Canada was located, especially if they had somehow found themselves in a different world. There was no rational way to tell these people what she suspected had happened to her and Beth. There had to be a way to answer this question without divulging any strange facts. Instead of developing some quirky answer, she looked to Devon for help.

"Perhaps Jenny and Beth could tell us about their hometown rather than having to try and explain its location."

"Yes, that might be easier." Jenny sighed and smiled at Devon. "What would you like to know?"

"Do all the people in your village dress in a similar manner?" Jemma asked. Her bright smile and long, pale hair gave her a youthful appearance.

Jenny looked at her clothes and then at Beth's, and laughed. They did stand out in a crowd of people dressed in elegant finery of jewels and silks. "Yes, I guess they do." Their jeans, shirts, and docks didn't exactly fit in with Wardell's attire. Everything about them screamed different.

"Odd clothing, I must say." Her pale blue eyes gleamed in the candlelit room. There was a certain kind of gentleness about Jemma. A kindness Jenny had rarely encountered.

"I thought the same thing when we first arrived in this village," Beth said, slightly offended by Jemma's remarks.

Jenny glared at Beth. They were, after all, guests in this castle. There was no need to be ungrateful.

"Yes, I suspect you would, but tell me, my dear, how do you find our humble village?" Jemma smiled, unmoved by Beth's remark.

"Different."

"In what way?"

Jenny looked at Devon, who nodded.

"Well, we don't have beautiful castles like this one in our town." Jenny's eyes surveyed with awe the elaborate dining room they now sat in. The large carved wooden table, the upholstered chairs, and the heavy curtains that fell to the floor, and pooled in a tumble of heavy crimson satin, gave credence to the wealth of this castle. The room was designed to impress, and it did its job.

"No castles?" Galfrid asked.

"Nope. None."

"Who rules the village?"

"Elected officials."

"Do you mean to say the people choose their leaders?"

"Yes."

"And it works?"

"Sometimes."

The doors to the dining room opened and servants carrying trays laden with food entered in the nick of time. Jenny took the opportunity to enjoy the fascinating talk going around the room as Galfrid and the other guests regaled them with tales of Wardell and the lifestyle she came to admire. They spoke of battles and of bravery, but the one topic no one seemed to mention was the whereabouts of Wardell's king and queen.

She looked at all the opulence of this room with admiration. When the servants placed trays filled with different meats, potatoes, and vegetables, she couldn't believe she was able to eat all she wanted. She relished the meal, but was still cautious as to how much food she should put on her plate.

She enjoyed the meal immensely. Not only was she full, but there was no one staring at her with disdain. This was the first meal she'd actually been able to enjoy in the past six years. She sat back and felt content. Why? Why was she experiencing such different feelings in Wardell than at home? Could it be she found a new place to call home? No. She had to stop thinking these foolish thoughts. These strangers were fine with her being a temporary guest, but it didn't mean she'd be welcome to move in.

The mood in the room continued to be jovial and uplifting. The ladies spoke of different projects around the kingdom and their children, while the men sat back and enjoyed some spirited talk of wars and games and their weekly hunts. This made for an enjoyable day for two lost girls.

"Father," Devon said when dinner ended. "May we have a word in private?"

"Yes, of course. Please excuse me." Galfrid took leave of his guests.

Devon escorted Jenny and Beth from the room. They made their way to Galfrid's office. Devon nudged the girls through the doorway and followed them into the study. He waited for his father to take a seat behind the dark mahogany desk and tried to find a way to tell his father about the girls' arrival in Wardell.

Galfrid sensed his son's hesitation. "Now then, son, what's troubling you?" Galfrid leaned back in the leather chair.

"Father, when you inquired where the girls were from, well, we weren't exactly forthright." He fidgeted in his chair.

"I don't understand." Galfrid leaned forward. His eyes locked with his son's.

"I failed to reveal many facts since I didn't think it was in the girls' best interest to disclose too much information before the others."

"What are you saying?"

Devon motioned for Jenny to tell his father about their arrival. "If you told my father your tale, he may believe you."

"Okay. Well, we didn't tell you everything about where we came from," Jenny said, beginning her tale.

"You are not from Morgansville?" Galfrid didn't understand where this was going.

"Yes we are, but what we never told you was Morgansville is not a part of this world." Jenny watched Galfrid's reaction.

"Devon, I don't have time for this." The Steward of Wardell attempted to rise but was stopped by Devon's next words.

"Father, please listen to what they have to say. After all, you've traveled through many lands and have you ever seen anyone dressed as these girls are dressed? And have you noticed Beth's hair? No, father, they are not from this realm."

Beth's hand flew to her hair. She didn't know what to say. She loved her layered cut. She pouted.

"Why don't you tell me everything from the beginning?" Galfrid put his elbows on the desk, his interest in their tale more than a little evident.

Jenny relayed their story, beginning with their walk through the catacombs and the disappearance of the glowing door. She didn't mention her aunt or her need to find a new place to live. She also failed to mention the voices she heard. The last thing she wanted was for anyone in this room to think she was deranged for hearing voices, even though the voices she heard guided her to Wardell.

Galfrid looked at Jenny with renewed interest. He took in her features, her brilliant green eyes, her long, dark hair, her full lips and pink cheeks. Jenny shuffled beneath the stare. Unabashed, he continued to study Jenny more intensely than before, rendering the young girl uncomfortable. "So, how did you come to be in Wardell?" More information was needed in order to properly assess this situation.

"We followed the stream," Jenny said. They had to find allies who had the knowledge, and perhaps the means, to help them return to their own world.

"So you entered our town through the meadow?" His eyes took on a faraway look.

"Yes. We went through a meadow and followed the stream through the forest." Jenny kept her encounters with the snake and the magnificent eagle to herself.

"I see." His curiosity piqued. He was about to question her even more, but decided against it.

"Father, they need a place to stay. I thought we could give them shelter until we decide what must be done."

"Yes, yes, by all means. Have the servants prepare two rooms." Galfrid was deep in thought.

"Sir, do you think you can help us find our way back home?" Jenny asked hopefully.

Galfrid looked at Jenny and then at Beth. "I don't know. I will do what I can to help you return to your home, but I cannot make any promises. Devon, we will discuss this further in the morning. In the meantime, I ask that you do not speak with anyone regarding this matter."

"Yes, of course, Father. I'll be right back," Devon told the girls, as he left the office to inform the servants to prepare rooms.

"Sir, have we crossed over into another world? Have you ever heard or known anyone who has done something like this before?" Jenny had to know for sure that this was a parallel world and not some weird dream.

"I have no answer to give you, at least not at this time. I must make some inquiries, and then I may have something to tell you. I ask for your patience and your silence for the time being."

"Of course. Thank you."

"For what, my dear?" Galfrid's smile was easy and charming, much like Devon's smile that stole her heart.

"I want to thank you for giving us a place to stay and for helping us."

"You are most welcome."

The door to the study opened and Devon entered. "Follow me. I'll show you to your rooms."

Devon led the girls out of the office and down a decorated hallway. They walked back to the large staircase. They climbed the stairs to the third floor where they walked down another corridor. Guards were posted at the end of each hallway and came to attention as the three friends passed by. Their attire matched the uniforms they'd seen on the guards standing by the dining room and the study.

Devon stopped and opened the door to the first bedroom. A large canopied bed draped in pale blue sheers faced a wall of windows. On either side of the bed, matching silk coverings concealed a night table. A loveseat decorated in cream and deep blue colors sat near a wall of windows. On the opposite side of the room a white fireplace had been lit.

Draped across the bed, a nightgown and matching robe lay in wait, while on a larger table surrounded by four upholstered chairs clothes were laid out for the room's occupant. This room boasted everything a young girl wanted and needed. Here, no one was in need of anything.

"This is your room, Beth. I hope you'll be comfortable."

"Are you kidding? This is so cool. Thanks, Devon."

"You're welcome. Goodnight, Beth." Devon smiled.

"Goodnight." Beth stepped into the room and looked around, amazed by its beauty.

"Jenny's room is next to yours and mine is across the hall. Please, let me know if you need anything."

"Thanks again, Devon. I'll be fine."

"Very well. Goodnight."

"Goodnight, Beth," Jenny said, with a wink.

Devon led Jenny to the next room. This one, although similar to Beth's, was decorated in pale rose colors. The loveseat boasted cream and burgundy flowers. A fire gave the room warmth and a sense of coming home. Jenny smiled, as a familiarity engulfed her the moment she stepped inside. She approached the table with a pile of clothes that had been laid out for her use. She ran her hand over the upholstery.

The covered nightstand next to the bed had a pitcher of water and a crystal goblet on it. Jenny walked around the room, fascinated by its beauty. She touched the soft robe, and glanced at Devon in appreciation.

"Thank you so much, Devon. I can't tell you how much I appreciate everything you've done for us."

"You are most welcome. It's been a long and trying day. You need your rest."

"Devon, do you think your father will help us find a way home?"

A hopeful look crossed her young features. She wanted to find a way to get Beth back to Morgansville. This wasn't fair to her. She knew Beth would go along with everything for a day or two, but eventually they had to return her to the other world where she belonged.

"I hope so."

"So do I. Goodnight, Devon."

She walked into her room and closed the door. Jenny thought about the day and all that happened to her and to Beth. She looked around the room admiring it for its beauty. What a difference between this and her room at Aunt Nora's! All she had there were a small bed pressed up against one wall and an old dresser that sat against the other wall. But here, in Wardell, she felt like a princess living in a fairytale land. This was something she'd never had the opportunity to experience before.

Here she had the opportunity to live in a castle and stay in a beautiful room. In truth, she never wanted this feeling to end. More than anything, she'd love to be able to make Wardell her new home. Only she didn't know if that were possible.

CHAPTER 9

A CUP OF HOT CHOCOLATE

An hour later, Jenny's eyes opened as sleep eluded her. She looked around the unfamiliar surroundings and felt lost. It took her a moment to realize this wasn't a dream. Moonlight filtered through the curtains allowing her to better view the room. Memories of the day overwhelmed her, but caused a smile to curl her lips.

How wonderful to wake up in such splendor. She didn't have the sinking feeling she usually did whenever she woke up in her small bed in Aunt Nora's house. Jenny lay back against the many down-filled pillows and enjoyed the feel of the crisps sheets. She wondered what time it was. She didn't think she'd slept long, but she also knew there was no way she'd be able to fall asleep again. The excitement raging through her attested to that fact.

She left the comfort of the feather bed and went to the window to admire the amazing night sky. Back home the lights impeded a person's view of the twinkling lights, but in Wardell, a perfect picture of small dots twinkling brightly in the sky was her reward. She looked down and saw hundreds of small lights that seemed to float over the gardens below. She realized they must be fireflies flickering in the darkness. She sat on the sofa and looked out the window for a while longer, thinking how nice it would be to walk through the gardens below. Perhaps a walk might help her relax and fall back asleep.

Her rose colored silk robe covered her small frame perfectly as she placed her feet into the matching slippers. She left her room in search of knowledge where this castle and its occupants were concerned. She hoped to find more information regarding the missing royal couple. Perhaps some portraits of the royal family might disclose something she'd forgotten so long ago.

She left her room and reached the end of the hallway. Two guards came to attention at her approach and nodded as a sign of respect. They allowed her to pass unquestioned. Torches burned brightly in brass wall sconces and lit her way down the marble stairs. She chose a hallway filled with beautiful portraits and stopped in front of each one. She looked at them with such interest, and you might say with a sense of distant familiarity that scared her a little. She continued to study them with appreciation for the beauty represented with each stroke of the artist's brush. She moved from portrait to portrait and then stopped. She gazed at past members of the royal family and wondered at their history. Amazement flooded her with nostalgia when she looked into the eyes of the people captured within the gilded frames.

"Can't sleep?"

Jenny jumped and turned to face Devon. Her heart fluttered at the fright she felt, but also at the sight of her friend. "You scared me," she said, trying to still her beating heart.

"My apologies. I didn't mean to startle you. Can't sleep?"

"No. I guess I'm not used to my surroundings yet."

"Perhaps you're far too excited by all that transpired today."

"That too. What about you?" She asked, glad for his company.

"I was in the mood for a cup of hot chocolate. Would you like to join me?"

"I'd like that very much. Thanks." Jenny saw this as an opportunity to get to know this good-looking guy better. At the same time, she wanted to question him about the royal couple.

"I must warn you, though," Devon said quite seriously.

"About what?" Jenny feared his next words. She didn't know Devon that well, and most of the time she was the brunt of some nasty tricks played by the other kids in her class. So trust didn't come easily to her.

"I intend to question you." Devon's smile reached his blue eyes.

"Question me? About what?" Panic rose from deep inside. Had she somehow done something wrong?

77

"Your life." Devon watched her intently

"Oh." Jenny returned his smile and relaxed. She liked Devon. He was honest and kind, especially with her. "Alright, I'll answer whatever questions I can, but this better be really great hot chocolate or you're the one who's in big trouble."

They entered the largest kitchen Jenny had ever seen. She thought her bedroom was immense, but this was more than three times its size. She was thoroughly impressed by the grandeur of this castle. Never had she thought that one day she would be on an amazing adventure that took her from the cold house she was forced to reside in and bring her to a new world filled with wonders.

She sat here with the son of the Steward of Wardell, waiting for a cup of hot chocolate. Even if she wanted to dream this up, she didn't have this much of an imagination. She never imagined she'd visit a castle and actually spend the night. This was truly a dream come true.

A young woman dressed in a gray tunic, pants, and slippers rushed over to Devon and bowed before him.

Jenny snickered.

"Two of your very best hot chocolates, please."

"Yes, My Lord." She ran to do Devon's bidding.

"Let's sit down." He led her to a large wooden table. Jenny sat across from him. "By the way, I heard that little laugh of yours."

"Sorry." She blushed. The last thing she wanted was to ridicule his way of life.

"Do you find something amusing?" Devon arched an eyebrow as he waited for her reply.

"I've never seen anybody bow to someone else before now."

"Well, my father is a member of the royal family, as am I. The servants bow to show respect for our rank within the castle."

"You don't expect me to bow to you... do you?"

Devon thought for a moment. "And if I did?" A sly smile tugged the corners of his mouth. He enjoyed teasing her. She blushed so easily.

"I'd have to say no thanks."

Laughing, Devon said, "Then I guess I won't ask this of you. But just for your information, if someone doesn't do what is asked of them by a member of the Royal Family, they could face a sentence."

"What kind of sentence?" This bit of news appalled Jenny.

"They could spend a few days, or even weeks, in the dungeons, depending upon their offense against a member of the royal family."

"You're joking!" She looked into his blue eyes and tried to read him. She'd never heard of anything like this. Well, not since the old reigns of European royalty. She read enough stories about them in books at the library.

"No, I am not."

"Then, please don't ask it of me." Jenny couldn't see herself bowing to Devon.

The young servant returned with a silver tray and placed it on the table. First, she placed an earthen mug in front of Devon and after she served Jenny.

"Will there be anything else, Sire?"

"Are you hungry?"

"No, I'm fine."

"That will be all."

They waited until the servant left before Devon spoke again. "Jenny, you mentioned your parents disappeared six years ago." He took a sip from his cup, his eyes holding her stare.

"That's right." Jenny wondered why he'd ask about her parents.

"What happened to them?"

"Why?" Jenny didn't want to answer his question. Every time she thought of her lost parents, she was faced with thoughts that she would have to continue to live with Nora. She still didn't want to face the fact that her parents may be dead. In her heart, she kept hope alive.

"I warned you about my curiosity."

"Yes, you did." Jenny sipped her hot chocolate and grew pensive. "Alright, what would you like to know?"

"What happened to them?" Devon gently asked.

This was a touchy subject, and no one wanted to dive right in and discuss such matters, but when Jenny looked at Devon, she understood he was simply curious.

"I really don't know." Jenny stared at Devon.

"I don't understand."

"I was seven when it happened."

"What happened, Jenny?" Devon prodded her hoping she'd divulge her deepest secrets to him.

"I don't know. I remember being at home... I think we were at home. My parents left for the evening. They were going out to dinner. That was the last time I saw them. They never returned." Tears glistened in her emerald eyes when she looked at Devon who tried to reassure her with a smile.

"You were left alone?"

She wiped a tear that rolled down her cheek. "No. I think I was staying with my aunt and uncle for the night. They were really great back then. We used to play games, watch TV. I loved staying with them."

"Is this the same aunt you now live with?"

"Yes." Jenny tried to remember the events that preceded her coming to live with Nora, but as always, her mind drew a blank. There were so many unanswered questions. She wished she could remember the answers she so desperately wanted, needed.

"Where is your uncle?"

"I think he divorced Nora shortly after my parents disappeared. Aunt Nora took me in. No one really knows where Uncle Rob disappeared to, and even if Nora knew where he was, she'd never tell me."

"Did she ever tell you what happened to your parents?"

"No. She told me they died, but I never believed her."

"Why not? Surely she wouldn't tell you something that wasn't true."

"After Uncle Rob left, she wasn't the same. She hated me... hated everything about me. Maybe she blamed my parents for what happened to her. I just don't know how or when things changed, but they did."

"Did you ever find out what really happened to them?"

"No. All I was told was that they died. She never told me how or where. There never was a funeral so I never found out for sure if she was telling me the truth. Sometimes I think she lied to me just to be mean."

"Why would she do that?"

"I don't know, but—"

"But what?" Devon tried to make Jenny trust him.

"You're going to think I'm crazy."

"No, I won't. Please tell me."

"Okay, but you promise you won't think I'm nuts?"

Devon laughed at her choice of words. "I promise." He even raised his right hand and placed it over his heart, as though taking a solemn oath.

"I can sense them," Jenny said. A faraway look clouded her eyes.

"In what way?"

"I never believed they were dead. I see them in my dreams, and when I walked the catacombs, I heard voices." She spoke the words quickly, wanting the opportunity to divulge her secret thoughts to someone who would listen to her without judgment.

"What kind of voices?"

Jenny took another sip from her mug and continued. "I heard a soft voice telling me to find them. I thought that someone was in trouble, and I wanted to help them."

"Did you ever discover their identity?"

"I think it was my mother's voice I heard, but that's not possible."

"And then what happened?" Devon didn't want to break the momentum.

"I pushed Beth through the door, and that's something I shouldn't have done."

"Well, it's done and there's nothing you can do to change these circumstances." Devon took another sip from his mug.

"I wish I could. She doesn't belong here."

"But you do?"

"I don't know. What's crazy about this whole situation is that I don't feel any regret about being here."

"Jenny, there is no need to feel any remorse at all."

"Yes, there is. If it weren't for me, Beth wouldn't be here. She'd be at home with her family. I'm guilty of bringing her here."

"I understand Beth's predicament, but what about you? You didn't have a good life with your aunt?"

"No, I didn't, but she took me in when I had nowhere else to go. I owe her something."

"Perhaps, but you also have the right to find a better life."

"Maybe I do, but I involved Beth and that's inexcusable."

"Indeed, but I believe she'll be fine. She's strong and resilient, and I know she'll survive this ordeal."

"I just hope she forgives me."

"If she is your friend, she will. Why don't you tell me about your life with your aunt?"

"There's not much to tell. I lived in her house."

"Does she love you at all?"

Jenny laughed. "No. No, she never loved me. I don't think she's capable of loving anyone. She's very bitter, especially after Uncle Rob left her."

"So you don't miss her or your other life?"

Jenny thought for a moment. She thought about her aunt and Mrs. Parker, the students' cruel taunts, and answered Devon quite honestly and sincerely. "No. I can honestly say I don't miss any part of that life."

The young servant girl approached them when there was a lull in the conversation. "Would you care for anything else, sire?"

"More hot chocolate?" He was enjoying their time together and wanted to prolong their conversation.

"Well…"

"Two more hot chocolates," he told the servant girl.

"Yes, sire."

She returned a few minutes later and served the hot chocolate. This time she included some freshly baked scones with whipped butter.

"Thank you." Jenny smiled at the young girl.

She curtsied and returned Jenny's smile.

"Jenny, why do you think you were destined to open that door?" Devon took a scone and broke it. He slathered some butter on it and took a bite.

"I've been thinking about that, and to tell you the truth, I don't know. Nothing makes sense to me."

"Maybe you were sent to Wardell for a reason." He took another bite.

"What possible reason could there be for sending me to this world?"

"I don't know, but something pushed you toward the door, and something prodded you to step over the threshold. I believe things happen for a reason and you need to find out why you were brought to Wardell."

"How can I do that?"

"I'm not sure, but I'd like to help you discover the truth."

"Devon, I don't mean to sound ungrateful, but why are you being so nice to me?"

"Shouldn't I be nice to you?" Devon didn't understand her question. "I like you, and I believe your destiny may lie in this world. If it does, I'd like to help you discover your true path."

"Thanks. I'd like that." She smiled gratefully at her new friend, and then another thought hit her. "But what should I do about Beth?"

"I don't understand."

"She has to go home." Jenny would do just about anything she could to help her friend return to her own world and the life she loved so much.

"Do you know a way home?" He arched an eyebrow at her.

"No, but I'd like to try and find one." She worried her thumb over this latest predicament.

"Would you return to your old life as well?"

There were so many unanswered questions in this world. Where did Jenny fit in? Did she fit in to this life? If she did stay, where would she live? How would she survive? There were far too many ifs. But given the opportunity to stay here rather than going back to Aunt Nora's, Jenny would try to find a place here in Wardell. At least she'd have a chance at a good life. She secretly chided herself for having such strange thoughts. She shook herself back to the present, embarrassed she'd had such crazy thoughts. She took a bite of the scone she now held in her hand.

After what seemed like forever, Jenny looked at Devon. "Honestly? I don't know." She knew she wanted so much more than the life she'd left behind. She wanted a new life, and perhaps opening the door and stepping into this world was the beginning she'd hoped for.

"Then you must discover your heart's true desire. You need to find out where your destiny lies. If I can help you with this endeavor, I will."

"Thank you. I guess I need all the help I can get. Right now, I don't know which way to turn. Everything here is wonderful, and I'd like to know more about Wardell, but at the same time, I'd like to find out why I'm here. I need to know if this is where I really belong."

"I'm sure you'll find out where you belong. I only hope it's here."

Jenny smiled.

They finished their snack, and Devon led Jenny out of the kitchen and back to the stairs. Together, they went to the third floor and stopped in front of her room.

"Devon, I really appreciate everything you've done for us." Jenny looked at him still wondering why someone like Devon felt she deserved to be treated with such kindness. The only friend she'd ever had was Beth, but now she was proud to include Devon on her small list.

"Gratitude isn't necessary, Jenny. I consider you my friend, and as a friend, I'll do everything in my power to help you." Devon's words came from his heart.

"I think you deserve a little gratitude for helping me this way. I only hope I'll find a way home for Beth. She should go back. Well, goodnight Devon." She went into her bedroom and closed the door.

She walked into the lovely room and thought about their conversation. There had to be a reason for her arrival in Wardell. Was it possible her parents had something to do with this world and that was why the voices led her through the catacombs and through the open doorway?

Was her appearance in Wardell a mere coincidence, or did it really have something to do with finding the truth surrounding her parents' disappearance? There had to be a way to discover the truth hiding within the castle walls, and she hoped Devon would be there to help her out.

CHAPTER 10

A DAY IN THE VILLAGE

Morning came with a sound knock on Jenny's door. She sat up with a start and glanced around the room. Memories of the previous day came flooding back to her. She remembered Devon's kindness and the joy she felt at finding a true friend in him. She relaxed with a smile and stretched. She yawned and snuggled deeper into the soft mattress and comforter.

The knock sounded once more.

"Come in."

A young girl walked into the room. "Good morning, miss." She went to the windows and pulled the brocade curtains aside allowing the sunlight to enter and brighten up the room. A soft breeze flowed when she opened the windows.

Jenny left her bed and slipped into her robe. She went to the bathroom and took a warm bath set up by the young maid. When she returned, her bed was made and her old clothes were gone. New ones were carefully laid out for her.

She smiled, admiring the emerald green tunic embroidered with black vines around the collar and hem. This she wore over black tights with matching black slippers.

She picked up a beautiful silver hairbrush, passed it through her dark hair, and tied it into a ponytail with a green and black ribbon. Just as she finished her hair, Beth ran into Jenny's room dressed in similar clothing, only Beth's tunic was a lovely shade of royal blue over dark blue tights and matching slippers. Her freshly washed hair hung down in layers. "You look awesome, Jenny."

"You too. How did you sleep?"

"Great. What about you?" She passed a hand over the material of her tunic in wonder and amazement. She loved the feel of the smooth fabric. It felt so soft next to her skin.

"Not too good." She divulged the time she'd spent with Devon and the chat they'd had.

"The two of you are getting pretty tight." Beth wondered at the relationship developing between Jenny and Devon.

"He's nice. I like him."

"Yeah, I like him too. I think he's really cute," Beth told her in a conspiratorial manner.

"He sure is. Are you ready to go down to breakfast?" She didn't want to discuss her relationship with Devon. Some things were better left unsaid, and in this case, Jenny felt she should keep her feelings and her thoughts to herself.

"Lead the way." Beth followed Jenny to the door. "I'm starving."

At that moment, Devon stepped through his open doorway, wearing a white tunic trimmed with gold braids over black pants tucked into black leather boots. His freshly washed hair was tied at the nape with a white ribbon while his blue eyes shone with appreciation as he looked at the girls.

"Good morning. Did you sleep well?"

"I did," Beth said excitedly. "I've never slept in such a soft bed."

"I'm glad. What about you, Jenny?"

"I slept okay."

Devon looked at her. The dark circles beneath her usually brilliant green eyes belied that statement. "Are you ready for breakfast?" He held out his arms to the girls. Together they went to the stairs and made their way down. A young man opened and held the door for them. Devon gently nudged them through the doorway. "This is the breakfast room," he said.

Jenny went in first and smiled at the glamorous room with the large windows encircling it on three sides. Devon's parents were seated at the round table.

"Good morning." Galfrid returned their smile. "Please join us." He sipped his coffee and motioned for the girls to take a seat at the table.

Jemma smiled at the girls. "How was your first night in our humble castle?" Her pale eyes sparkled in the sun and brightened the room. A thin golden crown sat perched atop her pale hair. She wore a lovely pale pink dress with a golden braided rope around her small waist.

"Great," Beth said with excitement. "The bedroom's incredible. This castle is the best."

Jemma smiled. "And you, my dear?" she asked Jenny.

Jenny looked at Devon. "Very well, ma'am. Thank you for the clothes. That was very kind of you."

"You are most welcome, but please call me Jemma. Ma'am is far too formal and far too elderly." Jemma laughed.

"Okay, Jemma." Her good nature inspired Jenny to relax around Devon's parents. She never let her guard down when meeting new people. She never knew how they'd react to her.

"Now that you've had a good night's sleep, perhaps Devon could take you on a tour of the castle, or even better take you into the village for a proper tour of our town."

"That's a wonderful idea, Mother. Would you like that?" Devon asked the girls.

"Sounds great." Jenny's excitement encouraged him.

"Good, we'll go right after breakfast."

Trays laden with food were brought in, and the girls looked at more food than they ate in a week. They loaded up their plates and enjoyed every mouthful.

After breakfast, Devon led the way to the front doors of the castle. Through the doorway, over the moat, and past the gardens they went. The guards at the next set of gates came to attention as Devon walked by.

Jenny smiled, impressed by the guards. She looked these guards over and noticed the difference in the attire. Unlike the castle guards, these men were dressed in black leather tunics, pants, and leather boots. Large menacing swords hung at their sides and she understood these men were here for the sole purpose of guarding the entrance to the castle grounds.

A small roadway presented itself to them, and Devon led the girls down this road. Tall trees grew on either side of the roadway. Further out, flowers decorated the countryside and caused the area to take on the beauty of a watercolor painting.

Soon the village came into view. They stopped as the town spread out before them and admired the view. The market bustled at this hour. Booths of all sizes and colors lined the square. All around stores and pubs opened their doors for another day of business, but Devon was about to show them how this market boasted so much more than a simple shopping excursion.

They moved through the rows of merchants. Jenny stopped to admire some lovely dress robes when the seller turned and approached a customer. Eyes wide, she didn't understand what she was looking at. She grabbed Devon's sleeve. "That woman! She's a... a..." Jenny didn't know how to finish her sentence.

Devon looked at the woman. "She's an elf."

"You're kidding!" Beth pushed her way through to see this for herself. "OMG! I can't believe it."

Devon looked at the girls and laughed. "I don't understand what all the fuss is about."

"Are you kidding? We've never seen an elf before. This is spectacular. We never even knew they existed, except within the pages of books!" Jenny was in awe of everything she saw.

"But surely there are different types of people living in your world."

"Such as?"

"Well, obviously not elves, but perhaps fairies or gnomes?"

"Nope, nothing."

"What about magick?" He moved his hands like a magician would, but his eyes locked with Jenny's gaze. "Isn't there magick in your world?"

"No. No one can do magick. Gee, can you imagine what it would be like if you could do magick, Jen?"

"Yeah, that would be something." She turned away and looked at the lovely wares the female elf sold.

"Why?" Devon asked when he saw Jenny's nervous reaction to his question.

"Well, I don't really know. If anyone found out we could do magick, we'd become a sideshow." Beth didn't want to offend, but that's how she felt.

"I don't understand."

"It's nothing, Devon." Jenny tried to stop this talk about magick and such. The last thing she wanted was for someone to discover her deepest and darkest secrets. Jenny tried to make light of this topic, but she sensed she didn't fool Devon, who continued to stare at her. He nodded as though saying 'we'll talk later.'

"Very well, shall we?" He let them ahead of him as they walked farther down the row of merchants.

"This is outstanding. I've never seen so many cool things for sale before," Jenny said when she stopped before a booth where a dwarf sold handmade jewelry. "I've never seen anything like this before."

"That goes double for me. How do you explain all the characters we've seen?" She looked to Devon for answers.

"Characters? They are citizens of Wardell, and not characters." Offended, Devon looked from Beth to Jenny trying to gauge her reaction to this insult.

"Devon, I'm sure Beth didn't mean any disrespect. This is new to us. You have to remember in our world, elves, fairies, dwarves and magick only live in pages of fairytale books and stories. Nothing this fantastic lives in our world." Jenny didn't want to upset anyone.

"I didn't mean anything by it. Our world is quite dull compared to this one. Please accept my apology if I said something I shouldn't have." Beth blushed at his odd reaction. "I guess I'm still not used to being in a world so different from ours."

"I have no ill will toward you or what you said," Devon said in his usually jovial tone.

"I'm glad." She shyly moved closer to Jenny, still unsure.

Jenny stood quietly by. Her eyes took on a far off look. Ever since Devon mentioned true magick, she'd left them and entered another plane.

Devon watched her intently when he broke her concentration. "Jenny, is everything alright?" He touched her arm. Her skin was cold to his touch.

"What? Oh yeah, I'm fine."

"Are you sure?"

"Yes. I guess I got lost in my own thoughts for a moment."

Devon continued the tour into the heart of the market square where a crowd gathered and cheered all around them.

"What's going on?" Jenny stepped closer to Devon's side.

"Follow me." He made his way through the throng of spectators without resistance. The crowd parted for the son of the steward and his guests. He nodded his gratitude and moved forward. "I want you to see this display. I hope it will help you understand more about our way of life and our culture."

Groups of men dressed in black outfits entered the circle where the spectators stood. They saw Devon and formed a line in front of him. They raised their swords and saluted him before bowing. The first two men stood poised and ready to begin. They looked at Devon, who nodded. The mock battle began. Blade hit blade. The clang of steel echoed throughout the marketplace. The swordplay continued until the first opponent fell and a winner was declared. Then the next two and the next two fought, until only one fighter was left standing. Once the swordplay ended another group of men came into the circle. The display of hand-to-hand combat took place.

"Isn't this cool?" Beth whispered.

"I'm not sure if I like this. It's so violent."

"This is a part of our culture," Devon said.

"Do you use weapons as well?"

"Yes. I'm well versed in many of the arts of self-defense. Do people in your world use weapons?"

"Yes. The police."

"No one has mock combats?"

"We do have violent sports and competitions. I don't watch them, but they do exist."

"Would you like to leave?"

"No. I'd like to see this. If it's a part of Wardell, I'd like to experience it with you," Jenny said with a blush and a smile.

He relaxed. "Very well."

When the combatants finished their display, a juggler came into the circle. He held three torches, and with a fiery breath, he lit them. The audience clapped. The man bowed. He wore what Jenny considered to be striped pajamas, and began to rotate the flaming torches. Round and round the flames went.

Jenny watched in awe. She thought the spinning of the torches was too fast not to burn a hand, but the juggler seemed unaffected by the heat of the flames. Instead, the man fanned the torches into a full circle. Round and round it went only to break apart as he added another. He stopped when the flames had extinguished. He then began by lighting a single torch. He expelled another fiery breath, and within seconds the flame turned into a dragon's head that floated over the crowd and disintegrated.

The audience clapped and whistled. The man then sent a bouquet of flowers to disperse over the spectators. He bowed to the people. The girls laughed as the juggler continued to entertain them. All too soon the spectacle ended. People threw gold coins at the man who bowed and then collected his prizes. He walked around the crowd, hoping to collect a few more coins for his pocket. He went back into the circle to collect all the gold pieces that littered the stone floor. He smiled as he tried to collect every piece of gold.

"Shall we?" Devon said, wanting to continue the tour of the village. There were still things to see.

Just as they were about to leave, the juggler looked directly at Jenny. He approached her. From thin air, he produced a pink rose. He kissed the flower and handed it to her. With a bow, he retreated.

Jenny smiled and smelled the rose. "That was so sweet." Her eyes followed the strange man. This was quite an honor for her since no one had ever given her anything like this before. She was thrilled.

"Indeed." Devon looked from the juggler, who suddenly disappeared from view, to Jenny who showed Beth her prize. The air grew heavy. "We should return to the castle," Devon said as he raised his eyes toward the sky. He shuddered.

"Do we have to? This is so cool."

"Yes, it is time."

Devon led the girls through the market. From time to time they stopped and admired something a vendor sold. All too soon, the castle loomed ahead of them. He led them inside. Heaviness hung over them like an umbrella. Something hung in the air, and this worried Jenny and Devon more than either would admit.

"Are you alright, Devon? You got so quiet."

He simply smiled at her and led the way into the dining room for dinner.

CHAPTER 11

MAGICKAL JENNY

The hour grew late and Jenny was restless. She tossed and she turned in the feather bed. She thought back to the day they'd enjoyed with Devon. They were having such a good time and she was given a lovely flower, but the look on Devon's face made her wonder if something was amiss.

She turned on her side and pulled the comforter over her, but nothing she did allowed her to float away into a world of wonderful dreams. Her mind returned to the expression she saw on Devon's face when the juggler gave her a rose. She'd asked him if there was a problem, but he just smiled and led them back to the castle. She didn't understand why he behaved this way. There had to be a reason, but Devon refused to tell her anything.

She tossed and turned some more. This wasn't working. She was far too wound up to sleep. She needed something else. She needed some answers. She gave up trying to sleep and left the bed. She walked around the room, went to the window, and looked out at the gardens below. She returned to the bed and put on her robe. A walk around the castle was what she needed. Tomorrow she'd ask Devon if there was a library. At least when sleep eluded her she'd have a book to read.

Jenny left her room and descended the stairs. This time she turned right, wanting to explore an unknown part of the castle. She had just passed another corridor when she heard his voice.

"We must stop meeting like this."

Jenny turned around and smiled at Devon. "Can't sleep?"

"No. What's your excuse?"

"I was wondering if there was a library here. I'd like to borrow a book."

"Of course. I'll take you there. Jenny, is something troubling you?"

"No, I'm fine. But I was going to ask you the same question." Her thoughts jumped to their earlier discussion of magick, and she wondered if he'd discovered her secrets. Was that what troubled him? If he realized what she was that might affect the way he looked at her. She couldn't deal with his not wanting to have her around. She worried he'd want her to leave the castle.

"That's what you told me earlier, and I didn't believe you then, and I'm sorry to say, I still don't believe you." Devon tried to encourage trust.

Jenny feigned a smile. More than anything she wanted to tell Devon the secret she harbored, but she feared his reaction. No one knew about her deepest, darkest secrets, and perhaps it was best if she kept them locked up inside as she'd always done. There were some things she couldn't divulge no matter how much she liked the person who inquired about them.

"Jenny, I hope you know I'm your friend. If you need someone to listen, you can trust me to be here for you."

"I… it's nothing." For a brief moment, Jenny contemplated telling Devon the truth, but decided against it.

"Jenny, I know we only just met, but I consider you my friend. I'm here if you need me."

"Why are you being so nice to me?"

"I don't understand."

"No one, except for Beth, has ever been this nice to me."

"I like being nice to you, believe it or not." He paused. "I do care." He moved in closer sensing her volatile emotions.

"Is that the only reason?" She had to know the truth. Her heart fluttered at his proximity to her.

"I'm sorry. I don't know what it is you wish me to say."

"I want the truth."

"Jenny, I'm not lying to you." Devon was slightly offended by her words and stepped away.

"I'm sorry. I didn't mean to hurt your feelings."

"Perhaps if you told me what's troubling you, I might understand what it is you want from me." Devon pushed the door open and let Jenny inside first. He went to the wall and lit the torch in the sconce. He stood in the center of the room, and with a glance, a large crystal and gold chandelier descended. A fiery breath escaped his lips and touched each candle nestled within. One by one, they sprang to life, illuminating the room. He smiled at the shocked expression on Jenny's face.

"I did mention this was a world filled with magick, did I not?" He looked at Jenny and laughed.

"You did, but I didn't know that you could perform magick."

"I don't perform magick. I'm a wizard. Magick is what I am, not what I do."

"Aren't you afraid of using your powers?" Jenny was intrigued by this turn of events.

"Why should I fear them? They are a part of me... of who I am."

"I guess." Jenny walked around and looked at all the books lining the wooden shelves in an attempt to ignore all she'd witnessed. She slowly read each title. She wanted to be truthful with him, but she feared any repercussions her confession might bring on.

Devon walked over to the other side of the library and went to one of the shelves. He pulled out a large leather-bound book and brought it to Jenny. He placed it in her hands. Jenny took the book and read the title. *"Magick and Wizardry: The Legend.* Why this one?" Was her secret that obvious? She tried to keep this side of her all too herself.

"I think you'll find this book quite interesting. In fact, I guarantee it." Devon smiled at her.

"No, I don't think so." She tried to give it back to him. "I can't see myself reading something like this."

"Do me the courtesy of at least pretending to read it," Devon said, but refused to take the book from her outstretched hand.

"I prefer to be honest with you. I think I'd rather take this one." She held up a book and read the title. *"Warwick Castle: A History."*

"Why this book?"

"I don't know. It seems... interesting."

"Take them both, and please read them. Once you start reading the book I gave you, you'll understand why I want you to read it." The book held the answers to some of the questions burning deep within her heart. Perhaps she could then voice her own secret.

"I'm not sure I want to understand anything."

"Have faith in my judgment."

Jenny looked at the young man who'd befriended her in a land where nothing made sense. She trusted him, that much she knew, but should she trust him or anyone with the secrets that had been buried for the past six years? She wanted to talk to someone about this, but she feared losing her friend.

"Let's take a walk." Devon extinguished the candles with a single breath and led Jenny out of the library. They returned to the hallway where the marble staircase was.

"How about a cup of hot chocolate?" Jenny tried to act as though nothing out of the ordinary had taken place in the library, even though the books she now held belied those thoughts.

"I happen to know where we can get a great cup of hot chocolate."

"Lead on." Jenny grinned, even though her demeanor remained distressed.

Devon led her to the table they'd shared last night, and almost instantly a servant came over and bowed before them.

"Two hot chocolates."

"Yes, sire."

A moment later, the young servant girl returned and placed two steaming mugs of hot chocolate and a plate of freshly baked cookies on the table. Jenny smiled and thanked her. The servant quickly retreated.

"Now then, why don't you tell me what's troubling you?" Devon stared at her.

"It's nothing." Jenny looked away, ashamed of her own thoughts. She was afraid of something that lived within her heart, and she realized he would do whatever it took to draw that out of her. She wanted to tell him everything.

"Oh good. I love to hear talk about absolutely nothing. I find it most intriguing."

Jenny looked at Devon and laughed. "I don't know what you want me to say."

"Just tell me what's in your heart. I know there's something you wish to discuss with me, but you're afraid."

"I…" How could she be honest with him? This was something she couldn't tell anyone. She'd kept this to herself for so long, she didn't know if she should trust anyone. Even Beth wasn't privy to this secret.

"Jenny, what is it you fear?"

"The loss of your friendship."

Devon didn't know what to say. He stared long and hard at her, and she knew he sensed the sorrow within. "How could you think you'd lose my friendship if you told me what is troubling you?"

"I think you'll see me differently and maybe even hate me for it."

"I could never hate you. Please, tell me what it is you are hiding."

"I'm afraid." Tears threatened to fall from her eyes. More than anything she wished she could trust Devon. She liked him so much and she wanted to be closer to him, but what if he was repelled by her secret? What if he threw her out of the castle? What would happen to her and to Beth? So many disturbing thoughts floated around her brain causing her more distress than necessary.

Devon leaned in and looked at her. His eyes were kind and gentle as though he wanted to be the one to help her to learn to trust again. She gazed into the brightest blue eyes she'd ever seen and was drawn by them.

"Jenny, do you know why I want you to read that book?" He pointed to the leather-bound book.

She took a sip of the hot chocolate and swallowed before she even answered. "No, not really."

"Are you certain?"

She looked into his blue eyes and sensed he could read her thoughts, but she shied away from revealing her secrets. "I don't know anymore. So much has happened and I'm afraid."

"I guarantee there's nothing you can say that will make me take my friendship away. On my honor, I promise you this."

"You say that now, but when you hear what I have to say you'll treat me the same way Aunt Nora and the kids at school do."

"Were the other students mean to you?"

"Yes. They used to make fun of me."

Jenny said it so quietly Devon had to strain to hear her words.

"Why would they do that?"

"Well, Aunt Nora never spent any money on me, so I had a limited amount of clothes."

"And in your world this is important?"

"Very. The girls laughed at me for wearing the same thing every day. And my teacher was cruel. She took every opportunity to humiliate me in front of the other students."

"Why would she do that?"

"Her actions seemed to please her best friend, who unfortunately for me, was Aunt Nora."

"What about Beth?" he asked lightly, but Jenny saw his eyes harden. She assumed it was due to her secret.

"She's the best. She befriended me on my first day at Morgansville Elementary School. We're like sisters. I never would have survived school if it wasn't for her friendship."

"I can tell she cares very deeply for you."

Jenny smiled.

"Does she know this horrible secret you bear?"

"I didn't say it was horrible." Jenny looked at Devon.

"No, you didn't, but your silence leads me to believe that it must be horrible. If you refuse to share it with anyone, and you fear my reaction, then I must assume it is a dreadful secret."

A tear slid down her cheek.

He felt contrite. He hadn't meant to make her cry. He only wanted to help her say the words. "Jenny, please tell me what you're afraid of."

She looked at him. "Devon, this isn't easy for me."

"Only you can make the decision to trust me. I can't do it for you."

"I know, but if you start hating me because of it, well, it'll be your fault. I'll blame you." Jenny wiped her tears away.

Devon laughed. "I could never hate you."

"Fine. I'll take your word for it. Here goes nothing." She took a deep breath and tried to steady the trembling of her hands. She looked into Devon's eyes hoping he'd still like her. "I think I can do magick." She whispered the words, dreading the thought of being overheard by the servants.

A heartfelt laugh escaped Devon's lips when he saw the seriousness marring her features. He didn't mean to laugh, but he couldn't help himself. "You think you can do magick?" Devon finally asked when his laughter subsided.

"Shh. I don't want anyone to hear this."

"Why not?"

"Well…"

"Jenny, there's nothing wrong with magick. I have magick in my soul. I've shared it with you. Why are you afraid of your gift?"

"It's not a gift, Devon. Don't you understand? I'm even more different than I was told." She couldn't bear the thought of losing Devon's friendship.

"No, you're not different, you're special… very special. Never forget this. You can't allow anyone to make you feel less than you truly are."

"That's easy for you to say, but if anyone, including Nora ever found out I was capable of doing magick, my life would become a living nightmare."

"Only if you allowed it to become anything less than the kind of life you wish it to be."

"You don't understand. No one I know can do magick."

"Then perhaps you should consider staying in Wardell, where magick is accepted and revered."

"We can't stay here."

"I agree with you on only one point. Beth must return to her own world."

"What about me?"

"I'm not certain, but perhaps you are meant to stay here with us."

"What do you mean?" Devon's words piqued Jenny's interest. She wanted to hear more.

"Think about it. You have magick in your soul. The door only opened for you. You seem to be quite comfortable here, and I think you'd be happier living in Wardell than if you return to your aunt's house."

Jenny thought for a moment. "Where would I live?"

"You could stay with us in the castle." Hope lit Devon's eyes as he made her consider his words and his invitation.

"Are you sure I'd be welcome?" She feared no one would want her now that she told Devon about her magickal side. The lack of acceptance and the discovery of her secrets were something she spent her entire life fearing. This was something she spent her entire life fearing. Discovery was something she feared even more than Aunt Nora or Mrs. Parker. She feared discovery even more than she feared the other kids in her class and their cruel taunts.

"I cannot answer for everyone, but I know my parents and you'd be most welcome. At least you now have choice. Don't waste it." Devon watched the emotions flicker across her face.

Fear and delight shone in her eyes.

Was he being honest? Was there a place for her in this world? Could this be the beginning of a new life for her? Could she consider staying in this world, or should she fear making such a big decision. Nothing had ever been easy for her, and this decision was no different. If she stayed here, she'd never be able to search for her parents. Perhaps it was time to put that part of her life to rest.

She didn't know what to do. Well, at least she didn't have to make a decision right now. She could think about it. She tried to quell her excitement. She suffered so many disappointments in her life, and her greatest fear was to believe in something or someone and then having that trust thrown back in her face. She spent the past six years guarding her heart, and now she was in a different world with people she really cared about.

She really wanted to believe in Devon. As she gazed into his bright blue eyes, she sensed his honesty. Maybe it was time to start trusting someone, and maybe that someone could be Devon.

But what about Beth?

CHAPTER 12

THE SEARCH

The next morning, Jenny walked into Beth's room and found her crying. A lump stood in the back of her throat at the sight of her best friend's tears. This was her fault alone. Why had she insisted they open that door? It was her need for adventure that put them in a distant land with no way home.

"Beth, please don't cry. Everything will work out." Jenny walked over to the bed, sat down, and waited.

"I don't know, Jen. I want to go home. I don't belong here." She tried to push the tears away, but they kept falling down her dampened cheeks.

"I know you don't."

"Can you tell me when we'll be going home?"

"I wish I could, but I can't, at least not yet."

"We can't stay here any longer. We have to go back to our own world."

"Beth, I know this'll sound crazy to you, but I don't know if I want to go back." Jenny hoped Beth would understand her need to find a better life.

"What are you saying?"

"It's weird, but I think I belong here."

"No, you don't. You're just saying that because here you're treated better than you are treated back home. You're not thinking straight." Beth feared losing her best friend.

"Is there anything wrong with wanting a better life?" Jenny asked. "Shouldn't I find my own happiness no matter where I find it? Don't you think I should have the same opportunity as everyone else?"

"Of course I want you to be happy, but make sure you're doing this for the right reason, and not as a means of escaping the other world."

"I know it's hard for you to understand, but ever since our arrival, I've been at peace. I've never felt this happy before. Doesn't that tell you something?"

"I guess, but, Jen, I have a home and I have great parents. I miss them. I even miss my little brother, Josh, go figure. I'd like to see the little troll again."

Jenny laughed. "I know."

"Mom's probably having a fit by now. It's not right to put her through this." More tears trickled down her reddened cheeks.

"Devon's trying to help us."

"But what can he do?"

"He's gonna talk to his dad. Galfrid might be able to help us find a way home."

"He hasn't so far. What makes you think things will be different today?"

"I don't know, but Devon will do everything he can to help you get back home."

"I don't want to lose you."

"You'll never lose my friendship." Jenny's eyes glistened as her tears threatened to spill over. They hugged each other as a knock sounded on the door.

"That must be Devon," Jenny said, wiping her tears.

"Come in." Beth called out, drying her own. "I don't want Devon to see us this way. Are my eyes all puffy and red?

Jenny laughed. "No. You're beautiful."

Devon walked in and immediately noticed the girls' tearstained faces. "How are you feeling, Beth?" Today, he wore a chocolate brown tunic embroidered with a copper braid over dark pants. His long hair hung past his shoulders, while his blue eyes sparkled.

"I'm alright… I guess."

"I spoke with my father."

"And?" Jenny asked hopefully.

"I think I may be able to help. If we can find the door that brought you here, there may be a way to open it." Devon smiled at the girls.

"But how do we find it?" A small sense of hope crawled through Beth.

"We retrace your steps."

Jenny looked at Beth and smiled. Maybe they'd finally find a way back home. If not, at least Beth would have something constructive to do. She wanted to help Beth return, but now Jenny would have to make a choice. Should she stay in Wardell, or should she return to a life with no future? If someone had asked her this before, she wouldn't have hesitated to say she'd stay here, but now that she was faced with this decision, her thoughts went back to her parents. If they were in the other world, she should return and try to find out what happened to them. After all, the voices she heard had come from the catacombs. Perhaps they were trapped somewhere within the vast catacombs. If she stayed here, she'd never be able to search for them. She'd have to make up her mind before they found the door.

"So, when do we leave?" Beth asked with a smile.

"Right now, if you're up to it," Devon said.

"Could it be right after breakfast? All of a sudden, I'm starving." Beth smiled at her friends, feeling better than she'd felt since their arrival in Wardell.

Devon laughed. "Of course. Shall we?" He held out his arms to his friends.

"I guess you'll be glad to be rid of us," Beth said.

"On the contrary. I will miss you both very much."

Beth laughed. "You're just saying that to be nice."

"No. I've truly enjoyed our time together. Your world fascinates me." Devon spoke honestly to the girls. He looked at Jenny; it felt as though she could read his thoughts. She shrugged her shoulders; she still didn't know if she would leave or if she'd stay. She knew she'd miss Devon terribly if she left.

After breakfast, Devon led them to the front gates.

Galfrid stood just beyond the drawbridge. "So I take it you're going to try and find your way home?" He was handsome in a light grey tunic with black and silver braids on each shoulder. His hair was tied back with a silver ribbon.

"Yes," Beth said. "I hate the thought of my mom worrying about me. I want her to know I'm safe."

"I hope everything works out for you." Galfrid smiled at Beth. "It was a pleasure meeting you." He took Beth's hands in his and gave them a reassuring squeeze.

"Thank you for everything." Beth's sincerity showed when addressing the Steward of Wardell.

"You are most welcome, my child. Safe journey to you."

"We'd better go." Devon walked past the beautiful gardens, through the gate, and onto the roadway.

It was nice to see Beth so happy. Jenny was thrilled that Devon had the opportunity to see the real Beth.

"Jen, I can't thank you enough for this adventure."

"You're not mad at me anymore?"

"I was never really angry with you. I was just scared, but now that I'm going home, I feel a lot better."

"Beth, you do understand this is a long shot. There's a chance we won't find the door, and even if we do, we'll have to find a way to open it." Jenny felt bad telling her this, but she thought it was better than getting her hopes up and then not finding the door.

"There may be a way," Devon said.

"How?"

"First we must find the door." He kept his voice light so as not to worry them.

At the village gates, Devon waited for Jenny and Beth to show him the next step of the journey.

"This is up to you. I don't know where you were when you arrived."

The girls looked around and tried to remember their journey into Wardell. The forest loomed in the distance. They knew where they were, but the exact location was still unknown to them.

"I think we came out over there," Jenny said, pointing to the right side of the forest.

The darkened woods frightened the girls as memories of giant snakes and bewitched flowers overwhelmed them. They didn't want to go through that again. The only difference was that Devon was with them, and he gave Jenny a sense of strength she'd never felt before. With him, they were safe. Jenny didn't seem as nervous as she had before she'd met him.

"Then let's start there." Devon took their arms and led them into the woods. He stopped and waited.

"What's wrong?" Jenny asked.

Devon motioned for the girls to wait while he looked around the forest. He went into the forest as Jenny and Beth stood on the outskirts waiting to find out if it was safe for them to enter. A few minutes ticked by and Devon returned.

He smiled at the worried look upon the girls' faces. "We will enter here."

They entered the woods and it felt as though the dense trees surrounded them. Large roots cropped up out of the ground and crawled toward patches of sunlight beaming through the tops of the trees. The girls watched in fascination as the forest came to life once more.

"Can you tell me which direction you came from?"

"We followed the stream."

"Alright, I'll take you there."

When they reached the stream, Jenny and Beth looked around, but everything seemed the same to them. No matter which direction their eyes traveled, the majestic trees blocked their view. "Nothing looks the same, and, yet, everything looks exactly the same."

"I was just gonna say the same thing," Beth said.

"Don't worry; we will do this one step at a time. How did you arrive at the stream?" Devon forced them to remember their steps.

"Well, we're doing this backwards, so it's a little bit hard to figure out."

"How far up the stream did you walk?"

"I'm not sure," Jenny said.

"Alright. Let's follow the stream for a while. Perhaps you'll recognize the area when you see it."

They kept their eyes open for something, anything that would spark familiarity. The forest seemed denser. Nothing was familiar.

"I don't recognize anything, Devon. This is hopeless."

"No, it isn't. Take your time. Is there anything you can tell me about the meadow you were in?" Devon tried to draw all the information he could from the girls.

"The wild flowers," Jenny said, after a couple of minutes.

"There are a lot of flowers growing throughout the countryside. Can you be more specific?"

"Jenny, remember the flowers?" Beth asked, as thoughts of the spells the singing flowers cast upon them came to mind.

"What about the flowers?" This piqued Devon's curiosity.

"They were shaped like fancy colored bells."

"Were they blue?"

"All colors," Jenny said. "Oh, and... um... they seemed to sing. Please don't think we're crazy, but their song took over our movements. They tried to force us into the path of a giant snake that followed us into the forest."

"Giant snake?" Devon understood. He maintained a strong vigil and simply said, "I think I know where you were. Come on." Devon took the lead. Another hour and the forest was behind them. Up ahead was a lovely meadow where colors abounded within the expanse of the countryside greeted the travelers.

"This looks familiar," Beth said. "I can smell the flowers from here." Beth looked around, happy they'd found the meadow

"Let's go." Jenny wanted to hurry. Her excitement at finding the door and a way home for Beth was uppermost on her mind. She was ready to enter the meadow, but stayed by Devon.

* * * *

"Wait. We have to be very careful from here." Devon walked into the meadow. He kept his eyes open for trouble. He sensed they weren't alone, but he didn't want to scare the girls. His father had warned him the Dark One knew of Jenny's presence in Wardell. He closed his eyes and said, "May slumber render you harmless to those who would hear your deadly song." He blew on his hand and a sprinkling of colored powder floated across the meadow like a rainbow shower. Slowly the petals closed, as sleep overtook them. Jenny and Beth looked at each other, and then they turned their gaze on Devon who smiled at them.

Galfrid told him how to find the door, but he wasn't able to help them anymore than that. "Jenny, I think there's something you need to know."

"What?" Worry creased her brow, but her eyes never left Devon's.

"We'll never find the door unless you truly want to find it." It was time to tell her the truth.

"I don't understand. What do you mean, unless I want to find it?"

"You're the key. You've always been the key. Now you must decide whether you want to return to your old life, or if your heart's desire is to stay in Wardell."

"I don't understand. What key?"

"The door will appear if you truly need for it to appear. If you don't want to return, the door may not appear. You have control over its appearance or disappearance. Everything depends on you."

"But how that that be? I can't control anything."

"Yes, you can. Now you have a decision to make. Do you want to go back or not?"

"I want Beth to go back, but as for me?" She thought for a moment. "I'm not sure."

"You must decide. Without your decision, the door will never appear."

"Not necessarily," a baritone voice replied from behind.

A shudder waltzed through Devon who remembered, hated, and somewhat feared, the owner of that voice. He'd been warned about the evil one's presence, but had foolishly hoped the Dark One wouldn't find them here.

They turned toward the voice. A tall man with long platinum hair stood only feet away from them. He was dressed in a long and dark flowing cloak over dark clothing. He stood in place of the door. A strange smile curled his lips that caused a ripple to course through the three friends. Emotionless dark eyes centered on the girls. His gaze traveled over both of them.

Devon, on the other hand, worried this man would cause them trouble... trouble they didn't need. After all, he'd sworn revenge against those living in Wardell castle, and Devon hoped this wouldn't be the beginning of trouble for Wardell.

CHAPTER 13

MAELDOI

The stranger was intent on his approach, but Devon intercepted him before he reached his goal. Blue eyes locked with the man's dark gaze, but what caught everyone's attention was the staff he held in his hand, a silver walking stick with a large emerald sitting within the metal. The sun touched the top of the walking stick causing the green stone to shine in a menacing way.

"What do you want, Maeldoi?" Devon demanded.

"Aren't you going to introduce me to your delightful friends?" A wicked smile crept over his features.

"No."

"Devon." Jenny went over to the man called Maeldoi.

"Stay back. I'll take care of this." Devon put his arm out to discourage Jenny's approach.

"Good day to you. I am Maeldoi." The man brushed past Devon, almost knocking him down.

"Hello, I'm Jenny and this is Beth." Jenny wondered about his identity. His presence disturbed Devon, and she wondered why.

Maeldoi looked at both girls. He turned toward the lovely, dark-haired girl with the brilliant green eyes.

"What brings you to the Siren's Meadow?" Maeldoi asked, staring at Jenny. His stare upon her so intense, she shuffled.

"We have business here, Maeldoi. Leave us be."

"Careful, boy. You may find you've met your match."

"You will never be my match, Maeldoi. Now, remove yourself from my sight."

"You are trying my patience, boy." He smiled wickedly, anger colored his pale and aging face.

"Where's Ringwar? Is she still hiding out until you've done what you've been trained to do?" Devon smiled, trying and succeeding in raising the man's fury.

Maeldoi took a step forward, but Jenny placed herself between them. He stared with renewed interest at the girl before him. A sly smile curled his thin lips. "Are you seeking the door between our worlds?" he asked with a wry smile, trying to earn the girl's trust.

"Yes, we are," Beth chimed in, never dreaming that evil stood so close to them.

"And who is returning to the other world?" He tried to keep his tone friendly.

"Jenny and I are," Beth answered before Devon could stop her.

"I see." He thought for a moment and let his eyes travel over Beth. "Perhaps I could assist you."

"Don't bother, Maeldoi. We'll find the door ourselves," Devon said quickly before Beth shared more information.

"Perhaps, but I must warn you, Devon, if I so choose, I'll do everything in my power to stop the door from being opened." His eyes rested on Jenny.

"Can he do that?" Beth asked fearfully.

"Yes," Devon stated irritably.

"Why would you do that?" Jenny wondered what was going on between Maeldoi and Devon. She sensed the animosity.

"I don't want to see you leave." Another sly smile tugged Maeldoi's thin lips.

"Why not? You don't even know me." Jenny didn't understand what was going on here.

"I may not know you, but I know of you," Maeldoi responded wickedly.

"I don't understand." Jenny looked to Devon for an answer.

"In time, my dear, you will."

"What's that supposed to mean?" Why would a man she'd never met try to stop her from returning to her world? Who was he and how did he know her? There were so many unanswered questions.

Without uttering another word, Maeldoi turned, his dark cloak floating like and ominous cloud all around him. Much to everyone's surprise, the man vanished in a puff of black smoke. Beth and Jenny looked at each other and then at Devon for some answers.

"That's impossible!" Beth cried out. She shook her head in an attempt to stop her eyes from playing tricks on her? "How could he do that?"

"Many strange things can happen in Wardell." Devon's words were truthful, but his eyes continued to scan the area for signs of the wizard's return.

"Like what?"

"It doesn't matter, Beth." Jenny wanted to keep her secret a secret. "What matters is finding a way to leave Wardell and going home."

"That's true, Jenny, but once we find the door, and I want you to tell me what's going on here."

Jenny laughed. "Sure, but first let's find the door."

Devon led the way. He calculated the approximate location of the door based on where the siren's flowers bloomed this time of year. They had to reach the door before Maeldoi, or even worse, Ringwar returned.

"What about this area?" Devon asked. The soft tune of the sirens' song spread over the area. Slowly the petals shook and released their exotic songs.

"It looks familiar. It also sounds familiar." Jenny tried to figure out if this was the right location. "What do you think, Beth?"

"I don't know. Everything looks the same to me."

The gentle song of the sirens rose from the flowers and touched them. Would their song take over their movements once again?

Devon stepped forward and cast his spell upon the flowers before they ensnared the girls. Slowly, the flowers closed their petals and slept.

"Devon, how do we know if this is the right place?" Jenny asked.

"Only you can produce the door."

"I… I don't understand."

"The only way to summon the door is for you to want to return to your own world," Devon said seriously.

"But I found the door without even knowing about this world."

"I understand, but from what you've told me, you wanted to leave your old life behind. If finding another world helped you begin a new life, then the door freed you to pursue your dreams. You are the key to the door's appearance and its disappearance."

"So what you're saying is that I made the door appear because I hated my life?"

"Actually, yes, I would say that's how everything came to be. The door has been dormant for many years. It lay dormant until you approached it. Your feelings brought life and magic back into the door."

"So what happens if I don't want to go back to my old life again?"

"Jenny, don't even joke about this." Beth stared at her friend.

Jenny realized Beth expected her to come to her senses. Once they were out here and faced with the choice of going home or staying here, Beth believed she would choose the right thing and return to her own world. But Jenny wasn't convinced that was the right thing to do.

She looked at her friend. "I'm not joking, Beth." Jenny had never been more serious in her life. The thought of never having to return to Nora's house filled her with joy.

"What are you saying?" Beth's incredulity was written on her face.

"I'm not sure I want to go back and live with Aunt Nora." The more she said the words, the more she wanted to stay here and never see Nora or Mrs. Parker, or the other students ever again. The thought made her smile. She knew what she had to do, and she didn't think anyone, including Beth, would change her mind.

"But you have to go back."

"Why? No one wants me. There, I'm only in the way. You know this as well as I do. There's nothing left for me back in Morgansville."

"What makes you think this place will be any better?" Beth asked in desperation, as the fear of losing her best friend to a different world overwhelmed her.

"I don't know if it'll be better, but it can't be any worse." A chance for a different life stood before her. She craved a life where happiness was hers, and maybe Wardell was the right place to start a new life. "I'd like to give it a try, and I want you to be happy for me."

"Where will you live?"

"She'll live with us in the castle. My parents would love to have you stay with us," Devon said.

"Okay, but what about this Maeldoi character. He seems kind of mean."

"I don't know what he wants, but I'm sure he's already forgotten about me." Jenny tried to be brave, but even she didn't believe her own words.

"Beth, do not fear for your friend. I will protect her," Devon said with conviction.

"No, this isn't right. How am I supposed to go back home and tell everyone you're now living in a castle in a parallel world? They'll lock me up for sure."

Jenny laughed. "It won't be easy, but it's what I have to do. You don't have to tell anyone anything."

"Yeah, right. What if Nora wants to know where we've been and where you are right now? What do I tell her? What do I tell my parents? They'll want to know where we've been. Look how long we've been missing."

"I guess I never thought about it."

"Well, I have."

Jenny realized that Beth couldn't return alone and face all of the questions people would ask. She turned to Devon. "Maybe she's right. I can't expect her to lie for me. I should go back with her and try to explain this situation."

"No, you cannot. You see, you're the key, and now that Maeldoi has met you, you won't be safe anywhere except in Wardell."

"What are you talking about?"

"I can't tell you anything more, but, Beth, you need to return to your own world. I don't know what you should tell

Jenny's aunt, but you'll have to think of something to say in order to appease her curiosity."

"Like what?"

"I don't know, but she can't leave, at least not yet. Tell her aunt that Jenny's found a new home with people who care about her, and as soon as she's settled, she'll contact her and tell her all about her new life."

"Devon, I'm not sure I understand any of this," Jenny said.

"I know, but you'll have to trust me."

"Jenny, no. You can't believe you'd be happier living in this world."

"Why not?"

"Well... I... I don't know. This just doesn't feel right. After all, you've got a home."

"No, Beth. You have a home and you need to return to that home as soon as we find the door. But as for me, I'd like to stay here, at least for a little while longer. For some strange reason, I think I belong here and I need to find out why I'm feeling this way."

"You're serious?"

"I am. Ever since I found the door, I've had a desperate need to open it. Now, I have a need to discover my true self. Can you understand that?"

"I guess." Beth didn't want to understand, but she did.

"Go home, Beth. I don't care if you tell Nora anything about this, but as for me, I need to find out what's happening. I hope you can understand this."

Beth looked at her friend, and then at Devon. "I don't know what to say, even though I understand your need for a better life, but I hope you're not making a terrible mistake." Beth looked away from her friend and breathed deeply. After a moment, she relented. "I think you need to stay here and find your own happiness. I'll miss you. I can't be selfish."

"Thanks for understanding, Beth." She hugged her friend.

"Devon, I'm going to trust you to take care of my friend. She's as special as they come," Beth said sincerely.

"On my honor, I will look after her."

"I'm glad. Okay. So, how do I get home?"

"Jenny's the only one who can produce the door."

"And how do I do that? I don't want to go back to Aunt Nora's."

"That's something I don't know," Devon said with worry. "There must be another way to produce this door."

"But I want to go home," Beth said, stressing the point once more.

"And I really want you to go home. Don't worry, we'll figure this out," Jenny told her sincerely.

"How? I'm not sure I understand what's going on here."

"Join the club, but I believe there's a way."

"If you truly want the door to appear and take Beth home, it may be enough to make the summons."

"Do you think so?"

"No. It doesn't work that way." Maeldoi appeared once more in all his evil glory.

They turned and faced him. He stood still and held the walking stick in his pale hand. His dark cloak blew in the breeze, causing an ominous sight.

"What do you want?" Devon demanded. It was a mistake to have anything to do with the wizard. "Leave us be, Maeldoi."

He raised his staff and the door appeared. "There you go." His smile chilled Devon's blood.

Jenny didn't know what to make of this man. What was he up to? She pushed her bad thoughts aside. Beth would now be able to return to her world, while Jenny stayed here to build a new life. At Jenny's approach, a light traveled around and through the wood as it welcomed her back. She pulled the handle and the door opened.

Beth looked in and saw the torches ignite and light the passageway where the small paper balls still marked their trail. Everything was same as it had been prior to their arrival in this unknown realm.

"Follow the paper trail and you'll find your way back home," Jenny told her as tears glistened in her eyes.

"I'll miss you." She hugged her friend.

"Me too." Jenny's tears trickled down her cheeks.

"I wish you were coming with me, but I do understand why you'd want to stay here. I hope you find everything you're looking for."

"Thanks, Beth."

Beth turned toward Devon. "Thanks for everything, Devon. This has been the best adventure anyone could ever ask for."

"You are most welcome, Beth. Perhaps one day we'll meet again."

"I'd like that." She hugged him. Beth went back to Jenny and hugged her again. "I'll miss you so much. It's like I'm losing my sister." Tears fell down her cheeks.

"I know. I feel the same way, but we'll see each other again, real soon."

"Promise?" More tears gently rolled down their cheeks. This was possibly the last time they'd ever see each other.

"I promise. Now you'd better get going, and Beth, don't get caught by Mrs. Parker." Jenny smiled weakly.

Maeldoi watched the interaction and laughed. He looked at them, disgust clearly etched on his aging features. Jenny watched him and wondered about his true identity. She stepped back when he moved in closer and closer to the door.

"Hurry, the door will soon close." Devon's eyes never left Maeldoi.

"Good-bye." Beth looked at Jenny and stepped over the threshold. In an instant, the thud of the slamming door echoed throughout the meadow.

Jenny heard Beth scream her name. "Beth! Beth!" Jenny pulled the handle trying to open the door.

Devon looked at Maeldoi. "What have you done?"

Maeldoi laughed. "She is mine. If you want her, you must claim her. You know what I want and where I'll be." In a puff of smoke, he vanished and the door went with him.

Jenny and Devon stood rooted to the spot, the shock of what had just transpired still evident on their features.

"Where is she?" Jenny's face was panic-stricken as she pleaded with Devon for an answer. "What happened? Devon, where's Beth?" she cried out.

"I don't know." He tried to keep his composure.

"Maeldoi said you'd know where to find him."

"I think I do. Maeldoi has her, but don't worry, Jenny, we'll get her back," Devon said with assurance. He put his hands on her arms and tried to make her believe his words.

"I promise you, we will get her back."

CHAPTER 14

BETH'S DISAPPEARANCE

"**W**hy did he take Beth? And more importantly, where did he take her?" Jenny wanted the truth.

"The Black Castle."

"Where's that?"

"Several days walk from the village."

She didn't believe him. He couldn't even look her in the eyes. Where was this place? "Why would he want Beth?"

"He doesn't want Beth. He wants you."

"I don't understand."

"I think it's best if we return to the castle and speak with my father. He can answer all of your questions."

"I'd like you to answer them first." She couldn't believe this story he was trying to feed her.

"I can't. There's a lot involved here, and I'm not the best person to ask about Maeldoi and his doings," Devon said.

"Will he hurt her?" Jenny asked, as tears glistened in her eyes and fell from dark lashes.

"No. He wants to make a trade."

"What kind of trade?" Jenny didn't like the sound of that.

"You for Beth." Devon waited for her reaction.

"Then that's what I'll do. How do I get in touch with him?" Furiously, she wiped the tears away. She had to save her friend; after all, it was her fault they were in Wardell. If she had just taken a moment to think about Beth rather than herself, they wouldn't be here. They could have been back in Morgansville and Beth would be safe.

"Jenny, this isn't the best way to handle this situation."

"I don't care. It's my fault that Beth's in this predicament. I pushed her through the door. I wanted an adventure. I had no right to endanger Beth's life." Jenny was openly crying.

Devon went to her and put his arms around her. She leaned into his shoulder and cried even more. She cried for her friend. She cried for her life. She even cried for her parents. She cried for everything that rested upon her small shoulders.

Devon wrapped his arms around her and held her shaking form until her tears subsided. She finally looked up at her friend.

"Sorry. I'm not usually like this."

"I don't mind." Devon returned her smile. "But I think we should return to the castle before Maeldoi returns." He let her go. "Are you all right?" Worry creased his brow.

"I think so." She accepted the handkerchief Devon gave her. She dabbed her eyes hoping he didn't think any less of her for spilling so many tears. She wanted to be strong, but she knew very little about Maeldoi or this Black Castle. She didn't know what to expect.

"We should return to Wardell."

Out here they were in danger. The safest place for them was within the walls of Wardell and Wardell Castle.

Jenny blushed at her weakness. "Okay." It was all she could say.

* * * *

Devon took her hand, and together they walked through the floral-scented meadow until the forest loomed before them. He knew she was the chosen one. After all, Maeldoi wouldn't have taken Beth unless he also believed in Jenny's identity. He kept going, wanting to reach the stream where they would stop for a few minutes, and then continue their trek to the castle.

Finally, the village came into view. Jenny held Devon's hand as they came out of the forest, united by a common enemy and a common goal. Merchants bowed their heads toward the young man, while others waved to them. They passed many people who smiled and offered goods to the Lord of the Lands' only son as they made their way to the castle. He waved and thanked them, telling his people they were late and needed to return to the castle. Once inside, Devon decided to warn his father of Maeldoi's presence and the capture of their friend. He hoped his father could help them get Beth back. Devon brought Jenny before a large ornate door and knocked.

"Come." Galfrid's baritone voice beckoned them to enter.

Devon ushered Jenny into the room. "Father, we need to talk."

"Jenny, I'm pleasantly surprised to see you. I take it this means you've decided to stay with us for a while?" Galfrid looked from Devon to Jenny and sensed something was amiss. The smile left his face.

"Father, we have a problem."

"What's happened?" He pointed to the two chairs in front of his desk.

"We found the area where we believe the door to be."

"But?" Galfrid sat up in his chair and leaned his elbows on his large desk. He locked his gaze with his son's.

"Maeldoi appeared."

Galfrid's features darkened. Anger suffused his handsome face at the mere mention of this name. "What did he want?" Galfrid reigned in his temper, but it was a difficult feat.

"Me." Jenny said.

"I think you'd better tell me everything from the beginning."

Devon told his father the events that lead to their first encounter with Maeldoi.

"What happened next?"

"Maeldoi appeared once more."

"What did he say to you?"

"He was quite pleasant. Since we couldn't produce the door, he made it appear for us."

"Why?"

"I didn't want to return to my old life, and the door refused to appear. This was something even Maeldoi pointed out. He made the door appear using his staff. I decided to stay here, but I sent Beth home. She went through the door and it slammed shut. I heard her scream my name and then nothing."

"Are you certain she simply didn't fear the darkness when the door closed? Perhaps even as we speak, she is home where she belongs."

"No, Father. Maeldoi told us she was his, and if we wanted her, I'd know where she was and what he wanted in exchange. We must rescue her."

"Yes, of course. We will help the child, but first we must find out where she's being kept."

"I believe she's being held at the Black Castle."

"Yes, I agree with you. But, Devon, you and I both know that place is impregnable. The magick surrounding the castle and its land is dark and deadly."

"I don't care. She's there because of me," Jenny said. "I have to do everything in my power to help rescue her."

"I understand your feelings, but this is a dangerous journey. You cannot walk up to the Black Castle and knock on the door. He would kill you before you reached the black gates."

"I don't care how dangerous this is. I have to try. I can't leave Beth in the hands of that evil man. I don't know anything about this Maeldoi, but I can't bear the thought of him hurting her."

"I do not believe he will harm her, but we must find a way to help her."

"What should we do, Father?" Devon asked, knowing he'd do anything to help Jenny find her friend.

"I must seek out some information concerning the wizard and your friend. Once I've discovered that she is in fact being kept in the Black Castle, I will know what must be done."

"How long will that take?" Jenny asked anxiously. Galfrid's words were cryptic. She thought Galfrid and Devon were keeping something from her, and she didn't understand why they would think it best if they kept her in the dark.

"I do not have a timeframe. I will do everything in my power to save your friend. Please believe me, Jenny," Galfrid said.

Jenny looked into his eyes. Faith was something she possessed, but Galfrid was a stranger. "I don't know if I can just sit back and wait for you to discover whatever information you need in order to find Beth, but by the look on your face, I don't think I have a choice but to trust you."

"Thank you, Jenny. Devon, I must ask the two of you to remain close to the castle. I cannot take any chances where Maeldoi is concerned. You must, above all else, keep Jenny safe."

"Yes, Father."

"Sir, I'd like to know something."

"What is it, Jenny?"

"Why does Maeldoi want me?" She deserved answers, but at the same time she feared the answers she'd receive.

"I'm not sure, Jenny, but I will find out."

"I'm sorry, but I don't believe you."

"Jenny…"

"No, Devon. I can feel it. You know more than you're telling me, and with everything that's happened, I think I have the right to know the truth."

Galfrid shared a momentary glance with his son. He turned blue eyes on the young girl before him in wonder. "Jenny, tell me about your life."

"My life?"

"Please. Humor me." Galfrid watched her carefully. He leaned back in his chair and waited for her to begin her tale.

"Well, I don't remember much about my parents. I do remember we were happy." A sad look came over her as she thought about the two people she loved and missed more than anything in this life.

"Where did you live?"

"I don't really remember where we lived. Isn't that weird?" Jenny had a faraway look as she tried to remember her life before Aunt Nora.

"What do you remember?"

"I remember having fun with Mom and Dad. We used to go to a lake to have a picnic. There were tall trees and lovely flowers all around the area. I remember Mom used to pick them, and then we'd go swimming in the lake. Dad would throw me over his shoulder and we'd laugh and spend the day having fun." Jenny's eyes glowed with distant memories.

Galfrid smiled. "Where did you attend school?"

"I don't remember attending another school before Morgansville Elementary. I know I must have gone to school somewhere, but I can't remember where."

"Did you ever ask your aunt these questions?"

"I did."

"And what did she say?"

"She told me it wasn't good to dwell on the past. She'd tell me to move on and stop thinking about my parents. They were gone and they weren't coming back. She'd say things like "get over it." Actually, that was her favorite saying." Jenny wondered about the questions Galfrid expected her to answer.

"Sounds like you have a very peculiar aunt." Galfrid said these words carefully, but the fact that he was appalled by that woman's behavior was evident in his demeanor. Even the look in his eyes confirmed this to Jenny.

"I know."

"Alright, Jenny, but before you go, I need to test you." Galfrid smiled at Jenny and winked in his son's direction.

Jenny felt that Devon understood what Galfrid meant, but she wasn't sure what was about to happen here. "What do you mean, test me?" These words frightened Jenny.

"You'll see."

"Should I worry?" she whispered to Devon.

Galfrid leaned back in his chair. He stared at Jenny and smiled.

She didn't know what was about to happen, and this terrified her. She sat back and tried to relax, but her hands shook from the fear she felt. Jenny waited and played with the hem of her tunic. She didn't want to look at the steward for fear of having to do something she didn't want to do. There were some things that still scared her.

"Let's get started," Galfrid said.

CHAPTER 15

LIFE WITH NORA

"**W**hat am I supposed to do?"

"Why, magick, of course."

Jenny turned on Devon, panic stricken. She felt betrayed by the one person she believed in. She never should have trusted him. She'd told him something so personal, and he told everyone about it. She'd never trust another person again. She couldn't. No, never would she put her trust in anyone.

"Is there something amiss?" Galfrid asked Jenny.

She just shook her head.

"She won't admit that magick is a part of her life." Devon said the words in a conspiratorial manner.

"Devon! You promised you wouldn't tell anyone! I trusted you." Tears rolled down her cheeks. She'd been deceived… again.

"Jenny, I didn't tell anyone. I swear to you, on my honor."

"I don't believe you. I never told another soul."

Galfrid took a handkerchief out of his pocket and sent it floating gently across the desk to land in Jenny's hand.

She took it and dried her tears. Jenny stopped dabbing her eyes and looked at the handkerchief. She looked up at Galfrid, who smiled at her. She didn't know what to say.

Devon and Galfrid laughed at the shocked and frightened expression on her face.

"How?" She couldn't finish her question. Everything in this land was so different than what she was used to, and now this.

"Jenny, I think you know how I did this," Galfrid said.

She refused to answer him. She couldn't even look him in the eye. She feared her own powers let alone someone else's magickal prowess. Ever since she'd arrived in Wardell, she'd been discovering so many oddities, and she didn't know how to make sense of all she'd seen and experienced.

"Jenny, as you can see, my father sent you the handkerchief by magick. I think it's time for you to accept your own magickal side," Devon said without malice or sarcasm. He said these words in a calm tone and with a genuine smile.

But Jenny didn't think Devon's words brought any solace to her fears. She was still cautious where her magickal abilities were concerned. She didn't know what to think or how to react to this news. She expended so much energy hiding her magickal side from the world, and now everyone expected her to share what she'd guarded.

"I don't know what to do."

"Jenny, have you ever done anything you can't explain?" Galfrid asked. "Anything magickal?"

Devon spoke up sensing her feelings. "Don't be afraid to open up to us. We won't think any less of you no matter what happened."

"Are you sure?" Jenny feared losing Galfrid's respect once he heard her tale.

"Is that when you first realized you were different?" Galfrid asked, sensing Jenny's fear. He wanted to help her, but first she had to help herself.

"Yes."

"What happened?" Galfrid gently prompted her.

"I've always had problems at school."

"Why?"

"The town I live in is small. Everyone knows everyone, and I'm the newcomer. Aunt Nora warned her friends about me. She told anyone who'd listen to her that there was a serious problem with me."

"Does she know about your magickal powers?"

"No. I can't imagine what she would have done to me if she knew I could do magick. I couldn't tell anyone."

"Go on."

"One day, we were having lunch in the cafeteria and this girl who teased me walked by our table. She made some snide comments about Beth and me. A friend of hers followed behind and on her tray was a bowl of chocolate pudding and…"

"What happened?" Devon asked, enjoying where this tale was going.

Jenny laughed. "I don't know how it happened, but the pudding flew from the tray and hit Bridgette in the back of the head. Chocolate pudding streamed down her perfectly styled hair. She was furious and stormed out of the cafeteria."

Galfrid and Devon couldn't stop laughing. Their joviality became infectious and they made Jenny laugh as well. Once their laughter subsided, Galfrid asked, "Were there other incidents?"

"A couple. After that, I only used magick for simple things. I'd turn lights on and off, and a few times… I… well…"

"Go on, Jenny. You have nothing to fear from us. We will not judge you," Galfrid said.

She took a deep breath to steady her nerves. "Well, sometimes I'd wait until Aunt Nora went to bed and I would use my magick to make a cookie or an apple float upstairs to me. You see, I couldn't go downstairs. If Aunt Nora heard me, she'd accuse me of stealing, so I would have something fly up to my room."

"Why did you have to do that?" Devon asked.

"I was hungry." Jenny said this so matter-of-factly that her words shocked them. She looked at Galfrid and Devon. The last thing she wanted was for them to hate her for stealing food from the woman who took her in. Ashamed, Jenny turned away. She couldn't look at the two men.

"So your magick has increased?" Galfrid changed the subject.

"I guess."

"Can you show us what you can do?"

"How?"

"Can you levitate something?"

"Yes."

Jenny saw a quill on the desk. She looked at the object, and using her finger, the feather took flight and hovered in the air. The higher her arm rose, the higher the white feather floated. She brought her hand down and the feather gently glided back to the desk's surface.

"Very good."

"Thanks."

"Can you send it back to me?" Galfrid asked. It was time to see the extent of her magickal powers. Jenny would need to practice and develop her magick even more than she'd already developed it.

Jenny looked at the feather and motioned for it to take flight. The feather levitated into the air and gently floated around the desk and landed in his hand.

"Excellent!"

Jenny beamed at the praise Galfrid showered on her. She'd never had anyone's approval before. It felt… well, it felt great. "Thank you, sir."

"Devon, you must help Jenny strengthen her powers and teach her some methods of self-defense."

"Yes, sir. I'll take care of this." Devon leaned back in his chair.

"Good."

"Excuse me, but what are you talking about?" Something in their words frightened her. What were they talking about? She understood the magick part, but what about this self-defense?

"The journey to rescue your friend is perilous. You need to learn how to defend yourself."

Jenny swallowed hard, fearing what this entailed. "What exactly are you talking about?" She stared at Galfrid. She felt an explanation was in order.

"Exactly what it sounds like. You must be taught to protect yourself and to defend your friend should the need arise."

"I understand what you're trying to tell me, but I have to tell you the truth, I don't think I could harm anyone no matter what the circumstances."

"Devon will teach you. Don't worry, it's not what you think," Galfrid said quite seriously. "We are going to help you prepare to face and defeat the greatest evil out there—Maeldoi."

CHAPTER 16

LET THE TRAINING BEGIN

Devon led Jenny through an open doorway where they'd begin her training. Together, the two friends walked through the gardens admiring the colorful displays. A small conversation between them relaxed her, even though in the back of her mind she feared what was expected of her. They stopped before a stone wall where a large, wooden door opened with a wave of Devon's hand. He led her through the doorway, and together they stepped into the courtyard. Trimmed bushes and statues of past kings and queens surrounded a large stone floor.

"Come on." Devon pulled Jenny along.

"What is this place?" she asked, as her eyes surveyed the many statues.

"In ancient times the artists of this land used this arena to put on plays for the kings and queens."

"Really? What kind of plays?"

"Well, they would hold mock battles and put on theatre productions and dance recitals for the royal family."

"Wow! Sounds awesome."

"Yes, I suppose it was, but for now we have work to do." He led her to the center of the courtyard. "Are you ready?" Devon felt Jenny tense.

"Not really."

"Don't worry. I'm a good teacher."

"I'm sure you are, but I don't know if I'll be a good student." Somehow Jenny never pictured herself as a fighter.

Devon laughed. "You'll be fine."

"I'm not as certain as you are."

"We'll begin with something easy."

"Like what?"

"How about learning to use a bow and arrow?"

"I don't know. You don't know how much this scares me. I'd rather be doing anything else."

"I know, but once you get a feel for these weapons, you'll be fine."

"How do you know that?" She knew this was a land of wonders, but she wasn't sure she was prepared for everything expected of her. Now that she'd been told to learn how to use weapons, she wanted to shy away from everything Devon was about to show her.

"I can sense greatness in you."

Her mouth gaped at the compliment.

"Come on, let's give it a try," Devon said. He motioned to the young man in a white tunic and pants standing next to a target board to bring them two bows and two quivers filled with arrows. Devon took them and gave Jenny one of the two bows.

She took it in her hand and stared long and hard at its length, trying to will herself not to fear this weapon. She didn't have much luck. Just holding the bow in her hand made her panic.

Devon helped her put the quiver on her back. "All right, you look good," he said with a smile.

"I feel weird."

"After a few days, it'll become a part of your outfit. You won't even know it's there."

"I doubt it." Jenny couldn't believe what she was about to do. Never would she have believed that she would travel to a new world where magick was a way of life and frightening weapons were used to survive. She didn't know if she'd ever fit in.

"You'll see. Now, let's begin with your first archery lesson." Devon removed an arrow from his quiver and placed it with precision against the string. He centered his gaze, pulled back, and released. The arrow flew straight and hit the bulls-eye.

"Wow! That was amazing!"

"Would you like to give it a try?"

"Okay. I guess I can try." Devon's display gave Jenny the courage to learn.

"Good. Now then, take your bow and place your hand here." He placed her hand precisely on the bow. "Keep your hand here, and now I want you to take an arrow from the quiver and place it against the cord. Pull back and keep your target within sight. Relax. Take a deep breath… and release."

Jenny followed the instructions, but the arrow fell short of her goal. She looked at Devon's smile and smiled as well.

"Try again."

Jenny did as she was told, but once again, the arrow fell short. She placed another arrow in the bow and let it fly. It too fell short, but at least the arrow did find a closer mark.

"Again."

Jenny spent the next hour trying to hit the target. She didn't care where the arrow hit as long as it stuck to the board. So far she hadn't had any luck. The arrows began to pile up beneath the board.

The young man in the white tunic walked over to the board and looked at all the fallen arrows. He picked some up and placed them in Jenny's quiver. The others, he left where they fell.

"Don't despair, Jenny. You will hit the target," Devon said, encouraging her to keep trying.

"I don't know about that. I'm not very good at this." Jenny looked at all the arrows lying on the cement and smiled. She'd never learn to do this. It wasn't her. She wanted to find Beth, but at the same time she wasn't too keen on having to take time to learn how to use weapons she couldn't grasp. Learning how to fight didn't make any sense to her.

"It takes everyone time to learn the art of archery. Keep practicing and soon you'll hit the mark."

"I hope you're right."

"Don't worry, you'll master this, but in the meantime, why don't we try something else?"

"Such as?"

Devon walked over to the servant holding two leather belts with swords hanging from them. He took one and tied it around his waist. The second one he brought over to Jenny and tied it around her waist.

"I can't use this!"

"It's not as difficult as you think."

"Are you trying to tell me that fighting with a sharp knife is not as difficult as I think it is? Yeah right. That's something I'd like to see."

"You will. Learning will be fun, I promise."

"I guess I'll have to trust you on that."

"Good. Now remove your sword."

Jenny did as she was told. She removed the sword, amazed by its weight. "I thought it would be much heavier."

"This one is a little smaller than the one you'll use later on. For now, I think this size is best."

Devon began the lesson by showing Jenny the proper stance. He helped her understand the technique of holding a sword. "Once you master this, I'll give you one that's sharp. I don't want anyone getting injured on a sharp blade.

"This one isn't sharp?"

"Well, you can cut your finger, but you wouldn't be able to kill anyone with it."

"I don't want to kill anyone, period." Jenny's frightened expression made Devon laugh.

"You may never have to kill anyone, but I want you to be able to defend yourself against anyone, or anything, that might harm you."

"Who'd want to hurt me? I don't understand why I need to learn this stuff. I should be out looking for Beth."

"The journey to the Black Castle is filled with many perils. The road is long and arduous, and we must sharpen our skills to defeat the evil that will try to hinder our progress."

"What kind of evil?" Jenny didn't like the sound of that.

"Ah, that is yet to be determined."

"Do you really think me capable of using a weapon against someone?"

"Jenny, if our lives are on the line, I believe you'd be more than capable of using whatever weapon you must in order to save a life. This is why we must practice our skills. We don't have much time."

"Can't we send the palace guards to save Beth?" Jenny asked. They were just kids. Why should they spend so much time practicing with an array of weapons, when they should try to find a way to save Beth?

"No. This is something you must do... something we will do together. I won't let you face this alone."

"I'm glad. Devon?"

"Yes?"

"Thanks."

"For what?"

"For being my friend."

"I am honored to be deemed your friend." Devon gave her a mock bow causing her to laugh.

Jenny smiled and rotated her arm, trying to relax the muscles. "All right, let's try this again."

"Go." Devon taught her to thrust the sword and locate the vulnerable spots on the human body. He taught her to parry and block unwanted blows. He moved around as lithe as a cat.

Jenny complied with his orders and marveled at his skills, but deep down inside she didn't feel right about any of this. Since she was in another world, she had to adjust to their ways.

"Keep going, Jenny! You're doing great!" They continued their swordplay for another hour.

"My arms feel like they're gonna fall off."

Devon laughed. "You'll get used to it."

"Do I really want to get used to this form of pain?"

Devon's eyes twinkled with mirth. "It's a long and dangerous road. You must prepare yourself." He laughed at her fear.

"Devon, even if we practice the rest of the day, I'll never be ready to fight anything or anyone. I have to save Beth, now."

"You need to know the basics, the rest will follow."

Her impatience showed as her anxiety mounted. "But what about Beth? I have to help her before it's too late."

"Jenny, if you go out there unsuspecting and gullible, you'll only get yourself killed. You need to be fully prepared for this journey."

"How do you know all of this?" Jenny wondered what else he was hiding from her. She sensed there was so much more she should know about this so-called quest, but no one seemed to think she deserved to know the truth. She was tired of asking for the truth and not getting the answers she needed. Frankly, it was getting on her nerves.

"I just know."

"You won't tell me?"

"No. Telling you would be tantamount to altering the future."

"Maybe it would be better if you did."

"I don't know if it would be better or not, but I think it may be safer if you discovered some of this on your own."

"I still don't understand why I have to learn how to fight. We're wasting time. I should be going after Beth."

"I understand your impatience, Jenny. But this is what must be done to prepare you for your journey. Now, let's keep practicing. The quicker you learn, the sooner we'll leave." Devon held his sword in front of his chest, ready to continue the lesson.

"Are you sure Beth will be alright?" Jenny asked needing another moment to rest her weary arms.

What had she gotten herself into? At first, she thought this was nothing more than a joke, but standing here holding a sword in her hand made her a believer. There was so much more at stake than she ever thought possible. If only the kids back home could see her holding this sword, maybe she'd get a small amount of respect. Then again, they were probably too smug to have respect for anyone other than themselves. She smiled at the thought of watching her classmates' faces if they ever saw her here with someone like Devon.

"Don't worry, Jenny, Maeldoi won't hurt her. I'm quite certain of this." He stared quizzically at her.

"You see, that's what I mean. Why does he want me? What could he possibly want from me?"

"I'm not certain."

"Devon, I don't believe you. I think you know what's going on, but you don't think I have the right to know the truth."

"Jenny, there are some things I cannot tell you, but I do ask that you trust me and my father. We only want what's best for you."

"I understand that, but I feel as though everyone thinks only they need to know the truth about what's happened to me and Beth. I don't think that's right." She looked at the sword in her hand and suddenly felt as though strangers were writing her life, and the only part she had in this play was the same as before—to do what everyone wanted her to do.

Devon sighed heavily. "I know how you feel. I wish I could tell you everything you want to know. Believe it or not, there are some things even I don't know." His blue eyes searched her green ones.

"Okay. I'll let it go for now, but I want you to tell me something else about this journey. I don't want to be completely unprepared."

"If there is more to tell you, then I will."

"Is that the best you can do?" Jenny wondered what all the secrecy was about.

"For now, yes."

Jenny thrust her sword at Devon. He blocked her move and thrust his own sword at her, but Jenny's movements were quick as she blocked every move he made, just the way he'd taught her.

"Ready for a break?"

"Absolutely. I'm starving."

"Good, let's have some lunch," Devon said after they'd been practicing for several hours. He looked at her with admiration. When she began a new move, she didn't want to leave until she perfected it. She was a strong and capable companion. Devon admired her more and more.

"Come on." He led her from the arena and back onto the path. Together they returned to the castle.

CHAPTER 17

MAGICK TIME

How quickly a week flew by as Devon patiently taught Jenny all aspects of self-defense, archery, and swordplay. Although tired and battered, Jenny continued her studies. Only now was she beginning to understand the perils awaiting them on their journey to the Black Castle. Even though no one felt the need to include her in the dangers and the reasons behind this journey, Jenny kept her mind on her training, and from time to time, she'd pick up tidbits from palace gossip. It wasn't enough information for her liking, but she knew there had to be some truth to the rumors she heard bouncing around the castle.

Day after day, she came out here with Devon, and together they practiced their archery skills, as well as their swordplay, and every day Jenny wondered if she'd ever have to use these weapons to survive once they began this journey. She had to admit she did like the fact she grew stronger and stronger each and every day. Her body felt like she could handle anything, while her mind was clear and sharp. This wasn't a bad thing, just a scary thing for her.

"My father will work with you for a few days to help you develop your magick."

"I think I'm more afraid of that than this sword."

"Don't be. Magick is a lot more fun."

Jenny had shied away from her magickal side in the past, but she needed to embrace it and develop her skills. The only problem she faced was being able to delve into the magick living within her to learn all the many facets of magick. And yet, she still feared this part of her training the most. Jenny worried that once she opened her mind and heart to magick she'd never be able to go back to being who she thought she was. This would take her to such a higher level that she feared failing not only herself, but Devon and Beth who counted on her to save her from Maeldoi and Ringwar.

"I'll take your word for it." Jenny stopped another thrust from Devon's sword.

"You do that."

The clang of steel echoed in the morning air. "Don't worry, Jenny. If you're half as brilliant with magick as you are with these swords, you'll be just fine."

* * * *

The following morning brought sunshine and warmth to Wardell. Jenny dressed in a burgundy tunic trimmed with a cream colored floral pattern that she wore over black tights. She tied her hair into a ponytail with a burgundy and cream ribbon and let it hang in dark waves. She and Devon shared breakfast, and he escorted her to her first magick lesson. Galfrid waited in the great hall for their arrival.

"Welcome, Jenny."

"Good morning, Galfrid. I have to confess that I'm really nervous about this." The lavish room had tables set up with all types of knickknacks. The room was ready for Jenny's first magick lesson.

"I don't want you to be nervous. I only want to see what you can do."

"I'm not sure I can do much."

"How are her skills developing?"

"She's doing much better than I thought she would."

"So you're a natural, and that tells me something about your abilities." He walked around the long table and approached Jenny

"I don't think I have any real abilities."

Galfrid's black tunic was embroidered with silver thread depicting a griffon. "Of course you do," he said. "All you need to do is to have faith in yourself and in the magic living inside of you."

This man comforted her. It surprised her. She didn't trust many people, but here she stood, ready to share an intimate part of herself with Galfrid and Devon. One of life's many ironies. She walked the length of the table and admired the lovely wares. There were goblets, vases, plates, statues, and an assortment of cloths. She didn't understand why all these items were needed, especially those made of crystal and fine china.

"Come here, Jenny. We will begin with a simple task. I only want to know what you are capable of doing. Remember, I am not judging you, so you have nothing to fear from me," Galfrid said. "We have a lot of work ahead of us. Shall we begin?"

"I guess."

"Now then, Jenny, we've seen you levitate objects, so we'll begin with more simple levitation." Galfrid escorted Jenny to a table where different objects lay. He picked up a small bowl and looked at it. The bowl left his palm and floated into the air. A moment later it returned to the table.

"Your turn."

"Here goes nothing."

Jenny picked up the same bowl and held it in the palm of her hand. She mimicked Galfrid's movements, and with a look from her bright green eyes, the bowl gently floated into the air and then returned to the table.

"Again, only this time choose another object. Any object," Galfrid said. He looked at Devon and shared a gaze of hope and understanding.

The room was amazing. Large gilded mirrors were situated on the walls. She discovered the Great Hall was used for special occasions, such as royal dinners and balls— that would explain the long table and upholstered chairs tucked beneath, as well as the golden statues placed in corners. This room had large windows with heavy satin curtains that hung from brass curtain rods and pooled on the floor.

She took a deep breath. "Okay."

"And, this time, levitate it directly from the table's surface." Galfrid moved away from the table. He stood next to his son as they watched the young witch learn all that was inside of her.

"I'll try." Jenny focused on a white vase painted with colored flowers. It was heavier than the other objects, so this was more of a test for her. She watched it rise into the air. It flew up and around. Concentrating on the vase, Jenny made it fly around until it made a tour around Devon and Galfrid. Finally, the traveling vase returned to the table.

"She's pretty good," Devon said proudly.

"Yes, but she must relax and allow her magick to flow naturally," Galfrid said. "She's placed a rein on her powers and she needs to release them in order to achieve her true potential." Galfrid looked at his son. "Devon, I believe you are the only person who can help Jenny. There is a special bond between you, one based on the trust you have for each other."

"It may take some time, but I believe when the time comes she'll be fine," Devon said with confidence.

Galfrid looked at his son, a mirror image of himself. "As you know, she is running out of time. She must learn to develop her powers now."

"I know. I'll see what I can do." Devon watched objects leave the table and create an assembly line.

"Jenny, lift the entire table and its contents," Galfrid told her. "This will require you to concentrate even more." He paused and turned to Devon. "Such an undertaking will force her to use more magick than she's ever used before."

"I..." Jenny hesitated. She wasn't as sure of herself as Galfrid was.

"Jenny, go ahead. Embrace your powers." Galfrid motioned her to continue.

"I don't know if I can." She was scared.

"Search your heart and you'll find the truth in the power within."

"What if I break something?"

Galfrid and Devon laughed. "There is nothing to fear. Go ahead, Jenny, levitate the table."

Jenny turned toward the table and concentrated on the contents. Her arms rose, causing the table to levitate effortlessly and fly around the room. Laughter escaped her lips as she controlled the table with her mind. When the table touched ground, she ran to Devon and threw her arms around his neck. She hugged him. "I did it!" She laughed.

"Yes, you did." Devon returned her embrace.

"Well done, Jenny!" Galfrid said. "Now, do it again."

"Okay."

"Remember to concentrate."

"I will."

She levitated the table and stabilized it as it rose even higher. Laughter escaped her lips at the pleasure of being able to use her powers without fear or repercussion. The freedom she felt was nothing short of exhilarating.

"Jenny, keep that one in the air and levitate the other table." Galfrid watched her progress.

"I don't know if I can do that." Jenny worried she'd drop the table and break the lovely items on its surface.

"Never doubt your powers. Believe in yourself and you can do anything you want," Galfrid said.

Jenny held up the table with one hand and turned her head toward the other one. She lifted it into the air and made it fly. One table flew around the other. She laughed as they continued to fly all around the room. She put the tables down.

"Excellent work!" Galfrid said with a smile.

She ran and hugged Galfrid who was as surprised as she was by her emotional display.

"Sorry." Jenny blushed when she realized she'd hugged the Steward of Wardell.

"No need to apologize. I was feeling left out." Galfrid happily returned the hug.

Jenny laughed.

"I knew you could do it," Devon said.

Thrilled, Jenny inadvertently backed into the table where a lovely crystal and gold vase crashed to the floor. Jenny's cheeks burned with shame. Before anyone could react, she opened her hand and the pieces scattered across the floor shook. One by one, they floated upwards, and piece by piece the vase came together and landed in her hand. She returned it to the table's surface. It took her a moment to understand what had just transpired.

"Wow! I've never felt anything like this before." Jenny was as shocked as Galfrid and Devon.

"That was very good, Jenny. How long have you been able to do this kind of magick?" Pride shone in Galfrid's eyes.

"I don't know. This is the first time anything like this happened. I have to be honest and tell you that I'm a little frightened by all this power," she said. "I don't remember feeling this way before. It's an amazing feeling to know that I can do so much more."

"I can only imagine. Just remember you must never use these powers for evil. Your powers are a gift, and this gift must be used for noble causes. Once you begin this quest, you will understand more of what is expected of you. I believe you will need to use your powers to help free your friend, and that, my dear, is a noble cause," Galfrid said.

"I'll need to use magick to free Beth?" Jenny understood even less than she did before.

"There's a good chance you will. Magick will help you secure your friend's freedom. Don't forget, Maeldoi and Ringwar will use magick to try and prevent you from freeing Beth. You must be prepared to fight them."

"Okay, so what do we do next?" All of a sudden she wanted to use more magick. She was only now beginning to understand what was trapped inside of her. She'd spent so many years repressing her magick that she never really understood what she had. She wanted to release more and more magick.

"Anything you want to do. Jenny, only you know the extent of your powers. All we can do is to guide you while you strive to achieve your goals."

"I think I understand. I'm very grateful to you for everything. You've shown me that magick isn't something to be ashamed of. You made me realize that magick is who and what I am. I'll always be grateful to you both for this but—"

"But I sense you are still somewhat apprehensive and uncertain. You mustn't be. Uncertainty when the time comes could cost your friend her life," Galfrid said.

"I still don't know who or what I am. I wish you'd tell me more." Jenny searched Galfrid's blue eyes hoping he'd tell her something.

"And I promise you when the time comes, you will know everything there is to know."

"No offense, but that's all I've heard since my arrival. I think there is more to my magick and this trek then anyone is willing to tell me. I mean, why would I need to learn how to use a sword or how to fight? There are so many unanswered questions. I just wish someone would tell me more."

"I understand you feel we are keeping secrets from you, but you need to understand we only know what you do at this time. As I've told you before, I cannot share what I do not know," Galfrid said.

"'Hum." Jenny let Galfrid's words slide. She knew they wouldn't divulge anything more. She wished she knew why they were keeping such secrets from her. After everything she'd done, she felt she deserved to know at least as much as they did, but unfortunately for her, they didn't feel the same way.

CHAPTER 18

THE DRAGON

Evening came and the village market wound down. People milled about. The sounds of laughter rang out. Merchants closed their booths for the day, and life in the village ebbed. Flames were lit to cast an eerie glow in the windows of the pub in an attempt to entice men and women into its interior. The workday had come to an end, and it was time to spend a little of the gold the merchants had earned.

The pub was bustling as more and more patrons entered. Drinks flowed freely, as did the ale and food, when suddenly, amid the merrymaking, a distant rumble was felt long before it was heard. Closer and closer, a sound of something large approached the village. The merriment ceased. A quiet hush fell over the joyous raucous. Everyone stilled and waited for another sound, another trembling of the earth. Hearts pounded almost as loudly as the rumble heard moments before. No one wanted to move for fear of being injured by whatever was coming.

Suddenly, the tables shook with the force of an earthquake. Glasses fell over with a crash. Windowpanes burst and caused panic among the patrons as people ran in every direction attempting to safeguard themselves from the shards of glass flying in every direction. Rather than hiding, some of the patrons scrambled to the windows as a dark shadow fell over the quaint village. Curious, they stared out the broken windows trying to catch a glimpse of what had caused the distress within the village and the pub.

THUMP! THUMP! THUMP!

Closer and closer the unknown menace approached.

The guards sounded the alarm. "Close the gates!"

141

They scrambled to push the large doors together. With the closure of the large gates, the village was secure.

"Ready!" The shout from the guards sounded across the village. Suddenly, a large beam on the side of the door slid upwards and fell across the middle of the doors. Another beam crawled up and dropped across the top, followed by the last beam that secured the door from the bottom. The village was closed off to everyone as the guards prepared to fight whatever broke through the trees of the forest and came toward the village.

* * * *

Devon and Jenny stood in the courtyard wondering what was happening. The trembling beneath the ground was felt across the village and throughout the castle grounds.

Jenny touched Devon's arm. "What's going on?"

"I'm not sure." His eyes scanned the area. "We should return to the castle." He took her hand in his, and together they ran for the safety of the castle. Once inside, the drawbridge was raised to secure the castle and grounds against the approaching menace. Guards ran through the hallways making their way to the windows. Armed guards ran in every direction ready to defend their individual posts.

Devon and Jenny watched the drama unfold. "Follow me." Devon grabbed her hand and led her down one hallway and then another. They stopped before an ornate door. He looked around, and only when he was sure they were alone, he pulled it open and pushed Jenny inside. The door closed and darkness engulfed them. Devon felt along the wall until he found the sconce in which sat a torch. He lightly expelled a breath and ignited the torch. A bright flame illuminated their surroundings.

"Where are we?"

"The Tower. Follow me." Devon climbed the stone steps that wound their way to the top. He led her to a room surrounded by open windows. He touched the torch with its magical flame and watched as the flame took on a life of its own and began to jump from one torch to the other, until the contents of the room were revealed.

Jenny noticed the room had no elaborate decorations. No portraits graced these stone walls. No carpets lay upon the stone floor. Here, four barren stone walls encircled them, but what they'd come here for was the best view in the entire village. From here they saw every angle of the village and directly into the forest. This room was used for the sole purpose of seeing over the gates and walls of Wardell.

They went to the window and looked out. They searched the area hoping to catch a glimpse of what was terrorizing the village.

"There!" Jenny cried out at the sight of something she'd only read about in books.

Crashing through the trees of the forest a large black dragon roared. Large eyes surveyed the area while massive paws stomped heavily to announce its approach. The dragon expelled a fiery breath. It marched around the wall. Another fiery breath escaped the large jaw followed by a deafening roar.

From above, arrows flew and bounced off the dragon's scales; nothing could penetrate its hide. Large claws scratched the earth as the animal came closer and closer to the village. It let out another roar and followed it with a burst of fire from its massive mouth filled with huge teeth.

"Is that what I think it is?" Jenny asked in complete awe at the sight before them. She'd never seen anything like this before. What else would she see now that she lived in another world? She couldn't believe all the things she'd seen since her arrival in Wardell. How could she ever return to Morgansville and be happy living in that world again? She didn't think she'd ever be able to return.

"Yes, it's a dragon."

"Can they stop it?" Jenny was mesmerized by the sight below, never having dreamt of seeing a creature this magnificent before.

"No. It will terrorize the village for a while, and when it tires of this game, it'll return to the forest."

"How big is this forest?"

"It stretches out as far as the eyes can see. It could take us more than a week to walk the path to the Black Castle. Of course, that also depends on what's sent to attack us."

"But if Maeldoi wants me to come to the Black Castle, why would he send creatures to harm me?"

"I cannot answer that. I wish I could, but no one knows what Maeldoi has planned for you until you start your journey toward the Black Castle. I certainly have no idea what to expect when we arrive at the castle."

"That doesn't sound too good."

The dragon searched for a way into the village. Another great roar sounded and nearly shattered the windows as a burst of flames escaped its large snout. The flames scorched the ground and surrounding walls, but even the dragon's fire couldn't penetrate the magick protecting Wardell.

The dragon paced the length of the wall in an attempt to breach the barrier. He roared his anger and slammed his giant body against the stone wall. Again and again, he tried crash through, but failed to enter the village. Unsuccessful, the dragon moved toward the woods. After some time and effort, the dragon's large head, body, and tail disappeared between the giant trees.

Jenny looked at Devon. "What happened? Why did he go back into the woods?"

"I suppose the dragon couldn't find a way into the village, so he returned to the forest where he belongs."

"Has this ever happened before?"

"Yes. The dragon's been here a couple of times."

"And did he act the same way?"

Devon thought for a moment. "Yes, I suppose he did. I'm told each visit was similar."

"It sounds as though it's under orders to scare, but not actually harm anyone."

"Jenny, the magick protecting the walls is stronger than any dragon."

"You didn't notice them?"

"What?"

"That dragon has wings. It could have flown over the village and castle, burning everything in its path."

"Are you certain?"

144

"Yes, I am. I can't believe no one ever noticed them before."

"Well, to tell you the truth, this is the first time I've actually seen it." Devon couldn't meet Jenny's gaze. Ashamed, he turned away from her.

"But I thought it's been here on more than one occasion?" Jenny wondered what was going on. This wasn't like Devon to shy away from anything.

"It has, but each time it came here…" Devon sighed, embarrassed by his next words. "You see… well, my father sent me into the tunnels beneath the castle for safety." Devon's eyes were downcast in shame.

"Oh."

"Don't think badly of me. I'm not afraid of it, but my father fears Wardell will be left without a leader."

She placed her hand on his arm. Devon finally raised his eyes to look at her.

"Devon, I don't think you're a coward. I think your father did the right thing. This village needs someone like you to keep the peace. You'd make a great leader."

He smiled a genuine smile. "Thank you, Jenny."

"You're welcome."

"Let's get out of here."

With a single breath, Devon extinguished all the torches burning around the room, but kept his own torch alive as they made the long descent to the hallways of the castle.

"I must convince my father to allow me to escort you on your quest."

"Devon, I don't want to cause any trouble between you and Galfrid."

"I refuse to hide in the castle every time danger rears its ugly head. I need to prove my worth to my father, to my people, and most importantly to myself. This is something I need to do."

"Then tell your father how you feel. Let him know this is about you and not me."

"Perhaps this has something to do with the both of us."

"What do you mean?" She arched her eyebrow.

"I'm not certain. I think there's a reason why you were prodded through the door on that fateful day. I also believe I'm the one who must help you find the answers you seek. I also believe that I am the only person able to help protect you against the evils lying in wait once you begin this journey. I want to be there with you and for you, and I cannot allow anyone, including my father, to stop me from doing what I must do."

"I think you're right. Devon, you need to talk to your father about these feelings. Galfrid will understand. He's your father, and as such, he'll listen to you, and if you explain this to him, he'll help you out. I'm sure of it."

"Perhaps you're right. I'll speak with him."

"Good. Maybe you can get some answers for me as well."

"I believe the answers to your true identity and your path in life lies in the Black Castle. There is more to this quest than you think."

"What do you mean my true identity? The last time I checked, I'm Jenny Saunders, orphan." Jenny stopped before a large portrait in a golden frame. "Who is this?" She asked before Devon could speak.

"Queen Ileana."

"Is she the one who went missing?"

"Yes."

"She's beautiful."

"Yes, she is."

"I don't know why, but she looks familiar." Jenny admired the woman in the portrait. Long, dark hair encircled pale skin, while striking green eyes stared at Jenny. The queen posed regally in emerald robes. A jeweled crown sat upon her dark mane. There was familiarity in the green eyes… a memory from her past, perhaps. She didn't understand what was happening to her, but when she looked into the eyes staring back at her, she recognized those eyes. Jenny realized she had the same eyes.

"Is this King Morgan?"

"Yes."

In the next portrait, a man stood poised with a scepter in one hand and a jeweled sword in the other. He wore a purple and black tunic with a golden griffon emblazoned upon his chest. Blue eyes stared at her, and Jenny wondered where she'd seen those eyes before. Once again, a distant memory haunted her thoughts. She couldn't understand where this memory came from.

"I know these people, Devon. And yet, I know it's not possible. I've never met them, nor have I ever been to Wardell before. So why am I feeling this way about two strangers? What's wrong with me?"

"I'm not the right person to explain this to you."

Jenny wondered at all the secrecy. It wasn't as though she couldn't sense some of Devon's feelings. She saw he was fighting with himself as he tried to answer her questions without divulging information she wasn't supposed to be privy to. This irritated her more than anything else. If she found out exactly who she was and why she was sensing these odd feelings, perhaps she'd be able to use them as weapons once she reached the Black Castle. Keeping things from her could cause her more harm than good. She wished Devon would understand this and divulge what she sensed he kept inside.

"Then who is? Please, Devon, tell me the truth. I'd like to know what's happening to me."

"I honestly don't know."

"What about your father? He's the steward here. He must know something about the people in the pictures."

"How can he tell you why you find two portraits familiar? Think about it, Jenny." Devon was grasping at straws.

"I don't know. I only want to know why I'm feeling this way." Jenny continued to stare at the portraits, unable to take her gaze away. There had to be a connection.

"Devon, there used to be something hanging next to the portrait of King Morgan. What was it?"

Devon didn't know what to say. He looked around hoping to find something else to draw Jenny's attention away from the missing portrait. Unfortunately, nothing presented itself. "The frame broke on another portrait of the royal family," he said, after a few minutes.

Jenny's intense stare made him look away. She wanted the truth, but he wouldn't divulge any information to her. Although she felt she deserved to know the truth, she realized Devon preferred to keep some things to himself.

For the first time since their meeting, Jenny sensed Devon lied to her. That portrait had been purposely removed, and she had to find out why. What was so special about this particular portrait

147

that her friend would find it necessary to lie to her? She wanted, and she felt, she deserved to know the truth, and one way or another, she would discover the secrets being kept from her.

CHAPTER 19

GALFRID'S DISQUIET

A distinctive knock sounded on Galfrid's office door. "Come!" The handsome man called out to his unknown visitor.

Devon entered the office, his sharp eyes scanning the room.

"Hello, Father. May I have a word with you?"

"Of course." He motioned to the chair across his large mahogany desk that was cluttered with maps and an assortment of papers.

Devon sat down and fidgeted in the massive leather chair. He looked at his father and tried to smile, but his eyes held the seriousness of the topic uppermost on his mind. He leaned back in his chair, and then he placed his elbows on the edge of the desk only to remove them and leaned back in his chair. The leather protested his movements, but Galfrid sat quietly. Devon noticed his father's eyes never left him. He made several attempts to begin this conversation only to sit quietly and search for the right words.

"Now then, what's troubling you, son?"

"Father, we must speak." Devon knew what he wanted to say, but sometimes it was difficult for him to discuss his feelings with someone as imposing and collected as Galfrid was. The son of the steward should never show weakness, and sometimes it was difficult for Devon to separate what was a respectable topic and what wasn't.

"Very well." Galfrid leaned back in his leather chair and kept a steady gaze on his son.

Devon bristled in his chair as he tried to form his words. The words were there, but he feared his father's reaction to his decision. "I would like to accompany Jenny when she begins her quest to rescue Beth from the Black Castle."

"No."

Devon was shocked at the finality in that no, but he wouldn't abandon his decision. "But I have to do this."

"My decision is made and my response is clear. I cannot grant you permission to escort Jenny on this quest. It is far too dangerous, and therefore you must remain in Wardell."

"I'm sorry, but I don't agree with your decision. I have to take her."

"Devon, the fact that you wish to attempt such a dangerous quest is admirable, but I have my reasons for not allowing you to leave Wardell."

"And I respect them and your decision, but I also know what must be done. I know what I must do."

"You are too young and reckless to understand the dangers inherent in this type of undertaking."

"You fear Maeldoi and Ringwar will capture me. You fear they would use me to take the throne. Do I understand your position? Yes, I do. But I have to do what I believe is right. You cannot take this away from me, Father."

Galfrid sighed. "I do not doubt your bravery or your sincerity. I only doubt your lack of common sense where Jenny is concerned. Devon, I am the Steward of Wardell, and as such, I have to protect the crown and my people. Allowing Maeldoi and Ringwar the opportunity to capture you would be a foolish gesture. I'm afraid I must stand firm on my decision."

"She cannot make it on her own. She needs my help."

"You do not know, or understand, what the Black Castle truly represents." Suddenly, Galfrid seemed to travel to another time, another place. Sadly, he shook his head and looked at his son.

"I have never been there, but I know I can help Jenny on this quest without being captured by anyone." Devon's tone was forceful.

"You may think you are strong enough, but do not doubt Maeldoi's power. The strength he holds in his staff is immeasurable."

"Perhaps, but there must be a way to destroy it, and once we discover its weakness, we can achieve this. If this comes to fruition, Maeldoi wouldn't be such a threat to Wardell and Warwick."

"No, Devon. I'm sorry, but my answer must remain the same. You cannot leave Wardell."

"Father, she saw the portraits of the king and queen. They were familiar to her." Devon had to find a way to change Galfrid's mind and allow him to join Jenny on her quest. He had to be the one to take her on this journey. He knew there was more at stake than simply rescuing her friend. This was a quest to prove his courage. He couldn't allow Galfrid to stop him from doing what he believed he should be allowed to do. One way or another, he had to prove his worth to Wardell.

"There are many reasons for these memories."

"But what if she is the one?"

"Devon, no matter what we suspect, we have no proof."

"No we don't, but shouldn't we try to discover the truth? If I'm allowed to escort her, I will be able to find out if we have the right girl or not."

"How? The child has no memory prior to being sent to live with her aunt. She told us as much."

"We do know there is a resemblance, and under the circumstances I think I should aid her with this quest. I would like your permission to leave the castle and escort Jenny on this journey."

Galfrid stood and paced the office. He stopped and looked at his son. He took a moment to digest Devon's words. He finally made his decision, and shook his head. Sadness clouded his eyes when he looked into Devon's bright blue gaze. "No, son. I'm afraid I cannot permit this. That is my final word."

Galfrid placed his hand upon his son's shoulder and left the office.

* * * *

"I hated saying no to Devon, but until I'm certain of the facts I cannot allow him to endanger himself. You know as well as I the consequences of capture at Maeldoi's hands.

151

This isn't something I can allow to happen, no matter who this girl is."

"But what if she is the one?"

"Even so, I cannot allow our son to travel through such a dangerous realm. He is our only child. He is my son."

"I understand, Galfrid. He's also my son," Jemma said in a gentle tone. "I also know you must allow Devon to choose his own path. He must decide on the man who will emerge, and perhaps, one day, sit upon this throne. Neither you nor I can make this decision for him. He must make this choice on his own, and we must support his decision, whether or not we agree with it."

"We tried that once before, remember, and now we only have one son."

Tears stood in Jemma's eyes as distant thoughts and emotions flitted through her mind and over her lovely features. "You cannot shield this son simply to protect him from harm. We cannot prevent Devon from proving his worth in whichever way he chooses. No matter what happened in the past, we need to understand Devon is not Tristan. I do not believe Devon's fate will be the same as his brother's."

Galfrid hung his head in defeat. "You speak the truth, but I fear for him. Maeldoi isn't someone to be trifled with. We know what that man is capable of, and I'm not willing to allow another son to fall prey to him or his evil."

"This is true, but if you stop Devon from choosing his own path, you could still lose your son. After all, he is just like his father. He's brave and smart, and he will prove himself in whatever manner he chooses. We… you must allow him to choose his own path."

"I know." Galfrid wanted to do whatever he could to help Jenny find Beth, but at the same time he wanted to keep his child safe. This was more than a dilemma. It was the difference between his son's honor and his life.

"Galfrid, my love." Jemma placed her hand upon her husband's arm and looked into his loving gaze. "I don't want to see our son leave, but I know in my heart Devon must make his own decisions. We cannot make them for him. He has been given the opportunity to walk his own path, and now he must be allowed to fulfill his heart's desire and his destiny, whether we agree with it or not. He must prove his worth to you, and most importantly, to himself. He knows what this quest entails, and no matter what obstacles he could face, we must allow him to face them with pride and honor. Our job is done. We raised him well. We must now step aside and allow him to travel life's path on his own terms."

"Your words speak the truth, but I worry. I cannot bear to lose another son."

"And we cannot prevent him from living simply to make life easier for us. We cannot confine him to this castle in order to protect him from harm. Tristan made his choice and there is nothing we can do to change that. All we can do is allow Devon to make his own choices and to prove himself. I believe he will return," Jemma said with tear-filled eyes.

Galfrid turned away and wiped a tear that trickled down his own cheek whenever he spoke or thought of his first born. "I need to do what is best for my son and not what is easy for me."

"If Devon chooses to leave the safety of this castle, then who are we to stand in his way. All we can do is love him all the more for being as brave as his father and brother."

"I fear for his safety and the safety of Wardell. If Maeldoi captures our son, he will use him to steal the throne. If I do not permit this to happen, we will lose him as well. Maeldoi could kill him before our eyes. I fear there is no solution here. I lose my crown and Wardell, or I lose another son."

"I've thought of that as well, but if Devon manages to find out what happened to the king and queen, he will return, and one day he may sit upon the throne as your heir. If Jenny is who we think she may be, then he will help protect her and bring the rightful ruler back to Wardell."

"I suppose my fear is that Maeldoi will kill Devon, capture and hold Jenny and Beth. What will we do then? There is too much at stake here. I cannot be flippant about the seriousness of this journey."

Jemma looked at her husband. "We have no other choice. We must allow him to leave. If his destiny brings down the evil that has haunted Wardell for many years, he will return as someone who could one day rule this land."

Defeated, he went to his wife. "You're right, my love." Galfrid smiled and kissed Jemma's lips. He knew what he had to do. He understood what fate had made him do. With that thought on his mind, Galfrid left.

CHAPTER 20

THE QUEST

Morning peeked over the horizon casting a soft, pink glow across the waters and Wardell Castle. Serenity reined over the charred land. Jenny responded to a soft knock, and to her surprise, Devon stood there dressed in a black tunic over black pants and a dark cloak. On his back was a bow and quiver with an abundance of arrows. At his waist, a leather belt and sheath, holding a jewel-encrusted sword, was cinched. In his hand, he held another bow, quiver, and a belt with a jeweled sword.

"May I come in?"

"Yes, of course." Jenny closed the door behind him. "Where are you going?"

"With you, of course."

"Devon, your father wants you to stay here."

"I know, but I want to be the one who takes you to the Black Castle." He smiled at his friend.

"I don't want you to get into trouble for disobeying your father." She remembered her talk with Galfrid. He'd asked her to release his son from his promise to escort her to the Black Castle. She told Galfrid she would do whatever he wanted.

"Don't worry about me."

"I can't help it. I know how your father feels about you taking me to the Black Castle."

"Jenny, you need me. I'm the only one who can guide you safely to the Black Castle."

"I don't know about this." She struggled with her conscience. "You don't have to prove anything to me. I know who you are."

155

"Yes, you do. Don't look so worried. Everything will be alright, Jenny." Devon looked at her and hesitated. "Have you changed your mind about wanting me to escort you?"

Jenny looked at her friend and smiled. She wanted to do what Galfrid asked of her, but what she really wanted was to go with Devon. She didn't feel she had the right to tell Devon he wasn't welcome. That would be a lie.

"I really didn't want to go without you. I'm safe when we're together." She wanted to share this journey with her friend. She knew he would do everything in his power to keep her safe from harm.

"Good. Shall we?"

"How do we get out of the castle unseen?"

"We'll leave through one of the passageways lying beneath the castle. I've put sacks of food and water there for us." Devon placed a dark cloak over Jenny's dark green tunic and fastened the quiver and bow onto her back. He smiled as she cinched her waist with the leather belt and sheath.

Jenny removed the sword and took a moment to admire the handle. Rubies and emeralds were woven into the intricate designs of the hilt. "This sword is incredible and so light." She placed her sword into its sheath and showed herself off to Devon, who smiled with appreciation.

"It belonged to a member of the royal family. The metal was made and carved into a sword by elves. I thought it might bring you luck."

"Thank you. I'll cherish it."

"We have a long road ahead of us. We should leave." He opened the door and looked up and down the hallway. The coast was clear. For some strange reason, there were no guards stationed on this floor today. He motioned for her to follow him as he led her toward the back stairs.

Devon and Jenny ran to the back of the castle. He pushed a panel in the wall and it slid open to reveal a staircase. He removed a torch from the wall sconce and ignited a flame to illuminate the stone steps. Further and further into the bowels of the castle they went. He picked up two large satchels and handed one to Jenny who placed it across her chest in the same fashion as Devon.

"How much further do we have to go?" The passageways reminded her of the catacombs beneath her school, but where those were dank and moldy, here, these passageways were cleaner and easier to walk through.

"We're almost there. We have to be careful. We can't afford to be caught."

"Devon, you don't have to do this."

"Yes, I do. Come on we're almost there."

Devon opened a large, wooden door and as daylight greeted them, he blew out the flame. After a quick look around, he waved for her to join him. Together, they ran for the forest.

"Don't we have to go through the village?" Jenny looked around trying to figure out where they were. This was new to her, and when she didn't recognize this area, she worried about their location. They were supposed to start their journey to the Black Castle through the forest.

"No. Not too many people know of this passageway, but I'm an explorer, and when I was younger I found several corridors under the castle and village. Whenever I wanted to sneak in or out of the castle unseen, I'd use one of these tunnels. I used to sneak out whenever I wanted to meet up with friends from the village, but my parents wanted me to learn history."

"Cool."

The hour was early and darkness still held the forest within its grasp. Devon stayed close to Jenny to make certain she didn't injure herself. The forest was filled with hidden dangers and his job was to make sure Jenny stayed away from these dangerous areas.

Their adventure began. They walked around large trees and over thick roots. Devon was pleasantly surprised to see that Jenny proved a sturdy companion able to keep up with him. Time passed, and soon the sun's rays filtered through the trees, illuminating their route. He kept up a trying pace in order to make good time. The forest was still safe, but once they left their realm, there was no telling what dangers would greet the two travelers.

"So, how long will it take us to get to the Black Castle?" Jenny had no concept of distance in this land. Everything seemed vast and a great distance away. There were no cars, buses, or cabs.

If you had to travel, you had to use your own feet. She wasn't used to this.

"It'll take a week at the very least." Devon's eyes moved to survey the area. His senses were on alert. There were things hiding in the darkness of the woods, and it was his job to make sure they stayed safe.

"You mean it could take longer?" Jenny worried they'd arrive too late to rescue Beth.

"Yes, it could take much longer."

"But you're not sure?"

"No, I'm not."

"You've never been there?"

"No, I haven't, but don't worry, we'll get there in time to save Beth."

"If you've never been there, how can you be so certain?"

"I will do everything in my power to make sure we arrive in time to save your friend. I won't let you down."

Jenny looked at him. His striking good looks made her heart flutter, but it was the deep blue of his eyes that could captivate anyone. Still, she sensed more than he knew. She sensed he kept some information to himself, but at the same time she knew that he would keep his word to her. She believed in his words and in him. By his side, Jenny was safe.

CHAPTER 21

THE BEAST

When the sun was high in the sky, Devon took a break. He found a couple of fallen logs and set up a small campsite. He took out bread, cheese, and fruit and handed Jenny a metal cup filled with water. They had a small picnic in the woods. On another occasion, this would be an otherwise exciting way to spend the day.

They ate and drank their fill.

"We won't stop again until nightfall," he said.

"Why not?" Jenny didn't like the sound of that.

"This part of the forest is still quite safe, but once we enter the Dark Forest, we'll find ourselves in dangerous territory. That's where the real danger begins, and I'd like to walk its length as quickly as possible."

"I take it we have no other choice but to travel through the Dark Forest." Jenny hoped she was strong enough to make the journey. Back in the castle, this trek seemed like a breeze. She thought a short walk to another castle would be exciting, a simple outing, but now those they were out here where thoughts of giant snakes came to mind, she wasn't as confident as she let on.

"You're learning."

"I don't have much of a choice."

"That's true, but you're being a good sport. You're facing tremendous odds, and yet your spirit hasn't wavered."

"Actually, I find this very exciting." Jenny smiled conspiratorially.

"I hope you still feel this way after we've fought some hungry beasts."

"Gee, I can't wait." Jenny's eyes searched the horizon, but she wasn't sure if Devon was saying it in jest or if he really meant they would have to fight beasts. She couldn't wrap her mind around it.

Devon laughed. "Don't worry, we're safe here."

"This isn't so bad… I think." Jenny bit into an apple.

"For now we're safe, but it won't last."

"Always the optimist," Jenny said teasingly.

* * * *

The day continued with a long walk. The forest darkened the deeper they went. Soon, Devon removed the torch he'd packed and ignited it to lead the way. Always on guard, he claimed responsibility for Jenny's safety. When they entered the Dark Forest a while later, Devon looked around and said, "Be on guard. There are many dangerous creatures lurking in the shadows of this forest. Watch your step."

"Don't worry. I'm sticking close to you." She sidled in closer to Devon for emphasis.

Trees lined the area in abundance, and small plants carpeted the ground. From within the lush greenery, an odd plant shook and released a long vine that crept along the forest floor. Slowly, it wound its way like a serpent hunting for a fresh meal. Red thorns sprung from the thick, green vine and aimed its deadly venom at Jenny's legs.

Devon saw the creeping vine long before Jenny did, and with a quick slice of his sword, he cut the vine in half. The plant squealed and retracted its length. From the underbrush, another length of vine wound its way along the forest floor. Devon tried to cut the vine in half, but this time it crept to a nearby bush and waited for the right moment to strike. From the other side, the vine crept out and tried to wrap itself around Devon's leg.

Jenny jumped in front of Devon and cut the vine at the base with her sword. She watched in horror as a red glaze oozed from every thorn as the plant died. "What was that?"

"A carnivorous plant."

160

"That vine had thorns!"

"Yes, it did. That particular plant digs its thorns into a person's leg and feeds on the blood it draws."

Jenny looked around to see if anything else was trying to crawl toward her. "And I take it that would hurt."

"It would, but only for a moment. The thorns hold a deadly poison."

A twig snapped somewhere behind them. Devon stopped and motioned for Jenny to stay still and listen to the sounds around them.

"Now what?" Jenny wasn't sure she was ready for this. She wanted to be back at the castle safe and sound instead of being out here not knowing if they'd survive.

"I'm not sure."

The minutes crawled and all seemed calm as a light breeze touched them. Maybe their imagination was getting the best of them. Jenny thought it made sense that they were hearing things after the attempt on their lives by the poisonous and carnivorous plant that tried to attack them.

"Let's keep going."

A few more feet and another twig snapped.

"I heard that." Jenny inspected the surrounding foliage.

Devon handed her the torch and removed his sword, ready to battle anything that might come out and attack them.

"Stay behind me, Jenny." Devon stood poised, his sword locked in his grip.

"What is it?"

"I don't know."

Their eyes never wavered from where the sound emanated. Another rustle and Devon turned but kept his eyes fixated on one spot, as if mesmerized by the sheer terror of what was hiding within. He released the breath he held when he thought they were safe. They had taken one step away when, from the bushes, a large, brown rabbit jumped out.

"Well, that scared me," Jenny said, and tried to steady the trembling taking over her body.

"Startled me as well." Devon looked at Jenny. "I think it's time to leave this place. Something doesn't feel right."

Just as they were about to run from the spot, a large black bear, twice the size of a grizzly, burst through the bushes. His large yellow teeth dripped saliva and blood. Growling, he was on a direct path with the young pair. Large paws brought the beast closer and closer to them. Jenny screamed and dropped the torch. She grabbed her sword and waited for Devon's next move. She'd never seen anything this frightening; not even on TV had she ever seen such a monster. A large roar escaped the creature. It shook the forest floor with another roar. Devon backed away, but held his sword firmly in front of him. His eyes briefly scanned the area for Jenny and to his horror she was next to him, sword in hand.

"Jenny, what are you doing? Move away!"

"What is that thing?" Jenny's eyes never left the beast.

"A magically created beast."

A long and shaggy mane hid the beasts distorted features and covered its body. The creature began its advance. Slowly, it circled them ready to pounce as soon as it was able to attack the young pair. Devon pushed Jenny behind him, but the beast was after her. Devon knew he couldn't allow the beast to spring on them. He stood poised and waited for the beast's next move. He maintained his ground trying to protect his friend from harm, but the beast had other ideas. It moved its head from side to side as sharp claws scratched the dirt in a menacing manner. Jenny and Devon slowly backed away, knowing they only had seconds before the attack came.

"Be careful, Jenny." Devon lunged at the beast. Its roar echoed throughout the woods. The creature stood on hind legs and dropped back down on all fours. Devon sliced the air hoping to hit the beast with his sword, but the deadly claws swiped at Devon, knocking him to the ground. Another frightening roar escaped as Devon rolled only inches away from where the beast's claws landed.

To his surprise, the beast leapt over Devon and lunged for Jenny, who brought down her sword catching its paw. Standing like a giant man, a bloodcurdling howl escaped from between sharp teeth. Its rage spread through the air. Once again, the beast advanced on Jenny. Devon jumped to his feet as the beast's claws swiped at her. Jenny threw herself to one side, giving him the opportunity to spring into action and slice the beast's back. The scream that rent the afternoon air couldn't be called human.

"Devon, watch out!"

More saliva dripped from the beast's teeth as it jumped at Devon, ready to strike.

From behind, Jenny made her move. Just as the claws were about to shred Devon, she plunged her sword into its heart as a final roar escaped the hideous creature. Devon rolled away as the beast roared its final breath, and died only inches from where Devon lay.

"Are you alright?" Jenny ran to her friend.

Devon smiled at the concern in her voice. "I'm fine. Thank you for saving my life."

"I couldn't let it hurt you."

"I'm glad you did what you did." Devon took Jenny's extended hand and stood up. He hugged her; grateful she'd saved his life.

Pride shone. "Devon, that wasn't a real bear."

"No. It was one of Maeldoi's beasts."

"What do you mean one of his beasts?"

"He has his own zoo."

"Are they all like that?"

"Yes. Most of them have been magically transformed, while others have been mutated, through some form of black-magic, in order to look like these beasts."

"Jenny picked up Devon's sword and gave it to him. She couldn't believe what she was hearing. How could anyone do this to another human being?

"We need to leave. It's not safe here anymore."

"Okay."

Devon and Jenny ran through the woods. Distance was their savior. Finally, after what seemed like hours, Devon slowed his pace. "Let's take a moment and catch our breath."

"Sounds good to me." Jenny took out her flask and drank greedily.

Devon looked around. Large boulders covered the area. They sat next to each other on one of the boulders and kept their eyes focused on their surroundings, always searching for unwanted intruders.

"Maeldoi will be furious when he finds out we killed the beast. He'll send more to hunt us down. We should keep moving. I don't think it's safe here."

They continued the long walk until the forest darkened even more. Devon ignited a torch and led Jenny through the woods. Stones littered the ground creating a treacherous hike, and the darkness made it impossible to see the path they were forced to travel.

A while later, Devon said, "This looks like a safe place to spend the night." He looked all around the area.

"Are you sure?"

"Just to make sure, I'll have a look around."

"I'd offer to set up camp, but I don't know how to do that."

"Collect some wood and rocks to make a campfire. I'll take care of the rest."

"Okay."

"Here, take the torch." Devon handed her their only source of light.

"What about you?"

"If there's something out there, I don't want to alert it to my presence."

"Good thinking."

"Jenny, don't stray too far from here. I'll be back in a few minutes." Devon unsheathed his sword and ran toward the trees.

Jenny watched his catlike movements, impressed by his skills, skills that reassured her. She walked around and gathered wood, twigs, and rocks to form a circle to place the wood on the twigs. She sat back and wondered if she could do the same bit of magic Devon did with the torch. She concentrated on the fire, and closed her eyes as a breath escaped her lips. Soon a flame glowed. She stoked the flame until a beautiful fire burned. Proud of her accomplishments, she took out Devon's blanket, food and water, and emptied her own sack. She sat down and waited.

A twig snapped somewhere behind her. She stood and removed her sword. Her stance was poised and ready to defend the area.

"Who... who's there? Show yourself!" She was ready to fight anything or anyone that came into their campsite.

"It's me, Jenny."

"Devon. I'm glad it's you." Jenny breathed a sigh of relief.

"It's safe to spend the night here." Devon smiled at the sight of the camp. He walked over to it and looked at Jenny. "Well done."

"Thanks. I used my magick. It was more fun than fighting the beast," Jenny said sheepishly.

"I told you magick was a lot more fun than you realize."

"Okay, so I'll admit it. You were right."

"As always." He laughed.

She hit him for his impudent remark.

CHAPTER 22

THE TALE

Later that night, as they sat around the fire, Jenny nibbled on her dinner all the while enjoying Devon's company. She looked around the woods wondering how she came to be here. Only a few days before she'd been in Morgansville living in a house with Aunt Nora, dreaming of having an adventure, and now, all of a sudden, she was in the middle of the biggest adventure of her life. She wondered what the next few days would bring. She hoped she'd be capable of facing everything that was being thrown at her. She wanted to be strong enough to succeed.

Jenny looked at Devon, truly thankful for his friendship. If not for him, she didn't know what would have happened to her and Beth. After meeting Maeldoi, she realized she could have been the victim here. She could have been the one taken to the Black Castle, and if not for meeting Devon, there wouldn't be anyone to help her. Instead, she sat here with the son of the Steward of Wardell, enjoying some food by a campfire. She was thrilled to have a good friend like Devon in her life. She looked over the campfire and stared at this handsome guy.

"Tell me about Maeldoi." She wanted to hear more about the evil wizard.

"He's a very powerful and dangerous man." Devon spoke cautiously, never revealing too much information. This frustrated Jenny.

"I've gotten to know what kind of man he is, but where does he come from?" If she was to embark on a dangerous trek against this man, she should know a little something about him. It only made sense to her to know her enemy.

"Wardell."

"You're kidding?"

"No, I'm not. Maeldoi lived in our castle."

"How could an evil man like that live in your castle?"

"He wasn't always like that. There was a time when he served the present king's father. King Royce kept Maeldoi at his side as his royal advisor. He was true to the king, until one day he met a woman."

"Who was she?"

"Ringwar."

"I heard you mention that name when Beth disappeared."

"I did mention Ringwar to Maeldoi."

"Who is she?"

"Ringwar is an evil, old witch. She turned Maeldoi against King Royce."

"Why would she do that?" Jenny asked as a howl in the distance caught her attention. "What's that?"

"It's just a wolf. He won't come near the fire." Devon smiled at her fear.

"I… I believe you… I think."

"A lone wolf isn't a threat to us."

"Will you tell me the rest of the story?" She wanted to take her mind off the howling in the distance.

"I'll tell you what I can. Maeldoi was faithful to King Royce. He loved him like a brother, and the king felt the same way about the wizard. Then one day the beautiful and beguiling Ringwar entered the picture. Back then the witch was considered a very beautiful woman who used her beauty to lure men to do her bidding. She kept them at her side until she'd extracted all their goodness and only the evil she seeded lived within their souls."

"She did this to Maeldoi?"

"Yes. She controlled him. Ringwar wanted the riches of Wardell Castle. At first he fought her control, but her greed knew no bounds, and she used all her wiles to turn him toward the dark side. Once he was under her power, she forced him to overthrow the royal family."

Jenny was wide eyed as she listened to this tale.

"He tried to kill the king and the queen."

"But wasn't there a child?"

"Yes, the young prince. Now, in order for Maeldoi to take the throne and place the crown upon Ringwar's head, the royal family and their heirs had to be killed."

"Would he really kill that many people for his own gain?"

"Remember, Ringwar controlled him. He would kill anyone she asked him to. He was completely under her spell."

"Spell?"

"Yes. She controlled them with spells."

"If that's the case, Maeldoi can't be blamed for what he does."

"Not exactly."

"Devon, if Maeldoi is under her spell how can we blame him for what he does?" Jenny couldn't believe she was defending the man who'd taken her friend prisoner and sent wild beasts to kill her and Devon.

"When King Royce ruled, I believe Maeldoi wasn't in control of his actions, but as time passed, Ringwar's spells wore off. As she grew older and older her magic weakened, but Maeldoi remained loyal to her. And now he wallows in the evil that once held him prisoner."

"And you don't believe he can come back?" Jenny sipped her water.

"No. I don't."

"So what is he after?"

"With the king and queen missing, he wants to rule Wardell and place the crown upon his and Ringwar's head."

"But what about Galfrid?"

"My father is Steward of Wardell. He holds the crown and the rule until the true king's return."

"Did the king and queen have any children?"

Devon thought for a moment. She watched him struggle with his words. Why couldn't he just answer her question? Why was everything under such a cloak and dagger?

"Yes, they had a child… a daughter."

"Where is she?" The story of King Morgan and Queen Ileana piqued an interest she didn't quite understand.

"The child?"

"Yes."

"No one knows."

"Did the entire royal family disappear?"

"Yes. We're not sure if it happened at the same time, or if the child was taken at a different time."

"I don't understand."

"The royal family wasn't in Wardell at the time of their disappearance. They went into hiding."

"So what happened?"

"No one really knows, except perhaps one man."

"Maeldoi?"

"Yes, Maeldoi."

"Do you think he had anything to do with their disappearance?" Jenny wondered how one man and one woman could cause so many problems. What did the disappearance of the king and queen have to do with them? Something didn't feel right, and Jenny wanted to figure out how she was connected to everything she'd heard—if there was a connection. She believed there had to be a connection.

"Yes, I do."

"Has anyone ever tried to find out what happened?"

"We sent men to find them. We hoped someone in this realm saw them or knew what really happened the day they disappeared. Up until now, we haven't found any sign of them. We never found anyone who had seen them or had any knowledge of what happened to the royal family." Devon paused. He looked at Jenny and offered her a smile. "The road to the Black Castle is froth with danger. Not too many men ventured too close, for if they did Ringwar would destroy them. Only someone as strong and powerful as Ringwar could pit themselves against her and her black magick."

"And you think she has Beth, and she wants to trade me for Beth." Jenny's fear shone in her eyes.

"Yes, I do. If Maeldoi has captured her, then he would have taken her to the Black Castle and Ringwar." Devon took a drink from his metal cup and stared into the fire. "I wish I could tell you more, but for now that's all I know as well."

"I think you're holding back on me."

"It's time to sleep. We'll need to get an early start." Devon put his head down and closed his eyes. This conversation was over.

"Goodnight, Devon." Jenny relented. She'd try again in the morning.

"Goodnight, Jenny."

CHAPTER 23

THE DRAGON'S RETURN

The sun barely touched the two sleeping forms when Devon's eyes opened with the break of dawn. He sat up and stoked the fire, breathing life back into the dying embers. He allowed Jenny a few more minutes of slumber. He filled their canteens from the stream just beyond the trees.

Devon gently shook Jenny's shoulder. "Good morning, sleepyhead."

Jenny saw the sun barely made an appearance. She stretched her aching muscles. "What time is it?"

"Dawn. I've got breakfast on the fire."

"Oh, it smells great."

"Join me by the fire." Devon scooped up some eggs, bread and cheese and put the food on tin plates and handed one to Jenny.

"Where did you get eggs from?"

"I have my ways."

"What poor creature lost these eggs?"

Devon laughed. "I found a partridge nest. I thought we should enjoy a hearty meal before we set out. We have a long walk ahead of us."

"This is really good."

"Thank you." They ate with gusto, their hunger intense after all they'd been through the other day.

Jenny had never spent so much time running as she did yesterday following the fight with the wild beast Maeldoi had sent after them.

With the fire extinguished, Devon and Jenny continued to follow the trail.

171

"So, what's on the agenda for today?"

"We make our way to Warwick Castle." Devon waited for her reaction.

"What? Where did you say we were going?"

"To Warwick Castle." Devon smiled.

"Why are we going there?" Jenny remembered the book she'd borrowed, the *History of Warwick Castle*. She wished she'd read the book, but instead she read the fascinating book Devon gave her about magick. By the end of the book, all the questions haunting her about magick had been answered. Only now was she beginning to understand the hidden talents she possessed and how to tap into them. Her fear of using her gift waned. She tried many different spells, and they'd worked out for her.

"I believe we need to go there first."

"I'd like to go to the Black Castle and save Beth."

"And we will. Jenny, there are many reasons for us to continue on our path to the Black Castle, but I think we should visit Warwick first."

"Will you tell me why we have to go there?"

"Not really, but I think some questions will be answered there."

"Such as?"

"Let's wait and see."

"Devon." She put her hand on her hip and stared at him. She trusted him, there was no doubt about it, but Jenny wanted to get Beth.

"We can also pick up more supplies. We shouldn't continue without more food and water."

"Is Warwick on the way to the Black Castle?"

"Yes and no."

"That doesn't make sense." She wanted to reach the Black Castle, and without a plausible explanation for this detour, she'd continue to challenge his decisions. After all, Beth's life was contingent upon reaching the castle before Maeldoi or Ringwar caused her any harm. They had to rescue her friend before it was too late. She'd never forgive herself if she lingered at Warwick Castle and something horrible happened to her best friend.

Devon looked at Jenny, and she actually thought he would tell her everything, but instead he refrained from saying a word.

Frustrated, Jenny crossed her arms and stared at her friend. She wanted answers.

"I'm sorry, Jenny, but all I know is…"

She was just about to tell him that she knew he was hiding something from her, when from a distance a familiar rumble was felt.

THUMP! THUMP! THUMP!

Devon and Jenny frantically looked around. The ground beneath their feet shook with the strength of a thousand men. Desperately, they clung to each other trying to maintain their balance. Devon pulled his sword free from its sheath and waited.

Jenny followed suit. She was poised and ready to fight whatever was heading their way. "Devon, what is it?" Jenny feared Maeldoi had sent an army of beasts to hunt them down and kill them.

"I don't know."

"Shouldn't we run?"

"Good idea!"

They ran, even though they didn't know what followed them. Based on the rumbling beneath the ground, it had to be something large and dangerous. Small stones caught their every step. Leaves fell all around them as the creature pounded its way through the trees. Branches scratched their skin. They kept a harried pace knowing this was the only way to escape the clutches of whatever hunted them. Finally, the beast broke through the trees.

Devon looked back. To his horror, the creature chasing them was the same beast that wreaked havoc on Wardell only days before. "Dragon! Run!"

Jenny looked back and saw the large creature heading toward them. Dark scales covered its face. Frightening spikes protruded from both sides of a large snout. Long, sharp teeth were visible through its grin; the dragon closed the distance. He was stronger and faster than the young pair.

"It's catching up to us!" Jenny shouted.

"I know! Keep running!"

A cave loomed up ahead. Devon saw it and took Jenny's hand in his. He pulled her along, hoping to reach the cave before the dragon caught them.

"What are you doing?" Jenny felt Devon pull her off the path.

Stones were larger now and impeded their progress. Jenny tripped, but Devon's hold helped her keep her balance.

"There's a cave up ahead! If we can make it inside, we can lose the dragon!"

Finally, the mouth of the cave came into view. Devon pushed Jenny down and they crawled into the opening. They moved away from the entrance. They waited and listened. They were able to sit back and wait. Devon used his keen senses to listen for a sign that they'd lost the dragon.

The dragon's steps faltered and stopped near the cave's entrance. It used its long and wide snout to sniff the air. The dragon's large eyes surveyed the area in an attempt to gain their scent.

Devon motioned for Jenny to stay quiet.

She looked down the length of the cave, but only saw darkness. A question sat upon her lips, but she refrained from uttering the words. What if the dragon found them and caused a cave-in? What would they do if they couldn't get out of here in time to reach the castle and save her friend?

A roar of frustration left the dragon as the thunder of its gait passed by the cave where its prey sat quietly by.

"Is it safe?" Jenny barely whispered the words to Devon.

"I'm not certain, but I think we should stay here a while longer. We can have something to drink."

"What about some food?"

"I don't recommend it. The dragon would smell our food and return. We should be much more careful."

"How far are we from Warwick?"

"Only a few hours walk. Tonight, we'll be safe within its walls."

"Then we should get going." The thought of being safe appealed to her. There was far too much danger out here in the woods. She wasn't used to it and she really didn't want to get used to the type of dangers lurking within.

"Wait here. I'll make sure it's safe for us to leave." Devon crawled out of the entrance and stood up. He listened for any sounds that would warn him of the dragon's presence. When there was no sound, other than the song the birds sang, Devon relaxed. If the dragon had been lying in wait, the birds and small animals wouldn't be scavenging for food. They would have fled the area.

He used his keen senses to detect any anomalies. So far everything seemed back to normal.

"Jenny, you can come out!" he called to her, and bent over waiting for his friend to emerge.

She crawled out of the cave and stood up. "Is it gone?"

Her eyes searched the area hoping they'd seen the last of the dragon. They didn't need anything else trying to hunt them down and eat them. She would like to have a little boredom in this quest they were on. If they managed to get to Warwick without any mishap she'd be only too happy.

"Yes, it's safe. The dragon's left the area. We'll continue our journey." Devon took her hand in his and led her back on the right trail.

CHAPTER 24

WARWICK

The town of Warwick came into view just below the rolling green hills. At the bottom, a road led to a large stone wall guarding the town from unwanted attacks, much the same as Wardell. Giant gates stood open, but heavily guarded against any and all menace.

"Is that Warwick?" Jenny was impressed by the size of the town spread out before them.

"Yes, it is."

"Wow!"

"Warwick is the largest village in this land," Devon said.

"Where's the castle?" Jenny walked down the hill trying to maintain her footing, as it slanted drastically downward, but somehow they made it to the bottom of the hill without embarrassing themselves.

"The castle sits beyond the town up on a rise. The stone wall encircles and protects the village and surrounding grounds. In case of attack, Warwick becomes a virtual fortress and guards all those in need of protection," Devon said.

"Protection from what?"

"That all depends on who attacks Warwick and its surrounding neighbors."

"Even Wardell?"

"Yes."

"But Wardell seems capable of defending itself against anything." The dragon couldn't penetrate Wardell's security.

"True enough, Wardell can take care of itself, but should the need arise, the people of Wardell could travel to Warwick.

And if needed, the guards of Warwick Castle could journey to Wardell."

"Has Wardell ever been abandoned?"

"No. Only the royal family has been sent here."

"Why?"

"The royal family has been the target of many assassination attempts. King Morgan and Queen Ileana were on their way here when they disappeared."

"And no one knows what happened to them."

"No. We never found out what happened, or where they disappeared to. That's what I'm hoping to discover."

"Why is this so important to you?"

"My father is Steward of Wardell. He cannot abandon his position to search for the truth. This duty has fallen upon me. I must find the truth behind their disappearance. It's my duty as the only son of the Steward."

"But I thought Galfrid sent some men to uncover the truth."

"He did, but not all of them returned. I think the dragon killed the men and with so many casualties, my father abandoned the quest."

"And now that we're out here, you're going to try and find out what happened to them?" Jenny understood why Devon wanted to accompany her on this quest. There was more at stake here than just saving Beth from Maeldoi and Ringwar. There were also many unanswered questions. There were questions surrounding the disappearance of the entire royal family.

"If I can."

"I'd like to help you." Jenny wanted to be part of every aspect of this journey.

"You'd help me with my search?"

"Of course I would. You've done so much for me. Besides, I'd like to meet this king and queen and maybe we'll find the missing princess. Wouldn't that be awesome? If you returned to Wardell armed with the knowledge of what actually happened to the royal family."

"Yes, it would be wonderful to finally know where our king and queen are. I would be honored to have you help me with my quest," Devon said with a sly smile.

"We're in this together."

Devon looked up and stared at the slow descent of the sun. "We should hurry. After dark, the guards won't permit us to pass through the gates. I'd like to spend the night behind the walls instead of out here."

They came upon the open gates where two guards dressed in dark pants and green tunics stood at attention. Over their tunics the men wore heavy armor and held large, menacing swords.

"State your business," the first guard demanded.

"Devon of Wardell Castle to see the Prince of Warwick."

"Enter."

Jenny walked next to Devon. Her eyes traveled in every direction, taking in all the sights. The town bustled with activity. Children ran around, laughing in playful abandon. Stone houses graced the perimeter of the town in rows climbing up into the hills surrounding Warwick. They walked down the roadway toward the center of town where a large market filled the square with colorful booths. Freshly baked bread, pies, and cakes enticed customers to purchase their goods.

"Where are we going?" Jenny's eyes traveled the perimeter. She wanted to see everything Warwick had to offer.

"To the castle," Devon said.

"Who are we going to see?"

"Prince Rainard, ruler of Warwick."

"I thought all rulers were kings," Jenny said.

"Prince Rainard's father is still alive. And as long as the king lives, his son remains a prince."

"But doesn't that mean the king rules Warwick?"

"No. King Theron has been ill and cannot rule his lands, and, therefore, the rule has fallen upon his first born son, Rainard."

"What happened?"

"We don't know."

"So why do you want to speak with the prince?" She looked him in the eye. "And before you tell me something I won't believe or say that I'm not supposed to know, remember I'm in this with you. I think I've earned the right to know a little bit more about what's going on."

Devon was about to give her another vague answer when Jenny's attention was drawn to some beautiful parrots for sale. She wanted to get a closer look at these birds. She looked around admiring the colorful birds when off to the side she noticed a bird more beautiful than any bird she'd ever seen in real life or on TV. She walked over to the cage in which he sat and gazed at his beauty. He sat on a perch in a gilded cage. He seemed sad. Jenny walked over to him. He was incredible.

"Devon, what kind of bird is that?"

"A phoenix."

"I've heard of them, but I've never seen one before. He's amazing." He was the size of an eagle. Gold plumage encircled his head and neck, but his body was decorated with lovely purple and golden feathers. A long, golden tail hung down giving the bird a magnificent coloring. Jenny was captivated by the phoenix's golden eyes.

"We should head for the castle."

"Yes." But, her eyes were fixated on the bird. If she didn't know any better, she'd swear he followed her every move. "Look at him. He's watching me." She stood mesmerized by the bird.

Devon also noticed the attention he bestowed upon Jenny. "Would you like to join me when I speak with the prince?" Devon asked, trying to draw her attention away from the bird.

Shocked, Jenny turned toward Devon and smiled. "Yes, I would."

"Very well, you may accompany me," he said with a smile.

"Thank you, Devon." She squeezed his hand.

"You're welcome. As you said, you have earned some rights."

She left with Devon, but not before looking at the bird once more. There was something so reassuring in his gaze, but, as always, Jenny couldn't understand the odd thoughts that seemed to appear out of nowhere.

Soon, the hill bearing Warwick Castle came into view. Jenny looked up the path and marveled at its size and beauty. Warwick Castle was a cream colored mound of turrets, draw bridges, and lush gardens. Much larger than Wardell, Warwick was the epitome of what a fairytale castle looked like.

They followed the path toward the gates where once again two guards dressed in the same manner as the guards they'd already encountered at the village gates stopped them at the entrance.

"We've come to speak with Prince Rainard," Devon said.

"State your name." The first guard spoke to the two youngsters.

"Devon of Wardell Castle."

The guards bowed and stood to one side allowing Devon and Jenny entrance to the castle grounds.

"You seem to know your way around." Jenny was impressed. She looked at the gardens that boasted more colors than a summer rainbow. She'd love to stroll through and admire the lush gardens.

"My father and I spent many summers here with the king and the prince, hunting and fishing together. Our parents spent a lot of time together until King Theron fell ill."

"How long has he been ill?"

"It's been a couple of years now."

"What about the queen?"

"She was ill for a very long time. The king did everything in his power to save his queen, but she grew weaker and weaker, and one day, about four years ago, she passed away."

"That's terrible." Tears glistened in Jenny's eyes.

"Yes, it was a shock to us all."

"So how old is the prince?"

"He's two years my senior."

"He's very young to carry the burden of ruling a land like Warwick. He lost his mother and now his father is ill. That's a lot for him to bear."

"He's been raised to rule Warwick. True, he never imagined it would be this soon, but he knows his responsibilities to the town and its people. Rainard takes his position as ruler very seriously."

They walked over the drawbridge and this time the posted sentries didn't stop them. Instead, they moved aside to allow the young pair entry. They entered the hall and saw servants walk by. Most of them only glanced at the disheveled pair as they walked through the marbled foyer toward a long corridor. Ornate frames had portraits of people she didn't know, nonetheless, she admired them as they continued to walk the hallways.

"This is the way to the throne room." Devon led Jenny down another long hallway.

She felt a little awkward and shy about meeting a prince. She and Devon had spent the night fighting a beast and sleeping on the ground. Today, they'd had to run for their lives as a dragon chased them through the woods, and then they had to sit in an old dirty cave. They weren't exactly clean and ready to meet royalty. She shared her concerns with Devon. He laughed. Her hair was tousled. Her cheeks bore signs of scratches and mud. Their tunics were torn and dirty. He understood how she felt about meeting a prince for the first time, but their attire was the least of their worries. They had some serious discussions ahead of them.

"Don't worry, Jenny. You look fine," Devon said. "Rainard isn't your typical prince. Trust me; he won't think anything out of the ordinary." Devon smiled at her.

"I have so far."

CHAPTER 25

PRINCE RAINARD

At Devon and Jenny's approach, two guards simultaneously opened the doors to the large and ornate room where the prince sat upon his golden throne. Devon sent word requesting a private audience from one of the servants. He stood in the back and waited for a summons to see the prince.

"This room is beautiful," Jenny whispered. Except for Wardell, she'd never seen such magnificence before. Pale marble walls surrounded the room in opulent splendor. Large windows showed views of lovingly cared for gardens, while deep crimson curtains fell to the marble floor and pooled beneath each window.

The beauty of the room and its size astonished Jenny. At the front of the room on a dais sat two golden thrones where a young man listened to his people. This was so new to her and yet it wasn't. She was suddenly feeling in ways she'd never felt before. Was it this quest that had her emotions in turmoil, or was it something else? She looked out at the throng of people speaking with the prince about one thing or another and felt a distant memory trying to break through walls erected in her mind. She wasn't sure how to explain the strange feelings, but she knew they had something to do with this place.

A minute later, a uniformed guard approached. "The prince will see you now. Please follow me." They went down the same hallway. The guard stopped and opened the door. "In here," he told Devon with a bow.

Devon and Jenny entered the office. The room was large and airy. Windows stood open and allowed a breeze to flow gently around the room. A young man sat behind an ornate desk. The brown leather chair protested his rise as he came around to greet his guests.

"Devon! Good to see you!"

"Rainard!" The prince approached Devon and extended his arm in friendship. Devon grasped it. Their smiles proved a longtime camaraderie. "It's been too long, my friend. How are your parents?"

"They're quite well. Tell me, how is your father?"

"Not well at all. He's aging rather quickly and no longer recognizes me. I've had to have him locked in his room under a healer's care, and I'm sorry to say, under constant guard."

"Have they found out what ails your father?"

"No. They say a dark spell has been cast upon him, but no one can tell me how to break the spell or how to save my father."

"And what do you believe?"

"I'm not certain. At first I thought the fever was upon him, but the rapid aging process that has taken over him belies this. I am left to believe someone has caused this illness."

"I think you are correct. We need to figure out who would have a motive to harm your father."

The prince was about to say something else when he saw Jenny. Rainard looked at her and smiled. "Where are my manners?"

"Rain this is my friend, Jenny."

"How do you do?"

"Hello," Jenny shyly said as she bowed her head to him, unsure as to the proper greeting she should bestow upon the prince.

"Please come in and sit down. It seems as though you've had quite an ordeal getting here." He noticed the worn clothes and their unkempt appearance.

"What? Oh, yes, we've had a rather busy morning." Devon led Jenny to a chair in front of the desk as the prince returned to his own.

Rain leaned forward and smiled. "I'm so happy to see you, my friend. It has been a long time since I've seen a friendly face."

Jenny studied the Prince of Warwick. He was tall with long brown hair tied at the nape of his neck, as seemed the custom in this land. His build, although still slight with the touch of youth, began to show the man who would soon emerge.

Rain's dark eyes were drawn to Devon's companion, rendering Jenny uncomfortable. Unfortunately for her, this was fast becoming a frequent occurrence. Wherever she went, people in this land took to staring at her to the point of being unnerving. She didn't like the feeling it gave her.

"I know it's been a while, but in these dark times, my father hesitates to leave Wardell."

"Understandable. So what brings you to Warwick?"

"We're on our way to the Black Castle."

Rainard's shocked expression made Devon laugh. "Why the devil would you attempt such a foolhardy feat?" The prince wanted to hear this story.

"Maeldoi captured Jenny's friend and is holding her in his castle. We're on our way there to rescue her."

"That is a fool's errand. You know better than I that no one who ventures into the Black Castle ever returns."

"We have no other choice," Jenny said. "I won't allow her to be killed by Maeldoi."

"Brave words, Jenny, but you don't understand who or what Maeldoi is."

"Yes, your Highness, I do."

"Please call me Rainard, or Rain. Devon and I have been friends for many years. We do not stand on ceremony."

"Thank you, Rain."

"I think you're making a big mistake. Maeldoi is only one problem. Ringwar is the one who must be watched. She is as deadly as she is ugly."

"I'm well aware of Ringwar's treachery," Devon said. "This isn't the first time I've had a run in with them, but I also know what they're capable of doing, and we cannot allow Jenny's friend to be harmed in any way."

Rainard turned his dark gaze on Jenny with renewed interest. He leaned back in the large leather chair. "Why did he take your friend?"

"I really don't know."

"Devon?"

"They want Jenny."

184

"What could Maeldoi and Ringwar want with you?" Rainard addressed his question to the one person who should have the answers.

"I don't know."

Rainard raised an eyebrow and looked to Devon once more for answers.

Jenny's stomach rumbled; they hadn't eaten anything since this morning. She turned a lovely shade of pink.

"Where are my manners? You've had a long walk. Come, we will have some dinner, and then I will assign you rooms to spend the night."

"Thank you, Rain," Devon said. At least for this night they'd be safe.

The prince escorted them from the office and traveled down a long hallway, all the while talking idle chitchat about the fun times they'd had hunting and fishing together as children. They entered a lovely room with a square table and eight chairs. A large buffet held numerous vases and golden goblets, priceless heirlooms, no doubt. They sat down and two servants appeared. They placed platters filled with chicken, fish, beef, potatoes, rice, and an assortment of vegetables on the table.

"So, Devon, why don't you tell me what's going on. I might be able to help you."

"I wish you could, Rain, but at this point, there isn't much I can tell you." He still harbored some secrets.

He looked at Jenny who smiled. "Don't feel bad. I've been getting the runaround ever since I arrived in Wardell."

"How long have you been here?"

"About three weeks."

"So how did you manage to anger Maeldoi and Ringwar in such a short period of time?" Rain asked, showing even white teeth.

"That's the problem. I've never met Ringwar, and I'd only briefly met Maeldoi."

"Why have they set their sight on you?" This heightened Rainard's interest.

"I don't know."

Rain glanced at Devon, who made the prince understand they'd discuss this matter in private. The look that passed between friends wasn't lost on Jenny. She watched them carefully hoping to catch some tidbit of information.

"Well, let's hope you figure this out before you reach the Black Castle."

"Rain, what can we expect when we get there?" Jenny asked.

"There are many dangers on the road to the Black Castle."

"We've already encountered one of Maeldoi's beasts," Devon said.

"Is he trying to kill you?"

"Not me," Jenny said. "But I think he may want to kill Devon."

"Oh, well, that's understandable." Rain winked at Jenny, laughingly.

"Ha! Ha! Ha! Very funny."

"Devon, if he sent one of his beasts after you then he obviously doesn't mean for you to survive. I wonder why." The severity of his tone caused a quiet to fall over them.

"I guess we'll find out when we get there," Devon said with a smile, trying to lift the veil of apprehension and fear that fell over the room.

"Something isn't right," Rain said.

"I know. I sensed the same thing."

"This should worry you. You could be walking into a trap. A very serious and deadly trap."

"I know."

"And yet, you are willing to risk all to enter the Black Castle?"

"Yes, we are."

When dinner ended, the prince suggested a tour of the castle. Devon opted for a hot bath, having been to the castle on numerous occasions.

"I'm sure Jenny would love a tour," Devon said.

"Yes, I would."

Rain and Jenny walked down one hallway after another.

"This is so beautiful," Jenny said when they entered the ballroom. "I have to admit, I've never seen anything like this before. You're so lucky to live in a magnificent castle like this."

"Thank you for your praise. I was born and raised in this castle, and I suppose I'm immune to almost everything regarding the beauty of this castle."

They left the ballroom and continued down another hall where Jenny admired the portraits, when she paused before a certain painting. She looked it over and wondered at the people who looked back at her. She recognized two of the three people in this painting. Her eyes never wavered from the faces of the people immortalized by a talented painter.

"Is this King Morgan and Queen Ileana of Wardell?" She admired the beauty of the painting.

"Yes, that's a portrait of the king, queen, and their daughter, Princess Athelina."

Jenny studied the picture sensing the same familiarity as before.

"This is so strange." Jenny was fixated over the portrait.

"What is?"

"I've seen a portrait of the king and queen before, but from the moment I saw it, I felt as though I knew them."

"What about the princess?"

"I've never seen her picture before. This is the first time I've seen what the child looked like."

"Do you recognize her?" the prince asked.

"It's weird, but she looks a lot like me. I mean, look at the eyes. They're the same shade of green as mine."

"I did notice. I also noticed the queen's green eyes."

"Do you think Maeldoi mistook me for Princess Athelina?"

"It's quite possible."

"He'll be in for a surprise when he realizes I'm not who he thinks I am." Jenny worried what he'd do with Beth when he realized his mistake.

"Are you certain about that?" Rain asked, as his eyes took in the portrait and then turned toward the young girl standing next to him.

The similarities ran quite deep—the green eyes, hair color, and age. Their resemblance was far too coincidental. There had to be an explanation for this. Both Jenny and Rain kept looking at the portrait. If Maeldoi did in fact mistake Jenny for Athelina, then Beth's life wasn't worth much to him. This thought worried Jenny

Janine Summers

more than she could say, but for Rain to think that she and Athelina were the same person was absurd.

"Yes, I'm sure." Jenny looked away from the prince's intense stare to glance once more at the portrait. Why did she feel as though she knew the royal family? She wished she could remember all she'd forgotten. Her head hurt.

"Shall we continue our tour?" Rain asked when he saw the frustration Jenny felt whenever she looked at the portrait.

"Sure."

Rainard showed Jenny the rest of the castle. Amazement shone in her eyes as they walked through the hallways. She was truly stunned by the beauty and the grandeur of the castle. The riches of the castles in this world, was unbelievable. She'd never seen anything like it before.

When they reached her room, he showed her inside.

"If you have everything you need, I'll bid you goodnight."

"Thank you, Rain. I appreciate everything."

"There is no need for thanks. Good night."

Jenny watched him leave. She liked the prince. He was sweet, but unlike Devon, Rain opened an area she never even considered. Was she in some way related to Athelina? She really wanted some answers, but for now she wanted to clean herself up before she went in search for Devon and some much needed and wanted answers.

CHAPTER 26

THE TRUTH

"I don't know what you mean."

"Devon, stop it. I know I'm only thirteen, but I'm not an idiot. That portrait... the child, it's me, isn't it?"

Devon looked at Rain, who nodded. It was time to reveal the truth about the princess and her family.

"Tell her," the prince urged.

Devon took a deep breath. "Yes, we believe you are the child in that portrait."

"What do you mean you believe that picture is of me?"

"All signs point to you being the child."

"And that child is Athelina?"

"Yes, she is Princess Athelina, daughter of King Morgan and Queen Ileana. She went missing about six years ago. She and her parents were never found."

"My parents went missing around the same time. That's when I went to live with Aunt Nora. Everything I remember starts six years ago." Had she finally discovered her true identity? She feared getting caught up in this fantasy only to wake up and find it had only been a dream and she was back in Morgansville at the mercy of her bitter aunt.

"That is why we believe you are the lost princess, Athelina," Devon said. It was good to finally tell Jenny the truth. "I hated keeping secrets from you."

"So what happened to my parents?" Jenny needed to know everything about her past life.

"We don't know," Rain said. "We've been trying to find out what happened to them for the past six years."

"We?"

"My father sent men to search for you and your family. We sent men to track you down, but the men never returned," Devon said.

"My father also sent some of his own men to join in the search," Rain told her. "We've never been able to amass any information concerning the king and queen. It's as though they simply disappeared from this land. We searched for you as well, but found no clues that would lead us to your whereabouts. Now we know you were sent to another world."

"Do you think Maeldoi and Ringwar had anything to do with my parents' disappearance?"

"Yes, I've always believed that they had a hand in your parents' disappearance. We've never been able to prove it, but I believe it to be true."

"As do I," Rain said, knowing how difficult this must be to hear.

"How can I find out what really happened to my parents?" It felt odd talking about her parents and trying to maintain her belief that they were still alive and living somewhere in this land. How could all of this happen? She had to find out what happened to them.

"We'll know more when we reach the Black Castle. I think all of your questions can be answered by questioning Maeldoi and Ringwar."

"Devon, do you think they'll allow Jenny to live long enough to ask questions?"

"Yes. They will want to hurt her as much as possible before they destroy her. I'm hoping this will give us a chance to find out what we need to know. If I can keep them talking, I'll gather information, get Beth and get Jenny out of there before it's too late."

"Be careful, Devon. Now that we know Jenny is the lost princess, Maeldoi and Ringwar will figure it out, if they haven't already. They'll destroy her before you can stop them."

"We have to save Beth." Jenny raised a stubborn chin. Nothing else mattered to her except finding and rescuing her friend.

"An admirable goal, indeed, Jenny, but trying to make them tell you what happened to your parents is nothing short of foolhardy." The Prince tried to reason with her.

"I don't care."

"You must care," Rain said. He spoke as though he was a teacher trying to make a student understand her responsibilities. "You are Princess Athelina, and one day you will rule Wardell. It will become your mantle and your destiny. You need to come to terms with who you are and what is expected of you."

"Until we find out what happened to my parents, I can't worry about being a princess, even though I still have no proof that I am Athelina." She pushed thoughts of her being some lost princess aside. Things like this didn't happen to girls like her. She spent six years under Nora's boot and that wasn't easy to forget.

"And you are under the assumption Maeldoi and Ringwar will sit down with you and tell you all about your parents? No, I don't believe they'll be that courteous."

"Rain, remember what this is all about." Devon said. "There is no need to scare Jenny into facing her fears and her future obligations as the true ruler of Wardell. We have to rescue Beth. If we can find out what happened to the king and queen, then we will, but my first obligation is to rescue an innocent girl from the clutches of evil."

Rainard looked at Jenny with remorse. "My apologies, Princess. I didn't mean to upset you."

"You didn't, but I have to admit I'm a little confused and scared," Jenny said.

"I understand how difficult this is for you, but don't worry. I'll do whatever I can to help you get through this. I give you my word." Devon squeezed her hand.

"I know."

"I wish there was something more I can do to help you."

"Rain, you told me the truth. Thank you for that."

"I'd like to do more. But for now you'd better get some sleep. Tomorrow will come soon enough, and no one knows what perils await the two of you," Rain said. "Come on, I'll see you to your room." Rain stood and escorted Jenny to the door.

"Goodnight, Devon." Jenny smiled and left with the handsome prince.

At the door to her room, Rain stopped her from entering. "Jenny, before you retire, I would like to make one last plea."

"What kind of plea?"

"I would ask you to reconsider."

"I don't understand."

"Now that we've established your identity, I think you should return to Wardell. If Maeldoi gets his hands on you, Wardell and its lands could be lost forever."

"Galfrid will defend Wardell."

"I know, and I have nothing but respect for Galfrid, but Maeldoi is royalty. He could claim the throne as the only living member of the royal house."

"I don't understand. I didn't know Maeldoi was royalty."

"Yes. Maeldoi is your father's second cousin. He has the right to the throne, but as long as your parents' disappearance remained a mystery, we have managed to keep the steward's rule alive. If they kill you, Maeldoi will take Wardell and the first thing he'll do is kill Galfrid, Jemma, and Devon."

"Why would he do that?" Jenny couldn't bear the thought of Maeldoi hurting her new friends.

"The Steward has far too many supporters. They'd fight with him and that is something Ringwar cannot allow. Galfrid would remain a constant threat to Ringwar's rule. They'll have no choice but to dispose of them."

"But only Maeldoi is royalty. What does the rule have to do with Ringwar?"

"As long as she rules Maeldoi, she has more power than the wizard."

"Rain, I understand what you've told me, but I have no choice. I have to go to the Black Castle and rescue Beth."

"Jenny, you could be hurt."

"It doesn't matter if I get hurt or not. I can't go to Wardell and claim to be Athelina if I have no proof of my identity. Devon will help me find out who I am. It's the only way."

Rainard thought for a moment. "I understand. Goodnight, Athelina."

"Goodnight." Jenny went into her room and closed the door. She leaned against it. Tears glistened in her eyes and trickled down her cheeks. She walked to the bed and removed her robe and slippers. She climbed in and pulled the comforter over her. She thought about the fact that she was Princess Athelina. No matter what happened, she couldn't allow anyone to capture her. She'd fight the Dark Wizard and his witch—she'd fight them both. With a determination she'd never felt before guiding her, Jenny extinguished the candle and allowed sleep to take her away from the nightmare she was living.

* * * *

Morning came and Jenny left her bed to take a quick bath, hoping to wipe the weariness from her exhausted body. Dressed in a fresh blue tunic left for her by a servant, she waited for Devon. She answered his knock and admitted him.

"Good morning. I see you didn't get much sleep." Devon also sported fresh clothes.

"Do I look that bad?"

"No. Just tired."

"How was your night?"

"Much the same as yours. I've been thinking about everything we discussed last night."

"And?"

"And maybe we shouldn't continue." Devon wanted to give Jenny the opportunity to turn back.

"How can you say that?" Jenny was horrified. She couldn't believe Devon wanted to turn back.

"Jenny, now that we know your true identity, I think we should return to Wardell."

"Devon, what are you saying?" This journey was meant to save her friend. She had every intention of finishing what she started. There was nothing anyone could say to make her turn back.

"Perhaps my father was right." He watched her intently. He knew what she would say, but perhaps this was the best thing for Wardell.

"No!"

"Jenny—"

193

"Devon, don't do this to me, not now. Not when we're so close."

"I'm not doing this to you. I'm doing this for you."

"No, you're not. I'm going to find Beth whether you come with me or not. I won't allow her to be killed because everyone thinks I need to be protected. What I need is to be allowed to fulfill my destiny."

"You don't think you need to be protected?"

"No, Devon, not if it means losing my best friend, the same way I lost my parents. I need you to help me find Beth. I know I can't do this alone. I'm not a fool. I know what dangers can and will be out there waiting for me, but I have to finish what I've started." Jenny's eyes pleaded with him. She took a breath. "Together we're strong. We can defeat Maeldoi and Ringwar and rescue Beth, but I need your sword and guidance." Tears stood in her eyes as she begged her friend to finish what they'd started. Frantically, she wiped them away hating her weakness.

Devon looked at her and smiled. He couldn't allow her to travel alone, and seeing her determination he knew that they would continue this journey together. He began this quest with her and he would see this to the end.

"I'm sorry, Jenny. I guess the thought of losing you to the Black Castle scared me, but I promised to take you there and I won't go back on my word. I'll do everything in my power to help you save Beth."

"Thank you." Jenny hugged him. She couldn't believe her luck in traveling here and finding such a good and kind friend. He meant everything to her. He was her friend, mentor, and protector.

"Come on. We'll have some breakfast and then we'll leave for the Black Castle." He led her from the room.

"How long will it take us to get there?"

"We haven't even left yet and you're already asking me how long before we get there?" Devon laughed at her.

"Just curious." She shrugged her shoulders and smiled.

"It depends. The more time we waste fighting the beasts Maeldoi and Ringwar send, the longer it will take us to reach the castle."

"But why send these beasts if they want to trade me for Beth?"

"No one knows what Maeldoi's plans are," Rainard said, as he caught up with Devon and Jenny.

"Rain." Jenny smiled at the handsome prince.

"Good morning. So I take it you've made your decision?" His freshly washed hair was tied with a dark ribbon and his frame was resplendent in a brown tunic, black pants, and leather boots.

"Yes. We'll continue on to the Black Castle," Devon said.

"I thought as much," Rain said.

"We have no other choice. Beth doesn't deserve to die. She's done nothing to warrant such a fate." Sadness crept into her eyes whenever she thought of Beth being kept in the Black Castle with someone like Maeldoi. She didn't think too highly of Ringwar either. The two of them sounded like what nightmares are made of.

"If you give me a list of what you need, I will see to it that you receive everything you require. I think you'll need all the help you can muster."

"Thank you, my friend." Devon placed his hand upon the prince's shoulder. "We understand the dangers, but I feel certain we will succeed.

"I wish you all the best. Now, come one, we will eat and then you must prepare yourselves to leave." Rain led them down the hall to the stairs.

They went down to the lower level of the castle and turned down one of the long hallways. He stopped in front of the breakfast room. They went inside and sat down at the table. They enjoyed their last meal together.

CHAPTER 27

PRINCESS ATHELINA

When a knock sounded on Devon's door he assumed it was Jenny with a million questions. To his surprise, Rainard stood there with a servant who entered behind the prince and placed a tray with tea and pastries on the coffee table.

When they were alone, Rain faced Devon. "Alright, my friend, who is she?"

"I don't know what you mean."

"Devon, this is me you're talking to. Jenny and I saw portrait of Princess Athelina."

"So…"

"Devon, the resemblance is a little more than uncanny."

"Are you certain?"

"Tell me who she is and what's going on."

"Rain, I don't know what you're talking about." Devon sipped his tea and bit into a fruit pastry chewing it longer than necessary, in a futile attempt to stall. He hadn't wanted to discuss Jenny with anyone, even if that person happened to be a prince and the ruler of Warwick.

"You don't expect me to believe Jenny and Athelina are not one and the same."

"I never said she was the lost princess."

"You never said she wasn't Athelina."

Devon looked around to make sure they were alone. "Rain, there are some things better left unsaid."

"Is this why Maeldoi wants her?"

"Yes. I think he believes her to be the real Athelina."

"And what do you believe?"

"I'm not certain."

"Devon, you've spent so much time in her company and you don't know if she is the princess?" Rain sensed his friend was hiding the truth.

Devon took a deep breath. "Okay, okay. Yes, I believe she is Princess Athelina."

"How long have you known?"

"At first, I wasn't sure she was the princess, but I recognized her eyes."

"Yes, she has Ileana's eyes and based on the resemblance between Athelina, Ileana, and Jenny, I believe her to be the princess."

"I'm of the same mind," Devon said with a heavy sigh.

"Does she have her mother's gift?"

"She is definitely a witch, but she hides her powers from everyone."

"Why?"

"She doesn't understand the nature of her magick."

"But surely she's been trained."

"No, she hasn't. She's been living with an aunt in the other world."

"And her aunt has helped her achieve her potential?" Rain questioned Devon.

"Not quite. Her aunt changed her name to Jenny, and she raised her to fear who and what she is. She has faith in no one. Her trust lies only with a couple of people. I am privileged to be included in that small group."

"You need to do everything you can to help her discover the princess hiding beneath this false identity."

"I'm trying to make her understand the special person she is and to be proud of who and what she is, but this is no easy task. I'm doing the best I can to help her face her fears and Maeldoi."

"She must have known about her powers."

"Yes, but she kept her gift locked up. If Jenny's aunt found out just how different she was, there's no telling what she would have done to her."

"Surely, Jenny has seen pictures of her parents."

"No. Her aunt told her it was a waste of time to dwell in the past."

"I'd like to meet this aunt of hers, and I would love for her to meet my dungeons," Rain said, as a smile tugged at the corners of his lips.

Devon laughed. "I relish the thought."

"We should arrange for a visit." Rain laughed and joked with Devon, but beneath the friendship, both Rainard and Devon wondered what would happen when they reached the Black Castle.

"If Jenny is Athelina, then Maeldoi needs her. He will destroy her and take the crown," Devon said quite seriously.

"Yes. But your father was appointed Steward of Wardell."

"This is true, but Maeldoi will send men to force my father out of the castle. Our only hope is to destroy Maeldoi."

"You'll never make it alone."

"I won't be alone."

"You mean Athelina?"

"Yes. She's already saved my life by killing one of Maeldoi's beasts."

"She actually killed a magical beast?" Rain was in awe of this feat.

"Yes, she did. She risked her life to save mine."

"She's obviously as brave as her parents."

"She is."

"Devon, tell me why you came here first. You could have gone directly to the Black Castle."

"I guess I wanted to gauge your reaction to Jenny. I trust your judgment."

"So, you wanted confirmation that Jenny is indeed the lost princess, Athelina?"

"Yes, I suppose I did… I still do."

"If you want me to agree with you that Jenny is Athelina, then yes, I believe her to be the lost princess. There's no doubt in my mind."

"I feel the same as you. I've thought Jenny was the lost princess ever since I started training her. It's as though all the old instinct had rushed back. She excelled in every aspect of her training, including magick."

"Devon, you do understand how much more dangerous this journey has become. Maeldoi wants her in order to perform the ritual. The ritual will kill Jenny, and Ringwar will take her powers."

"Why? Ringwar is a powerful, if not an evil, witch."

"Yes, once upon a time, she was. But now she feeds upon Maeldoi's powers. And with Jenny's death she will take her powers, her youth, her beauty, and strength. She will then sit upon the throne of Wardell. Once she's done this, she will set her sights on my throne."

"I thought as much. What about Maeldoi? What can we expect from him?"

"That all depends on whether Ringwar will want the evil one at her side or kneeling before her."

"I wonder if Maeldoi realizes this or is he so intent on getting Jenny that he's blind to Ringwar's evil ambitions?"

"I'm not certain. Ringwar needs Jenny's soul. That is the only reason she's still alive, but Devon, they don't need you. If given the chance, they'll kill you and take Jenny."

"I'm prepared to battle them. On my honor, I will protect her."

"You could turn back."

"No. Maeldoi has Beth."

"Who is Beth?"

"Jenny's friend from the mortal world. She accidentally came to Wardell with Jenny, and when we sent her back to her own world Maeldoi appeared and closed the door. He now has Beth and is using her to get Jenny."

"So he has her friend, and if you're not careful, he could capture you and use you to get Wardell."

"That's a chance I'm willing to take. We must save this girl. She is innocent."

"Do you think it's a good idea to bring the princess to them?"

"No. But if Jenny wasn't with me, I'd be dead and he'd get her another way. Jenny will do anything she can to save her friend, even venture into the Black Castle alone. This is who she is."

"I wish I could go with you. You could use all the help you can get."

"Thank you my friend, but you are needed here."

199

"Yes, I know. If this illness hadn't fallen upon my father, it would make all the difference. I would go on this adventure and help protect the princess," Rain told his friend. Longing was clearly written in his dark eyes. This quest was something he would relish, but they knew Rain had other responsibilities.

"You must stay here and protect Warwick and Wardell in case we don't return."

"Maeldoi will try to capture you and Jenny, and then he'll come after me in order to have two lands to rule."

"True. After all, my father rules Wardell. I'm disposable."

"I wouldn't want to be in your shoes, my friend."

"I'm not overjoyed with this predicament either, but I gave Jenny my word and I intend to keep it."

"Very commendable, Devon."

* * * *

Jenny looked around the room. It was slightly larger than the room she'd used in Wardell. This one also boasted a large canopied bed draped in pale cream sheers, with a soft cotton brocade comforter, and bedding a couple of shades darker than the sheers covered the bed. A darker shade of cream-colored drapes hung on the large windows, while the furniture contrasted the colors of the room by being created in a dark wood. A sofa sat near one of the large windows, but the large stone fireplace gave the room warmth.

She looked around and noticed two doors. The first one she opened revealed the en suite where a large claw-foot tub sat near the wall. Opposite to this tub, a large porcelain bowl completed this en suite. There were so many differences between this castle and her room and washroom back home. If she had to choose a place to live, she'd choose Wardell. She felt accepted in this realm and this was a feeling she liked.

Another door opened to reveal a walk-in closet filled with an array of clothes. Tunics, pants, robes, dress robes, and slippers in a multitude of colors lined the sides of the closet. Jenny even found a lovely pink floral cotton nightgown and matching robe and slippers to use tonight.

She took a long bath and washed her hair twice, needing to wash away the grime from their long trek. Once the layers of dust were removed from her tired and battered body, she felt ready to face anything that came her way. Dressed in her nightgown, Jenny sat down on the sofa and admired the room. She noticed a set of bookshelves on one wall.

"This is great," Jenny said out loud and went to the bookshelves to select a book to read. She settled in a large chair, but couldn't concentrate. She put the book down and stood. She left the room.

* * * *

A soft knock on Devon's door interrupted their conversation. He opened it and admitted Jenny. She was genuinely surprised to see the prince sitting with Devon.

"I'm sorry, I didn't mean to intrude."

"Nonsense. You are most welcome." Devon moved to one side and let her pass.

"Come in, Jenny. Would you like some tea?" Rain asked.

At that moment a young servant came in. "Will there be anything else, your Highness?"

"Jenny?"

"Hot chocolate, please."

"Three hot chocolates, Dina."

"Yes, my Lord."

Rain stood and pulled a wing-backed chair over to where they sat. "Have a seat."

"Thank you."

Tension filled the air. Rain and Devon looked at Jenny and then at each other. What kind of conversation had transpired in this room? Curiosity overcame her. Would they share their conversation? She wanted to know what they'd talked about. She sensed she was the main topic in this room and that bothered her.

Not that those two incredibly handsome men were discussing her, but that the two men refused to tell her what they spoke of.

Dina entered and placed a mug of steaming hot chocolate in front of each person. She straightened and looked at the prince, awaiting further orders.

"Thank you, Dina. That will be all."

Before anyone spoke, they waited for the servant to leave and close the door.

"Are you having trouble sleeping?" Rain asked, concerned.

"Ever since I saw the portraits of the royal family I haven't been able to think of anything else," Jenny said. She picked at the flower on her robe as though she could pluck its petals.

"What do you mean?" Had the picture brought back some distant memories?

"Devon, who am I?"

CHAPTER 28

ALWIN

"**I**'ll escort you to the edge of the forest," Rain told his friends, as he took his horse's reins. "I would offer you horses, but the animals could injure themselves upon the uneven terrain. You have a rough road to travel, my friend."

"I understand, and I thank you for your help," Devon said.

They walked together for an hour until they found the path they would follow to the Black Castle. Rocks strewn about made this road difficult to travel upon, but this was the only way to the castle. They spent the last moments together in friendship. They laughed and talked about everything except for the journey ahead of them.

"This is where I must leave you," Rain said before they stepped onto the uneven path.

Ahead of them, the path narrowed and large rocks made the path treacherous. They would have a difficult time walking this path.

"Once again, thank you for everything." Devon shook Rain's hand.

"Please return to Warwick on your journey home. You will always have safe haven within my castle walls."

"Thanks for everything, Rain." Jenny stood on tiptoe and kissed the prince's cheek. He smiled at his friends hoping they would see each other again, and soon.

"I wish you safe passage. May you conquer the dark ones and find all you search for," the Prince of Warwick told them.

Devon and Jenny waved to Rain as he galloped away.

"I like Rain." Jenny tried to lighten the dark mood that fell over them like an ominous cloud.

"He's a good man, just like his father."

"It's a shame what's happened to his father," Jenny said.

"King Theron is a great ruler. He is fair and well loved by his people. He doesn't deserve the fate cast upon him."

"How did it happen?"

"No one really knows."

"Is it a medical problem, or has it something to do with Maeldoi's magick?"

"Why do you ask?" Devon glanced at his traveling companion with wonder.

"I don't know. Just speculating."

"No you weren't." He had to draw everything out of her.

Jenny wasn't ready to admit the extent of her powers, be they magickal or observational. She still had very little confidence in herself. Perhaps one day she'd figure this out, but right now, the less she said the better.

"I—"

"Jenny, haven't you figured out that I'm not the type of person to make any rash judgments against you? We're friends and that means the world to me. I will always be your friend and I'd like to think that you are comfortable enough to tell me anything."

Jenny looked at Devon and understood how lucky she was to have met him. He was so much more than a friend. If only he really knew how she felt about him.

"Okay. I'll tell you if you promise not to think I'm going crazy."

Devon smiled. "I would never have such thoughts about you, Princess."

"Yeah right, and let's keep this princess thing quiet. I'm uncomfortable with it."

"As you wish, Princess."

Jenny made a funny face. "I sense something evil in the castle." She gnawed her thumbnail.

"Such as?"

"I don't know. There was something evil hovering over the castle. It was dark and wicked, like a black shroud. It surrounded Warwick. I don't think it was my imagination." A distant look crossed her features. "Are you sure Maeldoi didn't act against the king?"

"No, I'm not certain of anything."

"You felt it too."

"Yes. From the moment we entered the castle, I sensed the evil."

"Why didn't you tell me?" She placed a hand on her narrow hip.

"I didn't want to scare you."

"Does Rain sense it?"

"I don't know. He believes a powerful spell has been cast upon his father, but I don't think he senses the evil within his walls."

"If he thinks there's magick afoot, why can't he sense the presence we felt?"

"He isn't magical. He's a mortal ruler, as is his father."

"Is there anything we can do to help Rain and his father?" Jenny liked the prince and wanted to do everything in her power to help him.

"If Maeldoi is behind the king's illness, then there is only way to help him and that is to destroy Maeldoi."

"Then that's what we'll do," Jenny said as she surveyed the area.

The path took them deep into the woods where an eerie darkness greeted them. They stayed true to the path hoping the trees would thin out and the sun would light their way. Instead, the forest closed in on them rendering the area in darkness.

"Should we light a torch?" Jenny asked trying to see the animals she heard scurrying around in the darkness… a distressing sound when their identity remained a mystery to them.

"I'd rather not. I know walking in the dark can be dangerous, but at the same time lighting a torch could turn us into a moving target. I'd like to avoid being stalked as food by something living in these woods."

"I guess you're right."

Devon took her hand in his and led her through the darkened woods. The further into the interior they went, the darker the area became. Tall trees prevented the sunlight from touching the ground as they wound their way around the roots and plants of odd color and foliage. Jenny feared what she heard more than what she could see. The thought of some animal stalking them didn't sit right with her, and even though they were armed, she'd rather avoid the task of killing some animal.

Just as they approached a grove of midsized shrubbery, they were halted by a strange sound. They stopped to listen in an attempt to identify the sound. Animal? Beast? No one knew what waited for them. They had to tread slowly and carefully.

"Stop! You cannot be here!" a small voice hidden within the darkened shadows shouted, startling the young pair.

"Show yourself!" Devon called out and pulled out his sword.

The bushes rustled.

"What is it?" Jenny asked, drawing her own sword.

"I don't know."

"Leave! Now!"

"No! Show yourself!" Devon commanded.

More rustling. The bushes moved when the creature hiding within failed to reveal himself. Whoever, or whatever, was hidden within the shrubs refused to exit its hiding place, and this made the young pair quite nervous.

Devon took a step toward the bush, but was stayed by Jenny's hand. "You don't know what's in there."

"There's only one way to find out what's hiding in there." Devon charged the bush.

A small man ran out of the shrubbery. He ran straight for Devon and hit him in the leg. Devon smiled and jerked to one side. The small man fell over, looking quite comical.

Jenny laughed. She sensed they weren't in any immediate danger and put her sword away. She watched the small man roll over. Anger suffused his small face, turning it a bright shade of red. Devon lifted him up by the collar of his white shirt. His small feet dangled and kicked the air with indignation. Jenny laughed even more.

Devon set the small man back onto his feet. He wore green pants, a white shirt, red suspenders, and a green and red vest. White socks, green shoes, and a matching hat completed his outfit. The only thing that wasn't comical was the sword he held in his hand. Why this man would be armed and dressed the way he was, was anyone's guess. Jenny wanted to hear this man's tale.

Jenny went up to Devon. "Who is he?"

"He's a gnome."

"Is he dangerous?"

"Hardly."

"I can be," the gnome said.

"Alwin, what do you think you're doing?" Devon demanded of the small man.

The gnome's shocked expression told them Alwin recognized the voice. "Devon?"

"Hello, Alwin."

"My apologies. I didn't know it was you."

"I gathered as much."

"Devon, what are you doing here?"

"I was going to ask you the same question."

"Word has reached the gnomes that Princess Athelina is alive and on her way to the Black Castle." He dusted off his clothes.

"Who told you that?" Devon asked with a sly look at Jenny. He tried to make her understand that she shouldn't acknowledge his remark with an improper introduction.

She nodded her understanding.

"Tales of the whereabouts of the princess have traversed the length of the forest and reached the fairies. They also search for the lost princes and hope to bring her back to Wardell." He stood back and stared at Jenny. "Who is this?" Alwin asked suspiciously.

"This is my friend, Jenny."

"Oh. For a moment I thought this pretty, young girl was Princess Athelina."

Devon laughed. "What would I be doing out here with Athelina?"

Alwin went to Jenny and looked up hoping to catch a glimpse of her eyes, but Jenny had no intention of making this easy for him. She stood still and looked up at Devon. The last thing she wanted was for someone else to discover her identity.

"What are you doing here, Devon? This forest isn't safe for the steward's son."

"We're on our way to the Black Castle."

"But I thought you said she wasn't the princess."

"That's right. She's my friend, Jenny Saunders."

"Why are you going to the Black Castle?" The gnome stood poised with one hand on his hip.

"Maeldoi has captured Jenny's friend. We are on our way to rescue her."

"How do you know he has her in the castle?"

"Let's just say we were told by the Dark Wizard himself where her friend may be found."

"I cannot believe Lord Galfrid allowed this foolish quest."

"Alwin, we are doing what must be done."

"You should head for Warwick Castle," the gnome gravely told them.

"We just came from there," Jenny said. "We don't have much time. The longer we wait, the more chance there is of Beth getting hurt."

"She is correct, Alwin. By the way, what are you doing in these woods? You're far from home as well."

"I have come to look for Athelina."

"You came out here all alone?" Jenny asked, impressed by the gnome's courage.

"Yes. I know these woods, and I am not afraid of the creatures living within," Alwin said with conviction.

"Devon, maybe Alwin can help us reach the Black Castle."

"No, Jenny. These woods are far too treacherous, and Maeldoi will continue to send his beasts. I cannot ask this of him."

"Yes, you can, Devon. I would do anything for you and your father," Alwin said with pride, his respect for Devon evident.

"Thank you, my friend, but the road ahead of us is filled with danger."

"I know, Devon, but perhaps I can be of assistance."

"No, my friend. You may get hurt."

Alwin laughed. "Now you insult me."

"I'm sorry. I just don't want to see you hurt."

"There is no need to fear for me. I am armed and I will help protect the girl." He patted the long sword dangling from a leather sheath.

"I'm not sure that's a good idea."

"Devon." Jenny tried to change his mind. "Alwin could be of great help to us. He came all this way alone. Don't you think he could contribute something to this quest?" Jenny thought Alwin might know a shorter route to the Black Castle.

"I can't be responsible for you as well, Alwin. Please understand my position."

Insulted, Alwin responded. "I don't need anyone to look after me. I am quite capable of doing this myself. Do not insult me again, Devon. You're not too big or important for me to teach you a lesson you won't soon forget." Alwin took a deep breath and glared at Devon.

Jenny laughed at the image his threat produced.

"I didn't mean to insult you. I apologize, Alwin. You are quite correct. But I must warn you that Maeldoi is out to kill me. This trek is more dangerous than you think it is."

"I understand, but if you tell me I'm not capable of defending myself or my friends one more time, you will feel the brunt of my anger. Do we understand each other?"

For a gnome who stood no more than four feet tall, he held himself with honor. Alwin impressed Jenny. She felt more at ease knowing there would be another person joining their little team as they made their way toward the Black Castle.

"Yes, of course, Alwin. In that case, we would be honored to have you join us on our trek."

"Thank you." Alwin bowed before them with a smile.

"You can stop laughing now, Jenny," Devon said, as he threw her a look, when she failed to stop the laughter.

"I'll try, but I don't guarantee anything." Jenny continued to laugh.

CHAPTER 29

JENNY'S DENIAL

Evening descended upon the travelers and soon the moon was their only source of light. A dark cloud crept over, causing the area to enter a realm of dusk. If the darkness remained it could prove dangerous to the travelers. Jenny moved in closer to Devon for safety. She feared the strange noises coming from the darkness of the forest.

"I'll scout up ahead and try to find a proper place to camp," Devon said. "Alwin, stay with Jenny. I'll return shortly."

"Shouldn't we stay together?" Jenny asked. She didn't want to be alone with Alwin who made it his business to try and figure out if she was in fact the lost princess, or if she was, as Devon stated, just a friend. He sensed something, but she and Devon tried to keep her identity between them.

"I want to find a safe place for us to make camp. Alwin will take care of you."

"Okay, just be careful."

He smiled and squeezed her hand.

Jenny watched him leave and went to the rocks. She sat down on a large boulder to await Devon's return. She hoped he'd be all right. These woods frightened her. She wasn't used to this. She'd never gone anywhere back home except for school and back to Aunt Nora's. Everything she did in this land was new to her, and she hoped she'd be strong and braves enough to face whatever waited for them out there. She didn't want to let everyone, especially Devon, down.

Alwin joined her. His height made her look down at him.

"You changed."

"Yes, I cannot be inconspicuous in the attire I previously wore."

"True. You did stand out a little."

He laughed.

She smiled at the four-foot gnome. "So, you're really a gnome?" Jenny asked, for she'd only ever read about gnomes and only saw small statues placed in people's gardens. Other than the clothing, he didn't look anything like those gnomes. When he joined her, he no longer wore the traditional clothes. He'd changed into dark pants and tunic with boots. His sword still hung from his belt.

"Yes, I am. Haven't you ever seen a gnome before?"

"No. I haven't."

"How could you come from Wardell and claim to never have encountered my kind?"

"I'm not from Wardell."

"No? Are you sure?"

"Yes, but you already knew that." She wondered what he was up to. She didn't want to answer questions regarding her identity. She wanted to keep that fact a secret she shared only with Devon.

"Yes, I did." Alwin stared long and hard at her.

Much to Jenny's chagrin, their chatting gave Alwin the opportunity to study her features. She'd done everything she could not to show him her eyes, but for some reason she sensed that her green eyes and long dark hair made him understand the reason she was out here. The way he smiled at her, she knew he'd figured out who she was.

The gnome laughed. "Do not fear me, Princess."

"I'm not who you think I am."

"Yes, you are the lost princess." Alwin smiled, trying to make her relax in his presence.

She didn't.

"What makes you so certain?"

"I knew your mother well. Your eyes betray your true identity."

"I guess I can't hide that from anyone." She conceded the truth about her identity.

"No child, you cannot."

Devon returned before Jenny had to divulge any other information. She sighed heavily.

"The area is secure. I've found a place for us to make camp," Devon said when he approached his companions.

They walked to the area Devon found for them to spend the night. The campsite was nestled among the boulders with only one side open, giving the travelers a vantage point.

"I'll gather some wood," Jenny said.

"Maybe you should stay here," Alwin said, fearing for her safety.

"Why?"

"Well, you are... well now, you know. I think you should let us do all the work. This isn't something a princess should do."

"Alwin, there is much to do, and as far as I'm concerned, I'm simply Jenny, a friend of Devon's. Don't think of me as anyone else."

"No, I cannot do that. You are the princess, and as such, I must protect you."

"Stop saying that!" She stormed away from Devon and Alwin. She didn't appreciate being treated like a princess when she was out here risking her life. She was on her way to the Black Castle to save her friend and that was the only thing we wanted to think about.

A few minutes later, she returned with wood and twigs. She threw them on the ground and stomped away.

* * * *

Devon looked at Alwin and ran after her. He didn't want her wandering around this area alone. Sometimes he forgot where Jenny came from, and even though she adapted well to this life, he had to remember this was all new to her. He finally caught up to her.

"Jenny, you shouldn't be out here alone. It isn't safe," he told her gently, as he looked into her eyes.

She turned on him, tears glistening upon her dark lashes. She brushed them away, hating this display of weakness, but she couldn't stop their flow. "I need to be alone."

"Not a good idea."

"I don't care," Jenny said with a stubborn tilt to her head.

"Yes, you do. If not, you wouldn't be out here risking your life to save another."

She glared at him.

"Jenny, come here," Devon softly said.

She walked over to him. He took her hand in his and led her to a large boulder. They sat down. Jenny waited for Devon to begin.

"I know this is a shock."

"Devon, I was an orphan who lived with a woman who hated the mere sight of me. I came here and found out my parents are royalty, living in a magical land. If that wasn't enough, I find out I'm a princess, and you think this comes as a shock to me? Devon, I don't even know who I am." She was terrified by everything she learned.

"Jenny," Devon began in a gentle tone. "You are Princess Athelina. Your parents are Queen Ileana and King Morgan of Wardell. That's a fact you cannot change. You are who you were born to be. The circumstances that changed your life cannot erase who you were or who you must once again become."

"I don't know if I can deal with this."

"How you face this will prepare you to one day sit upon the throne."

"The throne! I can't take the throne!"

"Yes, you can. No matter what happens, one day you will sit upon the throne of Wardell. That, my friend, is your destiny."

"What about Galfrid?"

"What does my father have to do with any of this?"

"The throne is his. I couldn't take it away from him."

Devon couldn't help but laugh. She possessed such tenderness, it was no wonder he cared so deeply for her. "Jenny, my father is the Steward of Wardell. He holds the crown for the rightful heir. That heir is you."

"No, Devon. I'm not the heir. I can't rule anything. I'm only thirteen years old!"

"There have been many young rulers in the history of our land. You're smart, you're kind, and you're fair. What more could we want in a ruler?"

"That's not funny."

"It wasn't a jest. You will need to deal with all that's happened to you."

"I'm trying, but it's hard."

"I know, but for now all you need to worry about is Beth. You must concentrate on getting in and out of the Black Castle alive, and if we can discover what happened to your parents, then our journey will be complete."

"You're right. I've been thinking about myself and this princess nonsense. I'm sorry." Jenny regretted her earlier outburst.

"You're being a princess isn't nonsense. You were born into this privilege and responsibility. It's an unfortunate circumstance that took you away from the life you were meant to live, but this doesn't make you anyone other than who you've always been... Princess Athelina."

"All I know is that I resemble a picture. No one has shown me proof that I'm who you say I am."

"What does your heart tell you?"

"I don't know."

"Yes, you do. Now tell me."

"That everyone lied to me and I can't believe what anyone told me," Jenny said. She regretted her words when she saw the hurt settle on her friend's face.

"You can't be serious."

"I... I am." Jenny looked away, hating herself for hurting her friend.

"I've tried to be as honest as I could, but you must understand why I couldn't divulge your true identity. Only you can discover what's in your heart."

"If I'd known who I was then maybe Beth wouldn't have been taken by Maeldoi. She'd be safe."

"How could you have prevented him from capturing her?"

"I don't know. All I know is that it's my fault Beth's involved in any of this. If not for me, she'd be at home with her family."

He saw that she wanted to lay blame at her feet.

"It isn't your fault."

"I trusted you and you lied to me."

"Jenny, I never lied to you. True, I didn't tell you about Athelina, but I never lied to you."

"I guess I'm angry to learn my parents lived here, and yet I knew nothing about this side of my life. Now they're gone. It's just too much."

"I know." Devon placed his hand on hers. "I want to help you any way I can."

"I know you do. I'm just having a hard time dealing with everything that's happened. Devon, I didn't mean to say those things to you. You've been such a good friend to me. I'm so sorry."

"All is forgiven. I'll help you deal with being a member of the royal family. I'm sure in time you'll understand what it is you need to do." Deep down he knew she hadn't meant the words she said. Her fear was coming out and he allowed her to use him as an outlet.

"Somehow, I don't believe you."

"Are you trying to insult me again?" Devon tried to sound offended as he jutted out his bottom lip and pouted.

Jenny laughed, but the mirth didn't reach her eyes.

"Come on, Jenny, we should return to camp."

"I can't handle Alwin."

"What happened?"

"He figured out who I am, and now he thinks I shouldn't leave his sight. This is our quest, and I won't allow him to stop me from fulfilling what I believe is my destiny."

"I'll speak with him."

"No." Jenny sighed. "I have to deal with this myself. If I am Athelina, then I need to start acting like her."

"Bravo. So are you able to forgive me for not telling you about Athelina?" Devon asked worriedly.

Jenny heard the sincerity in his voice. "Of course. I could never stay angry with you. After all, here you are risking your life to save my friend, and at the same time, you're doing everything in your power to keep me safe. How could I feel anything but gratitude and friendship for you?"

"Good. I'm ready to go back to camp and have something to eat."

"Me too. I'm starving."

"I'm going to like Princess Athelina. She sounds strong enough to face Maeldoi and Ringwar, and she definitely sounds strong enough to free Beth." Devon smiled.

"Thanks." She hugged her friend.

When they returned to camp, Alwin jumped up and ran to greet Devon and the Princess. "It's about time you two returned. I thought something happened to you."

"We're fine, Alwin."

"Well, I told you not to wander around out there, Princess. You must stay close to the campfire where we can protect you."

Athelina looked at Devon. He shrugged his shoulders knowing Alwin was in for a serious dressing down from the princess.

"Alwin, maybe I am Princess Athelina, but out here it really doesn't matter. Out here, we need to look out for each other. And if that means having to leave camp, then that's exactly what I'll do, and I don't need any comments from you or anyone else. I can take care of myself. Is that clear?"

Alwin looked at her and turned his gaze to Devon who smiled proudly at her show of strength. She was changing before their very eyes. Perhaps they would win the war against Maeldoi.

"She does have spirit, Alwin," Devon said. He hoped Alwin would understand her position and acknowledge her courage.

Devon kept an eye on Alwin as he considered Jenny's words.

"Perhaps you are correct, Princess. My apologies." He bowed again.

"It's okay, Alwin. If we're to face the evil of the Black Castle then we need to stick together, and that means no more bowing."

"Yes, Princess, I'm in agreement. We will do this together." Alwin smiled at the young pair. Pride showed in his eyes and in his stance.

"Thank you. After all, we'll only succeed if we work together."

216

"Understood."

"Since that's been resolved, let's eat," Devon said, as he took out the food Rain gave them. He prepared a modest meal.

"Tomorrow I will hunt for fresh meat," Alwin said.

"As long as you don't kill any animals," Jenny replied.

Alwin looked from Jenny to Devon, his eyes large as his laughter bubbled.

CHAPTER 30

A SOFT TOUCH

Morning brought the next step of their journey. The sun rose, along with the three people on a mission to the Black Castle. Jenny, Devon, and Alwin hiked over rough terrain hoping to arrive at their next destination—the Forest of Doom. Here they would face their greatest challenges yet.

Warwick Forest was almost behind them, and the first part of the most difficult and dangerous trek lay before them. Only Devon and Alwin knew how dangerous this path was. Jenny still had no idea of what could hide within the darkest reaches of the forest and beyond.

"We won't find another stream until after we've reached the Forest of Doom. That's why we insisted on the extra bags of water," Devon said.

"The Forest of Doom?"

"Yes. That will take us one step closer to the Black Castle."

"I don't think I like that name, Forest of Doom. It sounds like a death trap," Jenny said, wondering what she'd gotten herself into. She hoped she was strong enough to face whatever was coming after them. No, she had to believe in her friends and in herself. She'd managed to keep up with Devon and Alwin no matter how difficult the trail was. There was nothing to stop her from achieving her goals except her insecurities, and she refused to allow them to win.

Alwin's high-pitched laughter seemed to carry on the wind. "No one likes this forest."

"True enough." Devon's worry at traveling the desert's length was evident. His eyes shifted in all directions causing Jenny to follow suit. No one knew if Maeldoi would send more creatures to capture them.

"How long before we reach this forest?" Jenny asked, looking across the vast expanse of nothingness. The early morning air, still cool, blew a slight breeze, but once the heat graduated it would impede their progress.

"A couple of days at the most depending on what sorcery we face along the way," Devon said. His blue eyes scanned the horizon.

"More surprises?"

"Yes. Did you think Maeldoi would leave us alone?"

"Well, I had hoped he might," Jenny said, knowing Maeldoi wouldn't ignore them.

"It's a nice thought, but he won't forget about us. Remember, things will become more dangerous the closer we get to the castle."

White sand as far as the eye could see glittered like diamonds. From time to time a snake slithered by startling Jenny who wasn't used to serpents roaming around her feet. Her thoughts traveled to the giant snake she and Beth encounter when they first arrived in this world. What if there were more of them? That was the last thing she wanted to face.

Devon laughed when he saw her jump out of the snake's way.

"It's not funny."

"Don't worry, they won't bite," Devon said, as she jumped in fear of another snake.

"How do you know?"

"They are not poisonous. These snakes usually stay close to the forest. We may encounter some deadlier snakes in the desert, but for now we are safe."

"Oh! Sounds like fun."

"You are not afraid, Princess?" Alwin asked.

"Terrified is more like it." She hated snakes.

"Perhaps we should turn back."

"No. I trust you to keep me alive."

"And so I shall," Alwin said.

"Don't you mean we will?" Devon said.

"Yes. I mean we will keep the princess alive." The gnome looked up at Devon with a sly smile.

The morning passed without incident. The trek, although difficult, remained unhindered by the many small creatures crossing their path. The sun was high in the sky and cast its heat upon the already sweltering travelers. With their cloaks safely tucked into their sacks, they tried to stay as cool as possible, but nothing helped.

"We'll stop here for lunch."

They sat on rocks and had a quick meal and a short break. They continued the journey deeper into the desert. The sun's ray bore down on the trio, but no matter how hot it got, they had to continue this journey. There was no shade or water for the weary travelers. Most who entered the desert rarely came out.

Jenny couldn't help but wonder what fate had planned for her. Never had she imagined being involved in such a dangerous situation. Although she spent her life dreaming of adventures, she never really believed she would leave Morgansville.

A small smile crept over her lips when she looked at Devon and Alwin. Who would've thought that she, Jenny Saunders, the girl most disliked in her town was in fact a princess? If someone had told her this a year ago, she would have laughed at them for their foolish thoughts.

"We should keep our eyes and ears open. From here on out we'll have to keep our wits about us." Devon removed the bow from his back and held it firmly in his hand. He armed himself. There was something out of the ordinary waiting for them.

Jenny watched Devon as he held the bow in his hand. Clearly, he sensed danger. "What's wrong?" She had that strange feeling in the pit of her stomach. The same one she felt when she had to fight the snake and then the beast. Now she sensed a malevolent presence she couldn't explain.

"Something's coming." Devon's gaze searched the area.

Alwin removed his sword and walked next to his two companions. There was an evil in the tranquility of the midday heat.

"Let's keep moving," Devon said, as he replaced his bow. Their pace quickened. He stopped when the ground trembled with the force of an earthquake. They ran hoping to put as much distance between them and whatever seemed to be lurking somewhere close by.

The ground shook once more. "Is it the dragon?" Jenny called out, breathless. She didn't think she'd be able to run any further. Her lungs were near to bursting. This wasn't something she was used to, but the thought of being eaten by some ferocious beast appealed to her even less.

"I don't know! Keep running!" Devon shouted also trying to keep his pace quick.

Alwin's short legs had trouble keeping up with Jenny and Devon's longer strides. Desperately, he tried to keep up with the young pair as the ground beneath their feet shook even more. He tried to outrun whatever was coming toward them, but it wasn't an easy feat.

Jenny stumbled over the uneven terrain and fell to the ground. Beneath her feet, the sand shifted. She tried to get up, but wasn't able to. Every effort she made was thwarted by the moving earth.

"Jenny!" Devon ran to her.

When she finally stood, a sinkhole softened the ground beneath her feet. "Devon! Help me!" Her scream carried across the desert when her feet touched air rather than sand. In a second of terrifying fear, she fell through the earth's crust.

Devon saw her disappear and ran to her aid. "Jenny!" He reached her, horrified by the sight before him. She clung to the edge of the gaping hole. Without any thought for his safety, Devon threw himself to the ground and crawled toward her. He grabbed her hand and tried to pull her up. A moment later, Alwin reached the site and lay down next to Devon.

"Give me your hand!" he called out. They would attempt to pull her up, but the ground wasn't very sturdy.

Jenny held Devon's hand and tried to catch Alwin's. Finally, Devon and Alwin held tightly to her hands. They tried to pull her up, but it was no use.

"Use your feet!" Devon told her.

Jenny used her feet to climb up the wall of the sinkhole as she held on to their hands. Finally, she felt Devon grasp her elbow and pull her up the rest of the way. They collapsed on the ground next to each other, their breathing abnormal from the strain and the fear felt only moments earlier. No one moved; they continued to gasp for air.

"I've never seen anything like this before. What caused the ground to open in such a manner?" Alwin asked breathless.

"I'm not sure, but I think we need get out of here and fast." He helped Jenny to her feet and looked into the gaping hole. "Are you all right?"

"Yes, I am. Thanks to both of you. What happened?"

The ground beneath them softened once more.

"Run!" Devon took Jenny's hand and pulled her along.

Alwin tried to keep up with their hectic pace, but fell short. His legs couldn't travel the same distance as Devon and Jenny's.

"There's something beneath us, and I don't think we want to be here when it decides to break through."

"Alwin, hurry up! We don't want to lose you!" Jenny called out to her newest friend.

The poor gnome tried to move his legs as quickly as possible, but the soft touch of the earth impeded his progress.

"Try to make it to the rocks up ahead!" Devon yelled. Boulders came into view. They could save themselves if they could make it to the rocks.

Their destination set, the trio centered their gazes on the boulders and willed their legs to move faster. Devon jumped up on the first rock and pulled Jenny up. She stood next to him. "Alwin, hurry! It's catching up!" Devon yelled over the pandemonium.

The gnome kept up his pace. His legs moved quickly, but not enough progress was made. Devon jumped down.

"What are you doing?" Jenny screamed. "It's coming!"

"I have to help Alwin!"

"Well, hurry up!"

The ground behind the gnome sank into a well of unknown dangers. Jenny watched in horror as Devon reached Alwin. The open ground created a trench as Devon grabbed Alwin and threw him over his shoulder. He landed several feet away. Jenny jumped down and helped Alwin to his feet. They climbed the boulders and watched Devon's attempt to outrun the cave-in. He threw himself into the air and landed on the lower rocks.

"I'm so happy you're safe," Jenny told her friend with a shaky breath when she jumped down and helped him up.

CHAPTER 31

SOMETHING'S COMING

The crevice sealed itself and created a smooth, sandy surface. The desert was solid once more. No evidence of what transpired remained. The smooth sand sparkled in the sunlight as though there had been no disturbance.

"What the devil is going on?" Alwin demanded.

"I'm not sure, but I also fear this will happen again."

They walked over the rocks, but another tremor gave them pause. They tried to keep their equilibrium as the boulders shook from the unknown force. They swayed with the movement of the soft ground. Even the boulders shook from the force beneath the hot, white sand.

"What do we do now?" Jenny's frightened voice rose over the din of the earth's tremor. She wasn't strong enough to fight this evil force. She wondered if it was indeed a force of nature causing the tremors, or if there was something alive and hungry beneath the diamond-cut sand.

"We wait."

"Shouldn't we climb over the boulders and make a run for it?" Alwin asked.

"No. The ground will open up and swallow us whole this time," Devon said. He had to find a safe way off these boulders and away from this area. The only choice they had was to stay where they were and become prey, or try and find their way out of this mess.

"This can't be Maeldoi's doing. Maybe we came upon some quicksand." Jenny rationalized the situation they were in. No one could be that strong, whether he was a wizard or not. It was too difficult to believe this was created by black magick.

"My senses tell me there's magick involved here. Maeldoi is indeed behind this wickedness."

"Why is he doing this?"

"Maeldoi wants the throne."

"But the princess is entitled to the throne," Alwin said vehemently.

"She is, but Maeldoi and Ringwar have other plans for the throne and for Jenny. Unfortunately for us all, that places us in constant danger."

"So what should we do?" Alwin asked. He was a proud gnome who much like his kin would fight the wizard and his witch to preserve the monarchy. The king and queen were loved by all, and that love would be transferred to the princess. All who lived in Wardell would fight, no matter what the cost.

"We keep Jenny alive and reach the Black Castle," Devon said.

"How can we do that if the earth keeps sinking beneath our feet?" They were trapped by the dark magick encasing this desert, the dark magick that seemed to go on forever.

"I'm not sure. I'll be right back." Devon jumped to the next boulder.

"Where are you going?" Jenny asked.

"I want to check something out. Wait here."

"Be careful."

"As always, Princess." Devon bowed before her with a sly smile and a wink.

Jenny laughed, but secretly she feared for her friend's safety. They had no idea what waited for them beyond those rocks. It seemed that Maeldoi was getting restless. His games were becoming more and more deadly. She didn't know if they would make it to the castle.

* * * *

Devon climbed even higher and disappeared from their line of sight. He jumped over the top of the large rocks and began his descent. He stepped onto a rock, but almost instantly it sank. He jumped onto another rock, but as soon as his weight touched the surface, the ground shook and softened.

"Devon!" Jenny's scream reached him. He ran across the boulders jumping from one to the other. He reached the highest boulder and froze. A giant ant had pinned Jenny and Alwin against a large rock. Two pincers snapped at the tasty morsels. Saliva dripped from its massive orifice.

Alwin and Jenny swung their swords, but the body of the ant stood ten times their size. Their blades were useless against this monster. A harsh click sounded as its pincers beat against each other. It tried to envelop Jenny, but every time it drew closer to her, she swung her sword. It turned toward Alwin who also tried to impale the giant ant on his sword.

Devon grabbed his bow and arrow and positioned himself. The first arrow flew with precision and penetrated the ant's body. A piercing cry escaped the beast as it reared and bucked trying to fling the arrow from its body. Another arrow was launched and the ant staggered. One more arrow and the ant collapsed. Devon jumped down and ran to Jenny. "Are you all right?"

"Y... yes, I think so. Alwin?"

"I'm fine, Princess."

"No, you're not. You're hurt." Devon spotted blood trickling down Alwin's arm. A crimson pool formed beneath his hand where blood dripped from his fingers and stained the sand. The ant must have pierced his skin during one of its attack on the gnome.

"It's only a scratch." He covered the wound with his other hand.

"Let me see your arm." Jenny came around and knelt in front of the gnome. She tried to look at it, but Alwin resisted.

"It's nothing, Princess. I am fine."

"No, you're not, and with the desert in front of us and giant ants below, you won't make it." She tried to grasp his arm once more, but was thwarted.

"I told you, I am fine." The last thing he wanted was to have someone, especially the princess, fussing over him.

Alwin tried to make light of his wound. Treating him like an invalid was a waste of precious time. But Devon knew something wasn't right. He refused to give up on the gnome, even though he sensed this wound could end his old friend's life.

"Roll up your sleeve and let me have a look."

"Princess."

"Don't argue with me. Just do as I say." Jenny's command shocked both Alwin and Devon.

"Better do as she demands, Alwin."

The gnome looked at Jenny and shook his head. "Oh, the humiliation." He grumbled these words under his breath.

"Stop complaining and roll up your sleeve before I cut it open."

Alwin unbuttoned his cuff and pulled his shirtsleeve up. The ant's fangs had cut a long, deep gash into his arm.

"There's poison in that wound," Devon said, as the odor of the poison assaulted his senses. "We must do something. The smell will attract the other ants."

Alwin knew what they had to do. "Devon, you must leave me here. Take the princess away from this danger. I will not survive the poison. It's the only way. You must protect the princess."

"No, Alwin. I will not abandon you," Jenny said.

"You must."

Jenny ignored them both. She closed her eyes and held her hand above the cut.

A soft glow illuminated her hand. Devon and Alwin looked on in wonder. A ray of yellow light shone from her hand and touched the cut on Alwin's arm. Slowly, much to everyone's amazement, the skin came together and sealed itself beneath her touch. When the radiance left her hand, Jenny raised it and opened her eyes. She removed her canteen and poured some water on a handkerchief and washed the skin where the cut bled only moments before. The poison had been extracted from the wound. Alwin's arm was healed by the touch of a magical princess.

Devon looked at Alwin's arm in amazement. His blue eyes traveled to Jenny, who stared at her hand in wonder. "How did you do that?" Devon asked, shocked by this display of magic.

"I… I don't know. When I saw the cut, I just knew what to do and I did it. I couldn't allow you to die," she said.

"Thank you, Princess," Alwin said, disbelief etched upon his face. He moved his arm and smiled.

"Your magick is developing at an incredible rate." Devon had never experienced such magick before. No one he knew had the ability Jenny just revealed.

"I guess it is." Jenny still stared at her hand with uncertainty.

"We should leave as quickly as possible. The rocks are beginning to sink. There is little time."

"Where do we go from here?"

"I don't know, but we'll be ant food if we stay here any longer. Follow me." Devon climbed higher onto the rocks. They traveled over a long strand of boulders. Although this path was difficult to master, it proved to be the safer route.

The earth shook beneath the rocks. No one had to say the words; they knew exactly what was about to happen. They leapt from one boulder onto the next and continued hoping they could make it to the end of the string of rocks.

"They're coming back!" Jenny cried out when she felt the trembling beneath her feet intensify.

"Keep moving!"

They leapt from boulder to boulder as the rocks sunk into the ground behind them.

"We're losing ground! Hurry up!"

The line of rocks thinned. If it continued, they'd have to jump down and walk the desert floor where danger would swallow them up. Behind them, the boulders disappeared into the sand. They jumped down and ran as fast as they could hoping they were fast enough to stay ahead of the tremors.

"Which way do we go?" Jenny asked.

"Just keep running! We'll worry about the rest later!" Devon called back to them. "Alwin, try to keep up!"

"I'm doing my best, Devon! My stride is not as long as yours!" he cried out.

"The ants don't care about the size of your stride. Speed up, man!"

Breathlessly, they ran. From behind, another giant ant burst through the ground and closed the distance with Alwin. He urged his legs to move faster, but the ant was quicker and closed the distance with the gnome. Before he could react, the ant was almost on top of him.

"Devon!"

"Keep running, Jenny!" Devon shouted and turned to answer Alwin's cry for help. He removed his bow, ran toward Alwin. He fired the first arrow. The gnome threw himself to one side. It caught the ant in the eye. The creature shrieked and convulsed. Another arrow flew and the ant collapsed.

"Thank you, my friend," Alwin said, his lungs near to bursting.

"Let's get moving. We need to find Jenny."

"Where is she?"

"I told her to keep running."

They came around another set of rocks.

"Do you think there are more of these creatures hiding underground?" Alwin asked when they caught up with the princess.

"There's probably an entire colony of giant ants," Devon said, knowing Maeldoi wouldn't just send one creature to attack them.

"Maeldoi must be desperate. We're getting closer and closer to the Forest of Doom, and he wants us dead before we reach the Swamps of Iliria."

"The Swamps of Iliria?" Jenny asked.

"Are you mad?" Alwin asked, as he tried to keep up with them.

"It's the only way to the Black Castle," Devon said with a smile. "It's also the most exciting way."

"Oh, I can't wait." Jenny returned his smile.

Before Devon could comment, a giant ant sprang from the ground and knocked Alwin and Devon down.

"Devon!" Alwin's sword lay on the ground too far for him to grasp the hilt. He tried to move closer, but couldn't reach his sword.

Jenny looked at her friends. Devon's bow lay on the ground. He was scrambling toward it. She started back in their direction. The giant ant approached Alwin, the easier target.

"Devon!"

"Get away from here, Jenny!" He held out his hand and the bow magically came to him, but it was too late to use it against the giant predator. The ant was on top of him and though he desperately tried, he couldn't reach his sword.

Jenny jumped up and down on the hard packed ground trying to draw the giant ant's attention, but it refused to turn its large head. She picked up a rock and threw it at the ant. She couldn't chance an arrow for fear of hitting Devon or Alwin. Finally, the ant turned and walked in Jenny's direction. Its pace quickened. Jenny backed away needing room to kill it with her bow. She tripped on a rock and went down hard. Useless, her bow laid a couple of feet from her hand. She rolled and grabbed it, but the ant was almost on top of her.

"Jenny, look out!" Devon screamed.

She threw out her hands and a white beam of light escaped. The light hit and engulfed the two ants. Their bodies glowed and convulsed. The magickal light overcame them. They disintegrated into a mound of ash. Devon stood and ran to Jenny. He extended his hand and helped her to her feet.

"That was amazing! I've never seen such a display of magick before." He stared at the mounds of ash and then Jenny.

"Thanks. Alwin, are you all right?" Jenny's concern was evident in her green eyes. She still couldn't believe what had happened.

"Yes, I am fine. Thanks to you."

"Good. Let's find a place to camp." Devon hoped the attacks were over. "I can sense the danger has past for now." The earth was still, but his thoughts were on the strength of Jenny's magick and what that would mean when they reached the Black Castle and Maeldoi.

CHAPTER 32

THE SHIMMERING ROCK

The Forest of Doom was visible ahead of the weary travelers. Yesterday's battle with the giant ants left them achy and tired. Only sheer determination pushed them forward. Jenny had never expended such energy before and wondered if she'd have anything left when they arrived at the Black Castle.

The desert was long and hot. They'd left the safety of their little nest and now traveled over the same white sand. Her feet burned in the slippers she wore. She hadn't planned on having to trudge through hot desert sand. This was definitely nothing like beach sand.

"Any idea what we can expect when we reach the forest?" Jenny asked, trying to break the ominous silence that had descended upon them.

"Remember, the closer we get to the Black Castle, the more dangerous things will become."

"You think it'll get more dangerous than the ground giving way beneath our feet and giant ants trying to eat us?" Jenny asked fearfully.

Alwin laughed.

Devon thought for a moment. "Yes, I believe yesterday was only a taste of what awaits us in the forest."

"Oh, it sounds like more fun for us." Jenny smiled, but worry creased her brow and clouded her eyes. She wasn't sure she wanted to face any more of Maeldoi's creatures. The fact that this wizard thought to send creatures like the beast, dragon, and giant ants made Jenny wonder how she would continue to show strength she didn't think she possessed.

The walk took them closer to their next destination, and no one was anxious to arrive at the Forest of Doom. If she had her way, she would have preferred to send the palace guards to find Beth. They were more equipped to fight the creatures than the three of them. Then again, they had managed to fight and stay alive. Perhaps she wasn't giving herself enough credit.

The sun began to set in the sky. Devon looked around the area. The desert stood behind them. The forest beckoned the weary travelers into its midst.

"I think we should camp out here tonight. I don't want to travel the forest until morning," Devon said. The idea of having to battle monsters in the dark didn't appeal to him. Besides, it would be far too difficult to protect Jenny.

"Where should we camp? We're out in the open here," Jenny said.

"I know, but inside the forest we'd be even more susceptible to danger."

"So what do we do?"

"You and Alwin stay here while I scout around and find a place to camp."

"Be careful, Devon."

He smiled. "Don't worry." He turned to the gnome. "Keep her safe."

"Of course." Alwin straightened.

Devon walked away. Half an hour later he returned and announced he'd found the perfect spot. A fifteen-minute walk toward the setting sun and safety for the night was theirs. He led Jenny and Alwin to their campsite. They sat around the fire and ate dinner. Their food was running low as was their water supply, but Devon knew a stream ran the length of the forest feeding the vegetation and the creatures living within. They would have to fill their water bags from the stream.

"We have a long day ahead of us. We should get some sleep," Devon said to his friends.

"Devon, I understand we have to go through the Forest of Doom and then the Swamps of Iliria, but why is Maeldoi making this so difficult?"

"I really don't know. Whether he kills me out here or in the castle, he'll never get my father to give up the throne in order

231

to save my life. I know my father, and as steward he took an oath and he will never relinquish Wardell."

"So Maeldoi doesn't really need you to get the throne?"

"No. I know that Ringwar wants you, but they have no need for me or Alwin. We're dispensable."

"I'm afraid for the two of you."

"Don't be. As long as we stick together, Maeldoi can't harm us. In friendship we are stronger than all the magick within the Black Castle."

* * * *

"Let's keep moving," Devon called out the next morning. "We have to reach the forest while the sun is still high. We need the light to find our way through the woods."

"It's funny." Jenny's eyes were fixated on the forest.

"What is?" Alwin asked.

"Well, it's like the closer we get the further the forest seems. Is it moving?"

"No, it's an illusion. This forest is difficult to enter. I know there's a way in, but no one can simply walk into this forest. I heard of a path that leads those who wish to enter into the forest. We must discover its location before we can enter," Devon said.

"So, where do we look for this path?"

"I'm not sure. Alwin, any ideas?"

"I think there is a way beyond the end of the desert." Alwin searched his memory.

"What do you mean?"

"I remember hearing the tale of a magical wall of water guarding the entrance to the forest. I do not remember its location or the way in, but I do remember that there is one."

"And do we know how to find the entrance?" Jenny hoped this venture wasn't doomed. They'd come too far to turn back.

"Theoretically, yes, I do," Alwin said uncertainly.

"Why don't I believe you?" she asked the gnome.

Devon laughed in the background as Alwin squirmed before the princess.

"I don't know, Princess. I will find the path into the forest." Alwin fidgeted beneath the princess' emerald gaze.

"Are you sure?"

"Yes. Although I've never been here before, I know there must be a way in. I will find it."

Jenny smiled, almost feeling sorry for the gnome who only wanted to please her. "I'm sure we'll find a way into the interior. You haven't let me down yet." She couldn't allow him to think he wasn't pulling his weight. He been there every step of the way and this amazed her considering Alwin's size.

"Thank you, Princess."

Devon and Jenny laughed at the gnome who seemed to turn a lovely shade of red that matched his suspenders.

"Come on, let's find the path." Devon smiled.

Alwin told them he believed a waterfall would lead them to the path winding its way through the Forest of Doom, but an hour later they still couldn't find a way into the forest. There was no clue as to where the entrance was. It felt like a futile search. They'd walked and walked for hours and still the entrance remained a secret.

"This is hopeless," Jenny said.

"No, it isn't." Devon tried to reassure her, but he didn't feel as confident as he sounded.

"We've been over this area twice. If there's anything here, I don't see it."

"I know, but the path must be around here somewhere." Devon tried to remember the stories and legends depicting the Forest of Doom and the location of the unseen path.

"It's not like you can hide a waterfall in a desert."

Alwin stepped away from them and closed his eyes. He tried to remember the waterfall's location. He thought and thought. Finally, he opened dark eyes and focused on the young pair. "I think I know where it is."

"Where?" Devon asked.

"If memory serves me well, we must find the Shimmering Rock."

"There are no rocks in this area," Devon told him.

"Yes, there are. I saw something when we arrived."

"That's right. I remember seeing something shining in the sunlight."

"Whatever shimmered must be the boulder. Come on."

The next hour found them retracing their steps. They combed the area in search of anything that resembled a shimmering rock. Whatever magick kept the threesome from discovering its location, Jenny refused to allow it to happen. They had to find a way into the forest.

"There!" Alwin cried out when he spotted the shimmering rock.

They ran toward the large, white boulder. It sat about eight feet high and approximately six feet wide. It had an odd glimmer that seemed to make it blend in with the granules of the white sand.

"So now what?" Jenny asked.

Alwin walked around the boulder searching for a sign that would tell them how to journey into the interior. He looked up and down... nothing.

"There must be something here," Alwin said scratching his head in wonder. "There must be some kind of mechanism that will allow us to enter."

Jenny looked at the rock, and then at the sun. The rock shone in the sunlight and cast rays in a multitude of colors. It was a beautiful area. She continued to look all around until she saw something that bothered her. She looked up at the sun and then once more at the rock. She stared at the same spot for several minutes. Then it dawned on her. The sun's rays landed on the same spot. No matter where she looked, the sun's rays illuminated only one area on the Shimmering Rock. She placed her hand on the spot where the sun shone and pushed it. The spot was a trigger. Jenny pushed it into the shimmering rock and the surrounding ground trembled. A bright light crept through every vein of the boulder. There was a great rumble. They backed away from the boulder, but just as suddenly as the rumble began, the boulder split in half.

"Devon! Alwin!"

They joined Jenny.

"What is it?"

"I found it!"

A large waterfall stood before them. The earth continued to shudder from the force of the cascade. Slowly, the waterfall parted to reveal a staircase. They looked down and saw this was the way to the forest floor.

"How did you do that?" Devon's voice was filled with appreciation.

"I noticed the sun's rays shone on this one spot. At first I thought it was my imagination, but when I pushed this happened."

"Bravo, Jenny."

She smiled at the praise, but noticed Alwin seemed somewhat saddened by this turn of events. He should have been the one to find a way into the Forest of Doom. His face turned pink with the shame of failing his friends.

When Jenny saw his expression, she went to him and looked down at her friend. "Alwin, we did this together. You should be proud of yourself. If you hadn't remembered the shining rock, we never would have discovered the waterfall."

"Really?" Alwin's eyes lit up at the compliment.

"Yes, of course. Thanks to you we can continue our journey."

"Thank you, Princess."

"So, what are we waiting for? Let's see what's down these stairs."

They had to reach the forest before nightfall. They'd lost too much time searching for the entrance. He led the way down the stairs and noticed that both sides of the waterfall were kept at bay by some form of magic. Devon reached out and ran his fingers through the water, but his hand was as dry as it had been before he'd placed it inside the waterfall. This was a guardian and not a real waterfall.

They went down one slippery step at a time, feeling as though the water would force a watery grave over them. Finally, Devon reached the bottom and jumped down. The last step sat about two feet above the ground. He held out his hand and Jenny took it. She hopped down. Devon then waited for Alwin, who also needed a hand. A two-foot jump was more than his capabilities allowed. With Devon's aid, Alwin was soon on the ground next to Jenny.

Ahead of them, a long stretch of barren land lay in wait.

"We have to cross the land and then we'll enter the forest," Devon said. "I'd like to reach the forest before nightfall, but I have no idea how long it will take to reach or what we might find inside.

"What are we waiting for?" Jenny said with a smile. "Let's get going."

Joined together by the bonds of friendship, they walked the path. A determination stronger than anything they'd ever felt before pushed them forward. Thunder rolled as they turned and watched as the two sides of the waterfall were joined together like the zipper on a jacket. Once again, a single, giant waterfall flowed freely hiding all evidence that anything out of the ordinary had occurred. The water guarded the entrance as it was designed to do.

The companions turned away and began the next step of the journey.

CHAPTER 33

THE FOREST OF DOOM

"This looks like the desert we just left," Jenny said.

"I think it is." The forest closed in on them. They wondered what was going on.

"Is it Maeldoi?"

"I don't know. I've never been to this part of the realm before."

"Why is he playing these games?"

"I think I can answer that," Alwin said. "He's testing you."

"Of course. He's trying to find out how powerful you are," Devon said. "With your powers growing steadily, Maeldoi will pit us against horrible odds to understand your strengths and weaknesses."

"Are you telling me he wants to find out how strong I am so he can figure out how to kill me?"

"I'm afraid so. We need to close the distance and enter the forest before sunset."

"Will we be safe inside the forest?"

"I hope so. I don't know what's waiting for us. This is all new to me too."

At the forest's edge the trees were withered and wilted. Branches crawled toward the sky with gnarled hands. They looked at the lifeless landscape.

"This is so creepy," Jenny said, as she looked around feeling death all around them. "Is the entire forest like this?"

"I don't know. This forest is engulfed in dark magick. Everything inside is controlled by Ringwar's evil enchantments. I don't know what to expect. The first thing we need to do is find a place to camp," Devon said, surveying the area.

Cautiously, they walked into the forest where all manner of life ceased to exist. Rocks, dust, and the distorted trees were the only signs that once upon a time life had existed here.

"Be careful, Devon." Jenny smiled at her friend.

"I'll be right back," he told the princess.

Jenny and Alwin watched their brave friend run ahead. Slowly, they continued to follow Devon's path.

"Come on. I found a nest where we can spend the night," Devon said when he returned. He led them off the path they'd been following, but soon large rocks came into view. Inside the formation a small clearing presented itself to them. "We should be safe for the night."

"You mean you hope," Jenny said, knowing there was no safe place out here.

"Yes, that too." A smile tugged the corners of Devon's mouth.

Soon, darkness engulfed the forest. They felt an ominous presence all around them. The hand of dark magick fanned out over them. A shiver crawled over Jenny as she sat down. A small fire illuminated their campsite. Dinner consisted of stale bread and water. Their supply of food dwindled with each passing day, as did their water supply. They had to find life within this forest if they were going to find food and water. Without either of these things, the trio would never reach the Black Castle.

"We'll have to ration the water. I don't know if the stream still runs free."

"What if there's no water? How can we continue our journey?"

"Don't worry, we'll find some."

"How many days before we reach the Black Castle?"

"About two days."

"Do you think we'll get there in time?"

"Yes, we will. I promise."

Jenny wondered how Beth was being treated. Was she hurt in any way? Was Maeldoi being nasty to her? After everything Maeldoi had sent to hunt after them, she wondered how the evil couple was treating her friend. They weren't exactly known for their humanity. On the contrary, if she were to choose one word to describe Maeldoi and Ringwar, it would be evil.

"Jenny, Beth will be alright." Devon sensed her fear.

"I have this terrible feeling something's wrong."

"You're just nervous. It's understandable."

"But you think she's all right?" Jenny wanted to believe Devon's words.

"Yes. He won't hurt her, at least not until he has you in his clutches," Devon said.

"And then what?"

"No one knows. Now get some sleep. We need to be well rested for tomorrow." Devon put his head down and fell asleep.

* * * *

"I think there's water over there!" Devon shouted as he ran back to his friends the following morning.

"Great, let's hurry." They caught up to Devon.

"Where's the water?"

"Listen."

True to his word, a lovely stream trickled through the woods. Ahead of them, color painted the forest. Greens and browns grew all around them. They stepped away from the barren landscape and found a lovely oasis.

"This is beautiful."

"Let's fill our water bags. I don't want to linger here too long. Every creature living within this forest will use this water source. We should keep moving."

They filled their canteens and followed the stream as far as it ran. Wildflowers bloomed all around them, creating a colorful painting. From somewhere behind them, something moved.

"What's that?" Jenny demanded fearfully for she'd seen a shadow move.

"I'm not sure. Just keep going. Maybe it won't bother us," Devon said.

"Yeah, right. When have we heard something rustling around us and not had to fight it?"

"She does have a point," Alwin said, stretching to catch a glimpse of what remained hidden.

"Thank you. Now let's get out of here." Jenny ran.

They had to stay one step ahead of whatever lurked in the shadows waiting to pounce on them. Devon looked back and saw a dark form running to the next bush.

"Something's following us. What's out there?" Jenny looked back.

"I'm not sure, but I don't want to stay here and find out," Alwin said.

"My thoughts exactly," Devon said.

They took off at a run. The path narrowed as they swerved around trees and kept up the pace. The forest stretched out before them. Lungs near to bursting, the trio kept up this hurried pace. Distance would be their salvation.

"Where do we go from here?" Jenny called out somewhat breathless.

"It doesn't matter, just keep running!" Devon called out, coercing his legs to comply with his thoughts.

"Is it following us?" Jenny had to know if they were still in danger, or if whatever hunted them had lost its appetite.

Devon looked back and saw dark shadows closing in on them. His senses alerted him to danger. Maeldoi had sent a new threat, but no one knew exactly what that threat was, and after everything they'd fought, it was anyone's guess as to what was sent to slow them down.

"Yes, they are! Keep running! We have to get away!"

Eight men dressed in black clothes with silver spikes protruding from dark masks drew their swords and jumped out at the three travelers. Their signature war cry rent the morning air.

"Watch out!" Devon's cry rent the air. Sword in hand, Devon jumped in front of Jenny. Above all else, the princess had to be protected and it was his job to make sure nothing happened to Athelina.

CHAPTER 34

MAELDOI'S VISIT

The first man drew his sword and launched the attack. Steel against steel clashed, as Devon raised his blade to block the blow. He parried and thrust his rapier at the dark guard sent from the Black Castle… just another threat.

Another guard, his features also disguised, approached Jenny. She removed her sword and took her stance. This would be her first fight with a real sword, her sword, the sword of a princess. She had to remember her lessons and control her movements. Devon taught her to fight and she had to make him proud. She waited. The guard lunged at her. She sidestepped him and thrust her sword at the guard who parried and thrust his sword at her. She turned around and kicked him in the ribs. He fell back. She kicked him in the chin and he stayed down. She turned and watched her friends fight the other guards.

Devon's bravery showed as he continued to fight. Two guards went down at the end of his blade. He stopped a blow from another guard. These guards didn't stand a chance against Devon's expertise. The man also went down upon his bloodied blade. He moved toward the last two, but they simply ran off in fear. Obviously, they weren't prepared to die for anyone, even if it meant facing the wrath of the Black Castle.

"Jenny, are you all right?" Devon ran to his friend.

"I'm fine. Not bad for a greenhorn."

Devon looked at the unconscious man and smiled. "Not bad at all."

"At least I didn't have to kill him."

"You did well."

241

She wasn't used to this way of life and so he commended her on her prowess and her sympathetic nature. The fight had to be difficult on her. She'd never had to fight against another human being, even one who tried to kill her.

"Uh hum."

"Good job, Alwin," they said in unison, when they saw the two dead guards.

"Let's get out of here." Devon returned his sword to its sheath.

They ran for the other side of the forest. Further and further into the woods they went. They kept a harried pace as the sun cast a pink glow upon the horizon. Soon it would be time to find a safe place to spend the night. They ran a little further and came across a nest made from lush grass, trees, and rocks. A small stream trickled fresh water several yards away—a safe place to spend the night.

"I'll gather some wood. Jenny, you and Alwin set up camp."

"I can help you collect the wood." Jenny wanted to keep busy.

Devon went over to her and put his hands on her arms. He looked into her green eyes and smiled. She was so brave. "Please don't fight me on this. I want you to stay here with Alwin."

She couldn't fault him for trying to protect her. She smiled at him. "Okay. I'll stay here. Give me your water bag and I'll fill it for you."

"Thank you." Devon handed her his water bag and left in search of wood. "I'll scout the area in case more guards are lurking in the shadows."

"Alwin, I'm going to the stream," Jenny said, as she picked up Alwin's water bag.

"I can do that. You should stay here," Alwin said worriedly.

"The stream is only a few yards away. I'll be fine. Just set up camp." Other than Beth, Jenny had never had friends like Devon and Alwin. She was indeed a lucky girl. "I'll be right back," she told him with a smile, knowing how much he cared for her.

"Very well, Princess. I'll find us some food." Alwin relented knowing she'd set her mind on doing this task.

"That's a good idea. We could use some decent food."

Jenny smiled as she went to the stream. She knelt down and cupped her hands around the crystal clear water. She splashed it on her face repeatedly, and then concentrated on washing her neck and hands, enjoying the feel of cool water on her warm skin. She felt better now that she had cleaned up a bit. She had to get back to camp before Alwin worried.

She filled the water bags and when she turned to leave she came face to face with the one man she feared most. A man who made her blood runs cold. She looked into cold dark eyes and shivered.

"So, we meet again, my pet."

"Maeldoi."

"Yes. I've been looking forward to your arrival," the Dark Wizard said.

"Why?"

"You wish to know why?" Maeldoi found this amusing.

"Yes. I don't understand any of this," Jenny said.

"I thought you knew why I wanted you in my castle."

"I'm here to get Beth and take her home. That's all I care about."

"And how do you plan on doing that?" His eyes carefully surveyed her.

"I'll find a way."

"What if I stop you?"

Jenny wondered what this man with the long, white hair was up to. His black eyes stared at her, causing nervousness deep within her soul, but she refused to show him the fear she felt. His long flowing black robes blew softly in the wind causing them to billow like an ominous cloud. A large pear-shaped emerald sat in the silver walking stick he held in his hand.

Jenny saw it and sensed it was something she should fear. Evil surrounded him. "I'll fight you." Jenny stubbornly jutted out her chin. She refused to cower before this man. He promoted fear and she sensed that if she allowed him to see her fear, all would be lost. She stood straight and never wavered as her gaze locked with his.

Maeldoi laughed at her. He seemed to be enjoying his encounter with the lovely princess. But Jenny held her ground and showed a great deal of courage and spunk.

"You are your mother's daughter."

"You knew my mother?"

"Of course I know her."

"Where is she?"

"Now that is a very good question." Maeldoi smiled wickedly at the young girl.

"And do you have a very good answer for me?"

Maeldoi thought for a moment, still smiling that annoying smile at the princess. "Why not leave these fools and come with me? If you do, I'll tell you all about your parents." Maeldoi watched her carefully.

She knew he wanted her in his castle so that Ringwar could take her power, her youth, and the crown they so desired. Although she couldn't comprehend how this would be accomplished, she pretended to know exactly what he wanted. She hoped to keep the upper hand in this little tête a tête.

"No, Maeldoi. I won't leave my friends no matter what you promise me in return. I sense your deceit." Jenny stood proudly and waited for his next move, which was sure to come. To her surprise, he simply ignored her insult and continued.

"The road to my castle is treacherous. I have many lovely surprises in store for the three of you."

"Why are you doing this?"

"You will know everything in time."

"Yeah, yeah. That's what everyone keeps telling me. Why don't you just leave me alone?" Jenny turned to leave when she felt rage flow from the wizard. She knew she'd pushed him too far.

Anger suffused his face.

"You will not speak to me in that disrespectful manner!" He raised the silver walking stick and the emerald glowed angrily. He aimed it directly at Jenny. A green bolt of rage erupted from the large stone.

She threw herself to one side, rolled, and stood up. Her sword tucked in her hand ready to fight this evil man. "I want you to get out of here and leave us alone." Jenny placed her blade at the base of his throat.

Maeldoi laughed his understanding. Jenny would indeed use her sword if she were given no other option. Oh yes, there was no doubt in anyone's mind that she would fight him.

"Jenny!" Devon's voice called out to her.

"We will meet again, Athelina."

Before Jenny could respond, Maeldoi disappeared in a puff of smoke. Jenny stood still and stared at the spot Maeldoi had vacated. A chill ran up her spine. They would meet again, and the next time they met she'd be ready for a showdown. She now understood it would come down to him or her, and she wouldn't go down easily.

"Jenny, are you all right?" Devon demanded when he noticed her pale features and the trembling sword in her hand. He went to her and took the blade from her hand. "What happened?"

"Maeldoi was here."

"Jenny, I told you to stay with Alwin."

"He wanted to talk to me."

"Just talk?"

"He would have hurt Alwin. This way, he only spoke to me." Jenny looked up at her friend.

"I think he did more than just talk." Devon took her hands in his to share his strength and warmth.

"How do you know that?"

"The remains of the power of the emerald still surround the air around you. You're pale and you're shivering. That tells me something else happened here. Did he hurt you?"

"He was really angry with me."

"I'm happy you stood up to him, but he could have killed you."

"No. He wants me in his castle. His goal was to scare me." Jenny still trembled.

"He seems to have accomplished this feat." He looked her over to make sure she wasn't injured.

"What? Oh yeah, I guess he did. Don't worry, I'm fine." Jenny tried to smile, but the shaking cold of her hands contradicted her words.

"Come on; let's get you back to camp. I don't want to leave Alwin alone for too long, just in case."

"Sure."

Devon tucked her sword into the sheath, and together they joined the gnome who stood watch.

"Princess, are you all right? I have been so very worried."

"I'm fine, Alwin."

"Come, Princess, the fire is warm and you are trembling."

Jenny sat down near the fire and accepted some food from Alwin who had some kind of bird roasting over the fire.

"Thank you." She didn't know what she was eating.

Devon sat next to Jenny. "Tell me exactly what Maeldoi said to you."

"Maeldoi? Maeldoi was here?" Alwin asked.

"Yes. He paid me a visit."

"Jenny, please tell me everything," Devon said.

Jenny related her encounter to her companions. When she was done, Alwin stood and looked around.

"Don't worry. He won't return, at least not tonight."

"Never underestimate the dark wizard, Princess," Alwin said. "I know how evil and deceitful Maeldoi is. We should never believe anything he or Ringwar say. Their greed knows no bounds."

"I won't. It's just, well, he had the chance to kill me by the stream and he didn't."

"No, he didn't," Devon said. "But that doesn't mean he won't try anything else."

"He told me he had many surprises planned for us."

"Did he mention what they were?"

"No. I guess since it's a surprise he doesn't want to ruin it for us." She managed a small smile.

"What a time to get a sense of humor," Alwin said and shook his head.

"We'd better get some sleep. Tomorrow we travel to the Swamps of Iliria," Devon said. "Jenny, one more question."

"Anything."

"When Maeldoi spoke of your parents, did he act as though they were still alive or do you think he's killed them?"

"Funny you should ask that." Jenny thought back to her conversation with the wizard. Something in the way he worded his words made her reflect on a happier outcome. He could have simply said they were dead and watch those words shatter her to the very core of her being. But he didn't.

"Why?" Devon continued to watch her.

"If I didn't know any better, I'd swear they were still alive and Maeldoi knows exactly where they are."

"Really? Do you think he was being truthful with you, or was that just another ploy to get you to do whatever he wanted?"

"I don't know, but if I had to guess, I'd say he was telling me the truth. There was something about the way he said it."

"I wonder what he's up to."

"I don't know, but I want to find out." With that thought fresh on her mind, Jenny lay down on her blanket and closed her eyes, hoping she'd save her friend and find her parents.

CHAPTER 35

MAELDOI AND RINGWAR

Maeldoi walked the corridor of the Black Castle. His long robes brushed the marble as he made his way to Ringwar and give her the news. The smile he wore was a mixture of joy and satisfaction. For many years they'd tried to find the lost princess, and now she was on her way here. Soon they would have her and all their dreams will come to fruition.

"Maeldoi, is it her?" Ringwar sat upon a golden throne. She'd always wanted one, and since Maeldoi could not give her the throne of Wardell, he'd had one crafted just for her.

"Yes, Ringwar. Athelina is on her way here." A smile curled his lips.

"She is not alone," Ringwar said, her eyes paled by many years gone by. In her gnarled hand, a glass ball filled with black and grey smoke twirled as it gave its mistress the news she desired.

"No, she is not."

"The steward's son is with her."

"Yes."

"I do not recognize the other one."

"I cannot say. She was alone when I spoke with her," Maeldoi said as he looked into the crystal ball trying to see what images were contained within the glass orb.

"No matter. They will never leave this castle."

"No, they will not. I will make certain they remain within these walls as your prisoner."

"Where is the girl?"

"In her room. I locked her in."

"Excellent. Soon I will have everything I desire."

"Yes, you will and together we will rule this realm."

248

Ringwar failed to agree with Maeldoi. She simply stared into her crystal orb.

"You will be young and beautiful again." He stared at her aging face and remembered a time when men would have killed for a glance of those ice blue eyes, and a toss of her lovely pale mane. Now, as he looked at what she had become, Maeldoi simply held on to the memories of beauty and cunning.

"Yes, I will. Once the girl arrives, I will recapture my youth, and in doing so my powers will return." Ringwar was pensive. "Tell me, Maeldoi, is she as lovely as her mother?"

"Even more so. Her eyes shine like cut emeralds. Her onyx hair is long and wavy. Her stature is lean and filled with the blush of youth. She will be the perfect muse for you to use."

"This news excites me."

"I do hope this pleases you, Ringwar."

"Yes, it does. But what about her powers?" Ringwar wondered as she looked at the man who had stood by her side for decades.

"I cannot say. She never used her powers when I was around, but seeing what she did with the beasts I've sent, I must say she is brave and quite capable."

"Excellent. She will be a challenge, but I will win her over. After all, she is but a child."

"That is true."

"Now leave me. I must meditate and discover the strength of her magick."

"Of course," Maeldoi said and bowed. He retreated down the hallway and entered his wing. He'd designed this as an independent sanctuary from Ringwar and her darkness. Sometimes it overwhelmed him, but once they had the princess in the castle, Ringwar would have youth and beauty, and he would have his love. Although, he worried that Ringwar would choose another to rule by her side, Maeldoi also knew that since he'd stayed by her side all these years, she would show her gratitude to him. Then he and Ringwar would rule this land together as their king and queen.

Of this fact, he was certain.

* * * *

Beth sat in her plush room hoping the door would open and she would be free to go home. She'd been here for such a long time, and as she stared out of the window, she saw the jagged rocks below and the waters that kept everyone who didn't belong to the Black Castle at bay.

How would she ever get out of here? She sat on the divan and looked around. For a prison, she wasn't being treated badly. She was fed regularly, almost too regularly, and she had a room that rivaled the one she'd been given at Wardell Castle. The color tones differed, of course. Her room in Wardell Castle was beautifully decorated with blues and creams, which gave the room a homey feel, but here in the Black Castle, the room was elaborate with a dark canopy bed, where pale sheers hung from each bedpost. The satin curtains that fell and pooled on the floor were black and gold. Although lovely, the colors always reminded her she was a prisoner. Even the bedspread, also in black and gold, mocked her in that fact.

The fireplace roared trying to ward off the chill that ran through the halls and rooms of the castle. She looked into the flames as tears burned her eyes and threatened to spill. She wiped them away, thinking how many times she'd sat in the same spot and cried. More than anything, she wished she were back in Morgansville with her family and friends. She hated being all alone in this room. This wasn't right. She didn't belong here. She belonged in school with the other kids and especially with Jenny

This place was so dark, and every time Maeldoi, Ringwar, or one of their weird servants came in, she shuddered. The first few days she'd tried to leave the castle, but there were some really strange characters roaming the halls and she'd been caught and reprimanded each time. The last time she tried to escape, Ringwar had made it quite clear—Beth would be jailed in the dungeons below. Beth never tried to leave again. All she could do was to sit in the room and wait. Wait for what she didn't know, but she prayed Jenny and Devon came for her soon.

CHAPTER 36

SWAMPS OF ILIRIA

The end of the forest loomed ahead where a barren wasteland waited to inflict more danger upon them.

"I think I preferred the forest." Jenny smiled.

"As do I," Alwin said.

"Let's get through this as quickly as possible," Devon said.

Jenny sensed something was hiding in the shadows waiting for them. She wondered if Devon's senses had also picked up the ominous feeling. Ever since they'd left the coolness of the forest, she'd sensed something wasn't right. She didn't how to explain all that she felt, but she sensed something was out of place.

"I'm not sure, but we've done pretty well so far and I think... no I know... we'll be okay." Devon smiled at the princess.

"I sense danger." Jenny put on a brave face.

"As do I," Devon said.

The ground was dry and hard packed beneath their feet. A long and painful road filled with heat and unknown predators waited for them. A full day would pass before they reached the Swamps of Iliria.

"What's in the Swamps of Iliria?" Jenny asked. "I've never been to a swamp before."

"It protects the Black Castle from unwanted intruders."

"Are the swamps at the end of this desert?"

"Yes, but stay on guard. We don't know what's out there," Devon said. "Maeldoi won't make it easy."

"There's always a chance more giant ants will come after us," Jenny said, trying to lighten the mood that settled over them.

"True, but I think Maeldoi will come up with something even more sinister."

"Such as?"

"That!" Alwin cried out.

Devon and Jenny turned around and saw something large and dark moving toward them.

"What is it?" she asked in a frightened voice. The shadow was massive, but its identity remained a mystery. It moved toward the unsuspecting trio. What kind of menace had been unleashed?

"I can't tell. It's too far away." Devon strained to see what kind of creature hunted them now.

They took off at a run, putting some distance between them and the creatures. They ran until their lungs threatened to burst from the pressure they'd been under the past several days. Finally, they stopped to rest. They were trying to steady their breathing, but it would take longer than the few minutes they had.

"Maybe we lost whatever is out there." Jenny gasped for air. She drank from her canteen, buying herself some time to rest her achy muscles. Never had she run this much or this far before. She didn't understand what propelled her to continue with this trek.

"What manner of creature was that?" Alwin asked, as he drank some cool water from his canteen.

"I don't know." Devon tried to steady his own breathing. He drank some water as well, but his eyes scanned the area for the unknown creatures. Whatever was out there wouldn't give up, especially if it had been sent by the Dark Wizard. "We shouldn't linger."

The winds picked up. Stronger and stronger they became. Jenny tried to keep her balance, but was being thrown around. Devon and Alwin had similar trouble as the gusts pushed them toward the forest.

"What's happening?" Jenny yelled hoping Devon could hear her.

The wind picked up the desert sand and turned it into a funnel cloud. Devon ran to Jenny and took her hand all the while trying to stay on his feet. The funnel cloud touched down. It missed the travelers by a mere few feet.

"Run!" Devon pulled Jenny who also took Alwin's hand. They had to stay together. The wind could send them in different directions. They couldn't allow that to happen.

Another funnel cloud touched down behind the trio causing them to flee to the right and then left and right again. The wind turned and turned until a series of funnel clouds touched the desert floor. All around them the wind wound its way across the desert floor. There was nowhere to run or hide out here. All they could do was try and keep away from the deadly winds.

Jenny held on to Devon's hand with all her might. Alwin kept his hand locked with the princess. They needed to figure out where the next wind tunnel would touch down and tried to run in the opposite direction.

"Where are we going?" Alwin voiced the question on Jenny's mind.

"We have to get away from this wind! Look out!" Devon's voice barely carried over the din of the storm as another funnel touched the ground in front of them, creating a gaping hole. It was huge. "We'll have to go around this area!" Devon continued to pull them toward the swamps.

After what seemed like an eternity, the winds dissipated. They slowed down and the travelers were able to see how close to the forest they were. Out here they could see whatever came their way, but inside they were at the mercy of whatever lived within the darkness. Maeldoi must have planned it this way. If they were trapped in the darkened woods, they wouldn't see what other creatures were sent. In the darkness, the creatures would be upon them before they were seen.

"What the devil was that about?" Alwin asked.

"I'm not sure, but for some strange reason Maeldoi is herding us toward the forest. I don't like that." Devon stepped in front of the princess and scanned the area. "We'll keep to the border as much as possible and go around the crater. Once we're away from here, we'll make our way toward the swamps.

"How long will that take?" Jenny asked. All these games that Maeldoi was playing, was getting on her nerves. She just wanted to see her best friend, and hopefully find out what happened to her parents. At this rate, they wouldn't make it to the Black Castle before tomorrow.

"I'm not sure. Let's see what happens." Devon took the lead. No matter what, the princess had to be protected.

"Alright."

They kept to the border of the forest, staying alert and ready for anything. After the windstorm, they knew Maeldoi was capable of doing anything he wanted. He had the power to make this trek even deadlier. The result of the windstorm was vast. The crater the funnel created was larger than they first thought. It crawled as far as the eye could see. They had to circle around it.

"We'll never get around it in time to save Beth." Jenny tried to see past the expanse of the hole created by the funnel clouds.

"Yes we will." The last place anyone wanted to be was where the wizard herded them. "We'll make our trek through the forest as quickly as they could."

"Is that wise?" Alwin asked.

"No, but we have no other choice."

They entered the forest thinking something would pop out at them, but so far, everything remained quiet until the dreaded rustling was heard. Louder and louder, the sounds touched them. Something lay in wait for the trio. No one knew what new menace the Dark Wizard sent, but they had no doubt this wouldn't be easy.

Jenny approached Devon. "What was that?" She was so tired of hearing sounds rustling all around them without knowing what would try to kill them.

"I don't know, just keep moving." Devon quickened his pace.

From behind a large arachnid slid down from the tree. All around the unfortunate travelers, large spiders slid down their silken vines to cause them more trouble. Large eyes and long furry legs came from the trees for a snack. Each spider touched the ground wanting a warm meal.

"Watch out!" Devon's voice rang out.

They tried to run, but the spiders refused to allow them to pass. They swung on their vines and tried to catch and eat the travelers. As soon as one touched the ground another spider slid down the silken web.

Jenny, Devon and Alwin removed their swords and swung at the spiders. Jenny cut the vine of one spider. It fell at her feet.

"They could be poisonous, watch out for their fangs. Whatever you do, don't let them get close to you." Devon's sword sliced through the spider approaching Jenny's legs. It disintegrated into a mound of ash.

Unfortunately, Alwin wasn't so lucky. His short legs made him a perfect catch for the spiders. He tripped over a long leg and fell upon the hard packed ground. He was about to become dinner for one of these creatures.

"Devon!" he cried out, as the spider approached him and stood above his tired body, ready to have its afternoon snacks. Large eyes surrounded the spider's head while exposed fangs attempted to catch the morsel on the ground.

Devon and Jenny removed their bows and let the arrows fly. Both arrows struck the spider. Another volley of arrows flew and the spider wobbled. It fell over just as Alwin rolled away. They launched another attack and hoped they could destroy the creatures. To their amazement, one by one the spiders fell over and disintegrated into a mound of ash.

"They're not real!" Jenny told her friends.

"No, they're not. They're created by black magick," Devon said, slicing through another spider.

They continued to fight the spiders sliding down newly created silk. Another spider jumped on Alwin. He tried to knock the spider from his back, but the creature was not about to allow its meal to escape. "Devon!"

Devon picked up a fallen branch and knocked the spider off the gnome. He then sliced it in half. He turned sharply and his blade cut through another one. Another mound of ash was left. The spider, although not real, could kill someone and that was the reason Maeldoi had sent it.

They watched in horror as the other spiders climbed back up the silken cords and vanished into the trees.

"Jenny, are you alright?" Devon was at her side.

"Yes. Let's get out of here."

"Yes, let's find the swamps and put an end to this once and for all," Devon said.

By late afternoon, the smells around them changed from the scents of grass and wildflowers within the forest, to the musty scent of the swampland. Murky, decayed waters filled the air around the swamp. Creatures skulked around the marsh as something dark and evil moved within those waters. The scent of decayed waters filled the air as they approached the last leg of their journey. They came upon the swamp where creatures skulked around the marsh. Something evil moved in the waters, and an alligator the size of a car slithered into the swamp and ate something for dinner.

"Don't tell me we have to wade through there?" Jenny asked fearfully, pointing toward the dark swamp.

"We must cross the swamp. The castle is on the other side."

"Devon, are you crazy?"

"No. This is the only way to the Black Castle."

"There are snakes and alligators in there."

"Yes, and there are black flies and bats that will bite you and suck out your blood. But if you want to reach the castle and save Beth, this is the only way." Devon swatted a large mosquito that landed on his arm.

"Through that swamp?" Jenny's frightened expression told them both how she felt about this plan.

"Yes."

She stared at the swamp, thinking the water moved in an unnatural way. Frogs croaked in the distance. A dense fog hovered over the water. A shudder tore through her as she watched Devon approach the water's edge. He looked around and took something from a hook attached to a signpost. He raised something else to his lips and she heard the sound of a horn, but this was no ordinary horn. This one was carved from the bones of dead men. Alwin provided her with this bit of information.

Devon blew the horn twice and replaced it. They waited.

"What's he doing?" Jenny asked, her eyes never leaving Devon's dark form.

"Watch."

Through the fog, the sound of a paddle cutting the surface of the water drew near. From the dense fog, floating across the waters, a dark figure emerged, cloaked from head to toe. A wooden pole cut through the water as the mysterious figure used its length to push a large raft from one end of the swamp to the other.

Devon reached into his bag and pulled out a small square swathed in tissue paper. He unwrapped the square and placed it on the bony hand that crawled out from beneath the long-sleeved cloak.

"Who or what is that?" she whispered to Devon.

"That is the ferryman."

"You mean to say there really is a ferryman?"

"Yes, of course there is. He takes passengers to the Black Castle."

"Devon, I always thought you had to pay the ferryman with a gold coin, but you gave him something else. What did you give him?"

"Chocolate."

"What?"

"Yes. This ferryman loves bitter chocolate."

"How did you know this?"

"I did my homework before we left Wardell. Rain provided me with the chocolate. He knew I'd need it. Get on board. Alwin, are you planning on joining us?" Devon asked when the gnome failed to move. He stood rooted to one spot, entranced by the sight before him. He'd only ever heard of the ferryman, but he had never before seen him.

"Of course, Devon. Do you think I'd let the two of you go alone? You will need my help." He grunted.

They laughed.

Devon jumped onto the raft and held out his hand for Jenny. Once she was on board, Alwin followed. He needed a small running start in order to make the jump onto the raft.

The ferryman placed his pole into the water and pushed off the bottom. Slowly, they cruised across the marsh. Snakes slithered by the raft, while alligators bumped it, hoping a fresh tidbit might fall into the water.

"You thought we'd have to wade through these waters in order to cross the swamp?" Devon asked Jenny.

"I did. You could have told me about this right away."

"I could have, but this was much more fun." Devon laughed at her.

"I don't believe you." Jenny punched his arm.

"Ouch."

The raft continued to glide through the smelly water, as frogs croaked in the distance. From time to time, the screech of an owl or crow startled the passengers, but the ferryman never missed a stroke with his pole. He kept the raft gliding through the water with skill and precision.

"Is that it?" Jenny asked, as the Black Castle came into view. Her eyes took in all the details from the darkness surrounding it, to the tall towers. Nothing about this place could be considered pleasant. This place was surrounded by darkness and death. Mesmerized by its menacing appearance, she stared at the castle and wondered if they'd leave this evil place alive.

"Welcome to the Black Castle, Princess," Alwin whispered.

CHAPTER 37

THE BLACK CASTLE

Bright lights flickered in the windows of the castle casting a gloomy luminosity that cut through the foggy darkness of the swamp. The closer the raft came to the end of the swamp, the more threatening the castle became. This was an imposing structure that promised tales of sinister plots and evil doings. The last time Jenny had ever seen anything like this, Dracula lived in it.

"That's the Black Castle?" Jenny asked in awe.

"Yes. What do you think?"

"Wow! It's totally wicked!"

"Yes, it is."

Never had she seen such an awesome sight. The castle stood majestically upon a mountain of rocks. Black turrets reached for the bright moon casting a sinister glow across the evening sky. She wondered how someone entered this place.

"Don't tell me we'll have to climb those rocks in order to reach the castle."

"Nothing so dramatic. I think Maeldoi will even leave his drawbridge down for us," Devon said. This was also his first visit to the sinister Black Castle. No one knew what to expect. Maeldoi wanted Jenny inside, and that meant they'd have little to no trouble making an entrance.

"I guess he's expecting us."

"Jenny, getting in will be easy. Finding Beth and getting her out won't be." She had to appreciate the dangers hiding within the castle walls.

"This is quite true, Princess," Alwin said.

"But what about my parents? What if they're still alive?" Jenny kept the hope of finding her parents alive in her heart.

"If, and when, the time comes, I'll figure something out. You mustn't worry about that right now. What you need to do is keep your wits about you. I don't want you to think of anything except the mission before us. You have to concentrate on entering the castle and rescuing your friend. Everything else will fall into place." His serious tone took her aback.

The ferryman landed the raft and waited for his passengers to disembark. They watched the ferryman disappear into the fog. When he was out of sight, they stepped onto the roadway leading toward the bridge. The rough and rugged terrain stretched up the side of the hill. It wasn't easy, but the trio managed to reach the top of the hillside. Now came the dangerous part.

"Shall we go in and greet our hosts?" Devon took her hand in his.

"Of course." Jenny felt better about entering the lion's den. Devon's courage was contagious.

They stopped when a rope bridge presented them with yet another challenge. Jenny looked around hoping there was another way across.

"We'll have to cross this bridge, but stay alert. There may be guards waiting on the other side."

"Isn't there another way into the castle?" Jenny asked, looking at the narrow bridge hanging by ropes over a dark abyss.

"No, Jenny. This is the only way into the castle." Devon looked at the obstacle before them.

"Just thought I'd ask."

Devon went first to test the strength of the rope bridge. He held onto the ropes on either side of the bridge and tested it for strength. He kept one foot in front of the other, and he slowly made his way onto the rope bridge.

"Jenny, Alwin, is you all right?" Devon called out to them when he felt the pressure of their weight behind him.

"Oh, I'm absolutely wonderful, Devon. I think we should do this more often." Jenny kept her footing on the narrow ropes.

Alwin laughed. "This isn't so bad. I think Maeldoi is slipping."

Devon laughed as well. "We can use some good fortune. Let's just get to the other side while we still can."

Jenny kept her eyes focused on Devon and mimicked his every move. She refused to allow herself to get distracted, even for a moment. They were so close to the castle, and she wanted them to arrive safely. Finally, she could see that the end was upon them.

"No guards." Jenny stared ahead at the ominous Black Castle.

"No. Maeldoi's waiting for you."

"I know he is. I can feel his presence all around us." The evil was overwhelming her senses. She'd never experienced such darkness before, but the evil she felt within the castle walls took her aback. She feared what they would find once they crossed the drawbridge.

They traveled together all the while searching the area for guards or other vicious creatures. They gave a collective sigh when the drawbridge loomed ahead of them. Once they entered Maeldoi's domain they'd be at his mercy. The entrance to the castle darkened as they stepped over the threshold where black marble floors led to a black marble staircase. The gold and silver marbled walls glittered all around. A large, crystal chandelier hung suspended over the foyer, illuminating the area and the abundance of marble used to decorate this castle. A star of marbled hallways branched off the entrance to the foyer.

Candles burned all around them, giving the threesome the opportunity to better view the interior. They looked around wondering where they'd find Beth, but no one greeted the visitors. On the contrary, they stood alone trying to use their senses to discover the right passage.

"Where do we go from here?" Jenny looked at the maze of corridors.

"I don't know," Devon said, as his eyes moved in all directions, refusing to be caught off guard by Maeldoi or one of his pets.

A door slammed shut. They jumped. A blocked hallway stood before them. A moment later, another door closed, and then another, and another, until only one remained open. They looked at each other and then at the lone hallway open to them.

"I guess we go this way." Devon took the lead.

Torches sat in wall sconces. They were magically ignited, shining brightly in the lovely hallway that led them to another door. Devon pulled it open. "Grab some torches," he told Jenny as he continued to stare at the darkness.

She went to the wall and pulled out two torches. She handed one to Alwin and brought the other one to Devon. He used it to illuminate the interior.

"What is it?" Alwin asked unable to see beyond the two tall people blocking his view.

"There's a staircase. It probably leads to the dungeons."

"So, what are we waiting for? Let's find your friend, Princess," Alwin said from behind.

"Ready?" Devon asked his friends.

"Not really," Jenny said. "What about you, Alwin?"

"Of course. Let's get him."

One stone step at a time they sank lower and lower into the bowels of the castle. Deeper and deeper they went. No light shone for them when they reached the bottom of the stairs. Only darkness welcomed them. A long and narrow hallway presented itself. Devon held the torch and made his way down the corridor.

"I don't like this," Alwin said.

"Neither do I. Maeldoi is somewhere in this castle. I'm surprised he hasn't made his presence known to us." Devon advanced a few paces and then stopped.

"What's wrong?" Jenny asked fearfully.

"Something moved."

"What is it?" Jenny went to Devon. A shudder tore through her as she sensed danger waiting for them.

"I thought I saw a dark figure. Come on, let's follow whoever or whatever is wandering around down here." Devon led the way.

"I don't know if this is such a good idea."

"Princess, we have no choice in the matter. We must press on." Alwin stayed behind to guard their backs.

The hallway ended and a remarkable area opened up. Catacombs were scattered in all directions. The tunnel ended with a large cavern where someone could easily lose their way.

"Stay close," Devon told his friends and removed his sword from its sheath.

"Do you think he's got Beth down here?" Jenny asked worriedly.

"Maybe."

"It's so cold and damp." Tears glistened in her eyes as thoughts of Beth sitting in a corner, cold and hungry. The images that flashed across her mind nearly drove her crazy. She had to find her and save her from this place.

"Don't worry, Jenny. I'm sure she's fine. He wouldn't hurt her. He needs her to get to you, so we have that advantage." Devon slowly moved forward.

"I hope so. I'm scared she's been kept down here all this time. Look at this place." Stone walls surrounded the room and blended into the stone floor. There was nothing comforting about the place. It was a cold dungeon where no one should be kept.

"I know, but first we have to figure out where he's keeping her. I don't want to enter this maze blindly. We could get trapped, and that is something I'm not prepared to do. We will move with caution."

"What are we waiting for?" Alwin stepped forward when no one moved.

"A sign."

One by one, torches sitting in sconces came to life, illuminating the right passage for them to follow. They followed the trail left by the torches in the hopes of finding Beth before they went too deep.

"Are you sure we should follow Maeldoi's trail?" Jenny wondered if they weren't making a big mistake. Maeldoi wouldn't just allow them to enter, find Beth, and leave. He wanted so much more, and Jenny knew she was what they needed.

"There's no other way."

"Then let's find an end to this once and for all." Jenny prepared herself to face the Dark Wizard.

The catacombs were a maze of honeycombs. Someone definitely could lose their way and perish within this labyrinth. They approached an open area when the torches behind them extinguished. Up ahead others burst into flames. This room differed from the other one. Here, rooms with steel bars, like a jail, lined the corridors.

Jenny looked in, but couldn't see anything. She went to the next cell and brought the torch close to the bars. A hairy creature slammed its weight against the steel bars. Her scream rent the thick air and echoed throughout the dungeon.

Devon removed his sword and pulled Jenny away from the cell before the beast's claws could slice through her. She fell back against another cell only to have another hairy paw land on her shoulder.

Another scream split the quiet of the dungeon.

"What are those things?" Jenny asked her heart pounding. She tried to calm her nerves, but the fear she felt was overwhelming. Nothing was normal down here. To her, these past weeks had been trying, but this place was something only a nightmare could create.

"Maeldoi's beasts, animals, people, poor souls transformed into these hideous creatures. Maeldoi is breeding an army to capture a well-guarded castle and village." Even Devon's voice shook. The reality of what they saw was sinking in.

"How could he do such a terrible thing?" Jenny felt ill at the thought of people and animals being tortured by the wizard. Her anger came to the surface and threatened to spill over. She felt as though she would be sick. No one could be that evil.

"He needs power in order to take Wardell. These creatures are strong enough to fight the guards and kill my family. He wants the throne," Devon said. They had no choice at this point—they had to destroy the wizard and his witch.

The only way they could save Wardell was to destroy Maeldoi and Ringwar. Did they have what it took to overthrow such evil? Somehow, a plan had to be mastered in order to save those who were trapped within these walls.

"Can we help them?" Jenny hoped these poor souls could be saved.

"I don't know."

"We can't leave them like this. We have to transform them back into whoever or whatever they once were. Without them, Wardell would be safe," Jenny said.

"When the time comes, we'll try to help them," Devon said.

"Thank you. Devon, something's not right," Jenny said, as they approached yet another large chamber. She sensed something, but didn't understand what it was. She'd been sensing odd emotions and feelings ever since they'd begun this journey.

They heard a rattle. Something was chained up in the next room. Jenny wanted to help whatever poor creature was trapped. No one deserved such a horrific fate. She wanted to free whatever or whomever was trapped down here.

"I know."

"I can feel another presence," Jenny said. She raised her hand trying to make sense of what she felt.

"Can you tell what it is?"

Jenny looked nervously at Devon.

"This isn't the time to be shy about your insight. Can you feel what's hiding in there?" Devon demanded. He pushed Jenny into using her gift without thought or remorse.

"No. I feel two separate sets of emotions coming from somewhere and they're not ours." Jenny held out her hand toward the cavern ahead of them. "I sense fear, anger, and strength. It's weird."

"So there's more than one creature hiding in there?" Alwin asked, drawing his sword when Jenny nodded.

"Be careful." Devon led the way. "Remember, Jenny, whatever is in there was created to kill. Don't make the mistake of pitying the beasts, for they won't offer you any sympathy. If given the chance, they will kill us."

"I know, but I have to try. If there's a way to help the poor trapped souls then I have to do whatever I can to help them."

They walked toward the sounds, swords held tightly in their hands. They were ready for whatever the dark wizard sent. Slowly, cautiously, they came to the entrance of a large chamber.

Jenny wanted to peer inside and see what was in there, but she stayed by Devon's hand. He put his finger to his lips and motioned for them to wait. They did. They waited for Devon to make the first move. He would never allow Jenny to enter before him. He paused and looked inside. He hoped this wasn't a trap, but he sensed there was something large waiting for them. Suddenly, torches all around the room sprang to life. This seemed to be quite the norm. They flickered and lit the room revealing the source of the rattling chains.

"Dragons!" they screamed at the same time.

With one breath, the larger dragon sent a fierce burst of fire at them, sending Devon, Jenny, and Alwin running to the other side of the room.

"Can we make it out of this chamber?" Jenny asked.

"I don't know. We may make it, but Alwin is slower."

"Don't worry about me. I'll keep up with you." Alwin sounded insulted.

"I think this is the same dragon that attacked us at Wardell," Jenny said. Her eyes took in the view before her. The first dragon was large and black with scaly skin and spikes protruding from his low jaw filled with large teeth and fangs. Dark wings were pulled to its sides, and its tail was long and menacing.

The other dragon was smaller and was lighter in color. Scales covered its body, and it possessed the same spikes all around its jaw. They were shackled to the wall by large chains, and were barely able to move.

"It is." Devon tried to find a way out of the room without being roasted by their fiery breaths.

"So what do we do now?" Jenny asked. She stepped forward and put out her hand. She felt something strange as she looked at the dragons. She stared at their spiky faces. Something familiar sparked a distant memory, a memory she couldn't fully remember. She sensed, for reasons unknown to her, she'd seen these dragons before. Slowly, she walked toward the two beasts. A familiar aura emanated from the dragons and touched her. Jenny felt a life force emerging from the dragons, a life force she never forgot.

"Jenny, what are you doing?" Devon whispered to her. He tried to pull her back to him.

"I have to go to them."

"You'll be killed."

"No, I won't. Just stay where you are. I know what I'm doing." Jenny approached the dragons and looked into their eyes. One pair of eyes she saw every time she looked in the mirror, while the other haunted her dreams.

"Mother? Father?"

The dragons looked at the child and roared. They pulled and pulled on the chains binding them to the cavern wall.

"Jenny! Get away from them!" Devon yelled to her.

"It's Athelina. Please, remember me."

Tears fell down her pale cheeks. She beseeched the dragons to remember her. A white light surrounded Jenny's hands as she reached out and touched the dragons' heads. Their scales were rough beneath her touch. Slowly, she allowed her magick to flow from her heart into theirs.

Devon and Alwin looked on in wonder. No one understood what Jenny was doing, but their fascination forced them to stand still and watch. When the light extinguished and Jenny's hands returned to normal, the dragons looked at the child. Recognition flickered in their eyes. Jenny sensed the change in them. She moved a little closer to the dragons.

"It's me, Athelina, your daughter. Please, remember me. Remember us as a family."

Athelina's magickal touch sparked a memory in the dragons' minds as they looked around the room. Jenny sensed the dragons were no longer mindless beasts, but her parents.

She'd found them. After all these years, she'd found King Morgan and Queen Ileana of Wardell. Jenny looked at them and sensed they now knew their true identity as well as her own.

CHAPTER 38

JENNY'S RESOLVE

Devon came up behind Jenny, followed by Alwin. He put his hand on her shoulder and looked at the dragons. He looked into a pair of blue eyes, kind and sad. He then gazed into a pair of bright green eyes—the same as Jenny's bright green gaze. He finally understood Jenny's discovery.

"Your majesties." Devon understood.

Alwin approached and bowed before the king and queen of Wardell.

King Morgan raised his head and let a fierce roar escape between sharp teeth. He turned his head and looked at his wife.

"We have to force Maeldoi to turn my parents back," Jenny said.

"That may be more difficult than you think. I don't believe they'll accommodate you, no matter what you say or do." Devon didn't want Jenny to get her hopes up.

"I don't care what they want. I spent the last six years without them, and I won't do it again." Jenny turned toward the dragons. "We'll come back for you."

Her father roared and pulled on the chains binding him and his wife to the thick, stone wall.

"No, Dad, you have to stay here. Please, trust us to do this."

The king relented.

"Come on, Jenny. We'll do everything we can to rescue them, but first we need to find Beth and free her from the wizard's clutches."

They ran from the room. Once out of sight, Jenny stopped walking. Her body shook as the realization of what had been done

268

to her parents overwhelmed her. She slid down the wall and allowed her tears to fall freely.

Devon looked around and saw Jenny slide down the wall. He ran back and knelt in front of her. He put his hands on her arms and helped her stand. She raised her tear-stained face and looked into his eyes. She wiped at the tears. This wasn't the reaction she expected when she found her parents.

"I'm sorry," Jenny finally said, amid the hiccupping that wracked her small form. Why should this affect her so?

"Don't be. You've had a big shock. Your parents are alive and they've been turned into dragons. I'd say you have the right to shed some tears."

"All those years I lived with Nora my parents were forced to live down here as beasts. Maeldoi took a lot from us. We'll never get those years back."

"I know, but at least you've found each other. Isn't that what truly matters?" With a finger under her chin, Devon made her look at him. He wanted to help her accept this situation.

"I guess. I'm just so angry at Maeldoi. It's not fair."

"No it isn't, but you need to remember the throne is the only thing that matters to him, but don't worry, we'll think of something. Somehow, someway, we'll find a way to rescue your parents."

"I know." Jenny smiled. "Thank you."

"You're welcome. I must tell you I wasn't sure you still believed in me."

"Of course, I do. Devon, you're the best friend I've ever had. You've been with me every step of the way. You've been the strength guiding me. I owe you so much."

Devon looked at the princess and knew she meant every word. It was up to him to make sure he never let her down. "You don't owe me anything."

"Yes, I do."

"No, Jenny. I'm proud to be your friend, and I helped you because I wanted to."

Jenny looked at him and smiled. "I know."

"Are you feeling better?" He pressed his lips to her forehead and smiled.

"Yes, much better."

"Good. Are you ready to do some work?"

"Yes, I'm more than ready to destroy Maeldoi."

"First we'll find Beth, and then we'll get the wizard."

"You're right. We'll get Beth, and then we'll get the real monsters living down here."

They caught up with Alwin who'd gone on ahead to scout the area. They found him near the entrance of another large chamber. He pointed inside, but feared uttering a word in case Maeldoi heard them.

"What is it?" Devon whispered and leaned in to peer inside.

"Maeldoi." Jenny instantly sensed his evil presence. "Beth." She wanted to run into the room, but was stayed by Devon's hand.

"No. It could be a trap."

"Jenny!"

"Beth! We're coming."

"I'm okay, Jen!" she called out to relieve her friend's fear.

"Let her go, Maeldoi."

Jenny stormed into the room, determined to face and defeat her enemy. She didn't stop to think if there was a trap set for her. All she wanted was to get to Beth. Devon and Alwin stayed behind her, in case it was a trap.

"Hello, Athelina. I've been waiting for you," a deep voice said from behind. He held Beth a few steps away from Jenny.

She turned on Maeldoi. "I know what you did to my parents. You're a monster."

"Oh, and what did I do that was so bad?"

"We saw them in the chamber chained up like animals."

"But, my dear, that is precisely what they are." He threw his head back and laughed a chilling laugh.

"Let her go!"

"No."

"What do you want?"

"You."

Jenny looked at him. "Why?"

"I want you to join your parents." Maeldoi smiled.

"Why?"

"So I can have the throne."

"It doesn't belong to you. Galfrid is the rightful ruler."

"No! He is not! Now, then…" He seemed to calm down. "You can save your friends, or you can all perish in my dungeons. The choice is yours."

Devon and Alwin stood next to Jenny. Devon took her hand and squeezed it reassuringly. She looked at him and saw the quick shake of his head. He'd never allow her to surrender. They'd find a way to defeat the wizard.

"Just let Beth go. She has nothing to do with this." Jenny pleaded for her friend's freedom.

"It doesn't matter. As long as I have her, your life is in my hands," Maeldoi said.

"No, it isn't!" Her voice raised an octave.

"Maeldoi!" A gruff, female voice called out from the shadows. An old, petite woman with long white hair that fell past her knees shuffled toward the princess. She wore long, dark robes and placed a gnarled hand upon Jenny's cheek. She gazed into green eyes and touched her soft, young skin.

Jenny looked into the old and withered face. Pale and vacant blue eyes stared back at her. Ringwar. She'd wondered what this woman who ruled men with her face looked like. From where she stood, Ringwar was old and quite pathetic. There was no sign of an immeasurable beauty.

"So, you are Princess Athelina."

Jenny jutted out her chin. "And you must be Ringwar."

"Yes, I am."

"I want you to let Beth go."

"No."

"Why not?"

"I want Wardell, where we will reign over all the lands, and the people will bow to us."

"Even if you take Wardell, the people will never recognize you as their true rulers. They may bow before you out of fear, but they'll never bow to you out of love and respect," Jenny said with confidence.

Ringwar didn't acknowledge Jenny's words, but continued with her speech. "Once we have Wardell, we will set our sights on Warwick, and then the people will understand the extent of our power," Ringwar said with pride. "No one will dare stand against us."

"You will never get Warwick."

"Yes, Princess, I will take Wardell and then I will take Warwick. You see, King Theron isn't strong enough to fight us."

"Maybe not, but the prince is strong enough to fight you, and I know he'll do everything in his power to protect his people."

Ringwar laughed. "No, child. He doesn't have the strength to defeat us. Our magic will rule the lands, and no one will stop us." Her withered face gave her a frail appearance and a cunning look. This was something they had to beware of. This woman wasn't as frail and old as she looked. There was something there... something Jenny sensed. She was a formidable opponent.

"Then we'll have to stop you here and now," Jenny said.

"How?"

"I'll find a way." Jenny raised a stubborn chin.

Ringwar glanced at Maeldoi and laughed. Not a hearty laugh, but an evil laugh.

Sword drawn, Devon moved closer to Jenny.

"So, the steward's son has courage. Very impressive. I may have you seated at my side. I could use a strong man as my personal advisor." Ringwar saw the determination and the sword Devon wielded in his hand.

"I wouldn't count on it." He flashed a defiant eye.

"Do not be so hasty, Devon. If you do not do as I wish, I will be forced to kill you all," Ringwar said.

"My father would never allow you to enter the castle. He would kill you first."

"Not if I have the princess and his only son as my prisoners." She enjoyed the banter.

Jenny looked at Devon. "What do we do now?" she whispered.

"Run."

The companions ran toward the entrance only to be stopped by a hideous beast. A monstrous creature she'd never seen before blocked the only exit with a scaly body, sharp fangs, and yellow eyes that glowed eerily in the pale light. Thick claws threatened them as the creature extended its wings.

"What is that?" Jenny leaned into Devon.

"A harpy," Devon told her, ready to destroy this hideous creature.

The harpy's wings blocked all possible means of escape. A shrill cry erupted from the beast.

"I will make you a deal, Princess." Ringwar pushed Beth in front of her.

"What kind of a deal?"

"No, Jenny. You can't trust her."

"Stay out of this, boy." She glared at Devon. Ringwar softened and looked at Jenny. In a pleasant voice, she said, "Take your friend's place."

"What?"

"If you take her place, I will release her and she will be free to leave the castle."

"Jenny, don't do it. You can't trust her." Devon read her like a book. He watched the emotions dart across her face.

"I have no choice," Jenny sadly told her friends.

"Yes, you do. We'll find another way to free her, I promise."

"No, Devon. There is no other way." The sadness in her tone told everyone she would concede. "I have to do whatever I can to save Beth."

"Princess, please listen to Devon. You cannot believe anything Ringwar says. She will never release your friend."

"Careful, little gnome. You are easily disposed of." Ringwar laughed at her own words and wit.

"If I agree, I want three things," Jenny said, knowing she had to do everything in her power to help free Beth and save her parents.

Ringwar looked at Maeldoi and smiled, believing she'd won this battle. Pride flowed through her veins and shone on her face. They noticed the smug look on Ringwar's face. The crown of Wardell would soon sit upon her head. She'd won everything.

Jenny watched them. She knew their greed would be their downfall. As much as she wanted to save everyone, she also knew deceit when she saw it.

"What are your terms?" Ringwar asked.

"First, you let Beth go."

"Next?"

"You change my parents back into humans."

"And third?"

"You let Devon, Alwin, Beth, and my parents return to Wardell or another town of their choosing... a place where they can live out their years in peace and safety."

"Agreed." Ringwar was elated at the prospect of finally having Athelina's youth and beauty.

"Jenny, she can't be trusted." Devon tried to change her mind. "We'll find another way."

"I know," she said. "I have to do this. It's the only way."

Ringwar pushed Beth toward Jenny. They hugged each other. "Are you all right?"

"Yes. Jenny, you can't do this."

"Don't worry. I'll be fine. Go to Devon."

Maeldoi came over to Jenny. "Remove your weapons."

Jenny did as she was told. She dropped her weapons on the floor. "What about my parents. I'd like to see them first."

Maeldoi took her arm and led her to Ringwar.

"Well? What about my parents?" Jenny asked.

"Silly girl. Did you really think I would let them go?"

"No, I didn't. I knew you couldn't be trusted." Jenny threw her foot out and kicked Ringwar in the stomach causing her to fall to the ground. She ran to Devon. "Let's go!"

They ran from the room and down a passage. Behind them, the distinctive cry of the harpy closed in on them. The wind created by the creature's wings touched them, but they kept their lead. Devon removed his sword and entered the large chamber where they'd make their stand.

The harpy flew into the large chamber behind them. Devon and Alwin used their swords to try and run the harpy through. They fought valiantly, but the harpy was too quick. The dragons spewed flames in an attempt to burn it alive. One large burst of fire after another left the dragons, but the harpy was able to move around the cavern where the dragons could not. They were still chained to the walls.

Devon had enough. He spun around and dispatched his sword across the room. He watched it fly straight and hit its mark. The harpy disintegrated. Devon walked to the mound of ash and retrieved his sword. "You took quite a chance in there."

"I had no other choice. I knew Ringwar wanted me more than anything. I hoped to use that against her."

"It worked."

"Jenny, what's happening?" Beth cried, terrified at the sight of the dragons.

"Don't be afraid, Beth. The dragons are my parents." Jenny turned and looked at them. She'd wanted to help them, but she didn't know if there was a way to break the spell. She had to try.

"What?"

"All these years, my parents have been living down here as dragons. They've been kept prisoner down here."

"That's impossible." Beth didn't know what to believe anymore. She'd seen and been a part of a different world where many strange things occurred.

"No, Beth, it's quite possible. I've come to realize anything can happen in this realm."

"How?" Beth didn't know what to say.

"Magic."

"I don't understand."

"I know. When we return to Wardell, I'll tell you everything."

Beth looked at her friend. She forced a smile to her lips. "Okay, but the minute we're out of here, I get an explanation?"

"I promise," Jenny said.

"Oh, and Jenny?" Beth's tone was serious.

"Yes?"

"Thanks for coming for me." Beth smiled at her best friend.

"Any time," Jenny told her.

CHAPTER 39

THE REUNION

"So, let's destroy Ringwar and Maeldoi," Jenny told her companions. There had to be a way to stop this evil from spreading across the lands. It was up to them to stop the pair from reining their kind of evil across Wardell and Warwick.

"How?" Beth asked.

"We have to go back in there and get them. We have to stop them from ever hurting anyone again."

"Jenny, I can't go after them." Beth still trembled with fear. "This is all new to me. I can't make sense out of anything."

"I know, Beth. I want you to stay here with the dragons. They'll protect you."

"Maeldoi and Ringwar are too powerful to fight alone," Devon said. "There isn't anything we can do."

"I have to try. We have to try," Jenny said correcting herself.

"And exactly what do you plan on doing, you treacherous child?" Ringwar barked from the entrance to the large chamber. Her hand lay upon her stomach to showcase the pain Jenny inflicted on her.

"Whatever it takes to stop you and save us."

Maeldoi stepped forward with his walking stick in his hand. The large emerald nestled within shone brightly.

"What would you have me do?" Maeldoi asked Ringwar.

"Turn the dragons back into King Morgan and Queen Ileana."

"What? No. I can't allow that to happen. We've worked too long and too hard to release the king and queen."

"Maeldoi, I want them to meet their daughter and then we'll kill them all." Ringwar laughed harshly.

"But we need the dragons."

"No. Galfrid will relinquish the throne to us. He will grieve the death of his only child, and while grieving he won't have the courage to fight us. The throne won't matter to him."

"Then you do not know my father," Devon told the wizard and his witch.

"It does not matter. I have more than enough beasts and harpies to achieve my goals. Now that the dragons are no longer under my control, they are useless to me. You know what to do."

Maeldoi pointed his staff at Jenny's parents. The large emerald shone as a burst of green light surrounded the dragons. They roared as their wings expanded and then they slowly disappeared. Their claws retracted. Their feet shrunk and showed signs of toes emerging. Their teeth returned to a normal size. The hard scales covering their bodies disappeared and pale skin replaced them. The king and queen stood in place of the dragons dressed in tattered garments. They looked around. They looked at their hands and at each other.

"Mom! Dad!" Jenny ran and hugged her parents. "I knew one day I'd find you."

"Athelina, it is so good to see you, to hold you. After all these years, we never thought we'd see you again. We'd lost all hope of ever being found." Ileana's arms tightened around her daughter.

"How touching. But now you must all die," Maeldoi said.

Beth hung on to Devon's arm, while Alwin stood next to his friend, poised and ready to strike. He, like the steward's son, would fight to the end.

Jenny left her parents' embrace and went to stand by her friends. They would finish this together.

"Jenny, stay back." Devon pushed her and Beth behind him.

"No. I won't leave you. We came this far together and we will leave together." She took Devon's hand knowing if they were to die they'd die together.

"Brave words, Princess. I believe I will kill you last. I want you to watch your parents and friends die slow, painful deaths. I will make you suffer for your treachery," Maeldoi said, his eyes on Ringwar as he waited for her signal. His obedience was Ringwar's to command.

"My treachery? You took my parents away from me. For six years I lived with a woman who despised me. I never knew what love was. I arrived in a strange land only to be hunted by a madman who simply wanted to satisfy his own greed. Don't you dare talk to me about suffering? You have no power over me, Maeldoi."

The emerald glowed angrily. A green light escaped and spread toward her parents.

Jenny threw herself in front of the light.

"Jenny! No!" they cried out in unison.

She held up her hands and a brilliant white light escaped from her hands and from her eyes. The pure light flew across the cavern and destroyed the emerald held within the dark wizard's walking stick. It then enveloped Maeldoi until his final cry was all that was left. He vanished in a puff of smoke, and the evil staff fell to the floor in a useless heap of metal and wood.

"We should go after Ringwar," Devon said when they saw her shuffle out of the cavern. "She must be stopped."

"No," King Morgan said. He approached Devon and his daughter. "She will never gain enough power to leave the Black Castle. Without Maeldoi and his black magic, she is powerless. She is no longer a threat to anyone."

"But I thought she was a witch?" Jenny asked.

"She is far too old. Her magick isn't as powerful as it used to be. In order to gain power, she had to combine her magick with Maeldoi's dark magick. Only then were they powerful enough to cause such turmoil. But now that she is alone, she will live out what little time she has left alone."

"So that's why she wanted you, Jenny," Devon said. "She wanted to take your youth and your powers for herself. They sent the beasts to determine just how strong and powerful you truly are, and with Maeldoi at her side, she would have become more powerful than any witch or wizard in this land." Devon finally understood the madness behind Maeldoi and Ringwar's plan.

Tears welled in Jenny's eyes as she looked at her parents. She didn't remember them, but without hesitation Jenny went to her father. He hugged her fiercely and kissed her cheek.

"Father, I'm so happy you're alive," Jenny told the king. She couldn't believe this horrible ordeal had finally come to an end. Her parents had been returned to her and she would do everything in her power to make sure she never lost them again.

"I am grateful to you and your friends. If not for your bravery, we never would have been freed from their evil spells."

"Before we go, I want to see if we can free the beasts Maeldoi created."

"No, Jenny. They disappeared when Maeldoi did. There never was much hope for any of them. His magick kept them alive," Ileana told her daughter.

"Then let's go home," Jenny said.

"I think that's a very good idea." Ileana put her arm around her daughter's shoulders. She kissed her cheek.

"I guess we have a long walk ahead of us," Jenny said, thinking of everything they'd gone through to get here. The thought of going back the same way didn't thrill her at all.

"No. There is no need to subject ourselves to such a long walk," King Morgan told his daughter.

"I don't understand."

"Athelina, you have the power to return us to Wardell," Ileana said.

"Me?"

"Yes, child. Your powers are strong enough to do anything you wish. You haven't even tapped into the crux of your powers. That is how you destroyed Maeldoi."

"Why can't you do it?" Jenny asked, knowing Ileana had powers of her own.

"My magick is only fair. No one has the potential you do, my dear. You are strong enough to return us quickly and safely," Ileana proudly told her daughter. "Now concentrate on what you want to happen."

"Where do we want to go?"

"The castle gates will be fine."

Devon went to Jenny. "You can do this. After defeating Maeldoi, you can do anything, Princess Athelina." And for the first time, Devon bowed before Wardell's rightful princess.

She smiled at him.

They gathered together and formed a circle around Jenny. She closed her eyes and concentrated on their departure. A small mist swirled around them. Slowly, it crawled toward the group and encircled them. The pale mist grew and encased them in a protective cocoon. The color of the mist darkened as her magick intensified. Fear made Beth hold on to Devon's arm with all her might. She closed her eyes, not wanting to know what would happen next.

The mist darkened even more and became a gray wall of thick smoke. A quaking beneath their feet told them something was definitely happening. They disappeared from the Black Castle and before anyone knew what transpired, the entire group reappeared in front of the gates of Wardell Castle.

"We made it!" Devon laughed, as Beth finally opened her eyes and released Devon's arm. He smiled at her. Beth saw the marks she'd left on his arm and blushed prettily.

"We should go inside. My father will be so pleased with your return." Devon bowed before the royal family.

"I think he will be pleased with your return, Devon. Thank you all for your help and your loyalty to me and to my family."

Devon and Alwin bowed before the king and queen of Wardell.

"Do not bow before us. You have proven yourselves worthy," King Morgan told them.

"It's so good to be home," Ileana said, as she gazed lovingly at her beautiful castle. For six years Ileana dreamt of the day she'd return to her home and be reunited with her daughter and her people. She'd spent so much time hoping and dreaming of their return, and now here she stood before her beloved castle. She wondered if the market still blossomed when the morning hours arrived. She turned toward her castle. Everything was as she remembered. For the king and queen, the nightmare was finally over. The spells cast upon them were finally broken.

"Yes, my love, we're home and we are a family once again."

King Morgan kissed his wife for the first time in six years. He wrapped his arms around her small form and held her close. She felt good within his strong embrace. Morgan would never let her go again.

Janine Summers

CHAPTER 40

THE CEREMONY

Morning light filtered through the windows, shining warmly upon the young princess who slept snuggled beneath the down comforter. She opened her eyes and smiled. They'd been back for two weeks now and she was still adjusting to life in Wardell and the upcoming royal ceremony.

The morning after their return, Athelina woke with her memory intact. Ileana explained the necessity behind wiping her memory. They felt it would protect her, but they never imagined Nora would be so mean to the future ruler of Wardell. The princess recalled all the happy times in her life and pushed her time with Nora to the back of her mind, never to dwell upon it again.

Athelina stood before the mirror, in a long silk dress with a matching emerald green and gold embroidered robe. A braided, golden rope cinched her waist as her attendant braided her hair, intertwining it with a matching green and golden ribbon.

A knock on her door and Beth ran into the room. "Jenny, I mean Athelina, how are you feeling? Aren't you just so excited?"

"Nervous is more like it. I'm glad your mother let you come here for the ceremony." She continued to stare at her reflection. Disbelief was clearly etched on her face. Today she would become Princess Athelina before the entire kingdom, and she was scared.

"When she met your parents and heard what had happened, she didn't mind. Even though she didn't quite understand or believe everything we told them. She's still trying to figure out if what she was told what really happened. But she did allow me to come here and celebrate with you."

"You should have brought your parents here to see the ceremony. It's going to be spectacular."

"She couldn't come right now, but as soon as she has some time off, she'd love to come here for a visit, if she's allowed."

"Your parents are always welcome."

"Good. I'll let them know." Beth smiled. She twirled around to show the princess her cream colored dress. Although similar to Athelina's, it was slightly less extravagant. Beth fit in nicely at Wardell.

"By the way, the school board fired Mrs. Parker. My mother complained about how she treated you and the fact that we disappeared while in her care. The school board reviewed her work, and they felt she wasn't keeping up with their standards."

"I'm glad. She deserved nothing less."

"Ever since your parents went to see Nora, she hasn't been seen or heard from again. We're wondering what happened to her."

Jenny remembered the visit to Nora's. She accompanied her parents when they went to see her. She walked up to the door and rang the bell. When Nora opened the door and saw the king and queen on her doorstep she paled two shades. As quickly as her face lost color, she looked at Athelina and shook.

"I see your back."

"May we come in?" Ileana asked.

"Why? You have her. Why are you bothering me again?" The royal couple realized their mistake.

"I don't ever want to see or hear of you again." They disappeared before Nora could respond.

Jenny shook herself back to the present, and with a sly smile, she told Beth the truth. "Let's just say she won't bother anyone again."

"Why? What did they do to her?" Beth asked in a conspiratorial voice.

"Just scared her. She decided to move away, but for some strange reason, she didn't want us to know where she'd gone." Athelina laughed.

"It serves her right." Beth never liked Nora and felt no pity for her.

"Well, this is it. Shall we go?" Athelina asked, taking one last look in the mirror, wondering if the people of Wardell would accept her as their princess.

"Lead on," Beth said, excited at being included in this ceremony.

Athelina walked down the corridor with Beth at her side. They met up with Devon and Alwin, and together they entered the throne room. They walked to the front of the room and stood next to Jemma. Galfrid stood next to the thrones.

She watched the guards open the doors for the king and queen as they made their way to the thrones. The people of Wardell bowed. The royal couple stood at the bottom of the stairs leading to the large, golden thrones where Galfrid waited on the steps, ready to make the presentation. He wore a gray tunic with a silver griffon emblazoned upon its surface. A thin golden crown encircled his dark hair. Upon each chair sat a lovely golden crown—the crown of a king and a queen.

Galfrid waited for King Morgan and Queen Ileana to step forward. They knelt before him. Galfrid took the first crown and held it over Morgan's head.

"I now relinquish my rule as the Steward of Wardell and return the rule to your rightful King Morgan." He placed the crown upon Morgan's dark head. Next, he took the gold and jeweled crown and held it over Ileana's dark head. "I relinquish my rule as Steward of Wardell to our queen." He placed the crown upon her head. "Queen Ileana. Let us greet and honor the return of the true king and queen of Wardell. May I present King Morgan and Queen Ileana? May their rule last a very long time?"

Everyone in the room stood and cheered for the return of the beloved royal family. This was an auspicious occasion, and all those invited to the coronation were resplendent in their finery. Silk and satins in all colors shone in the candlelight of the throne room.

Morgan was dressed in a black tunic with a golden griffon depicting his house stitched into the material. He stood next to his wife who was resplendent in a lilac colored silk dress. They waved to the people who had come to witness the ceremony.

"As my first official act as your king, I wish to thank Lord Galfrid and Lady Jemma for their loyalty and kindness in ruling and protecting Wardell during our absence."

Galfrid and Jemma bowed before the king and queen. They waved and smiled at the people knowing their time as rulers had come to an end, but they rejoiced at the return of the king and queen.

"Lord Galfrid, you are an honorable and trustworthy man. I ask that you and your family remain in the castle. I also ask that you serve as my personal advisor and most trusted friend."

Galfrid was surprised and delighted by the offer. "I am honored, your majesty. I accept your gracious offer."

"Thank you, my friend." Morgan and Galfrid clasped arms as was customary in this land. At that moment, the doors to the great room opened and to everyone's surprise, Prince Rainard walked in. Next to the prince, an older man wearing a golden crown perched on his salt and pepper hair proudly walked next to the prince.

Athelina moved closer to Devon. "What's going on?" Her eyes were centered on the two handsome men.

"Your majesty. Please accept our apology for this disruption, but my father and I have come to pay homage to you and to your wife, but most especially we wish to pay homage to your daughter," Prince Rainard spoke on behalf of Warwick.

"I don't understand," King Morgan said.

"When Princess Athelina defeated Maeldoi, the spell he cast upon my father lost its power. King Theron has regained his strength and rules Warwick once again."

Athelina went to Rain.

"Thank you, Princess." He took her hand in his and kissed it tenderly with gratitude.

"You're very welcome, Rain."

She turned to King Theron. He took her small hand in his larger one and smiled. "I owe you my life, Princess."

"Sire, I'm just happy to see you are well."

King Theron bowed before the princess who risked everything and saved his life. He pulled her toward him and hugged her fiercely. "I will never forget what you have done for me and for Warwick. I would like to offer you this small gift."

King Theron motioned for his servant to come forward. He handed Athelina a golden cage with the beautiful phoenix sitting on his perch.

She looked at the bird. He sang melodically for her.

"I am truly honored, sire." Athelina looked at the magnificent bird in the gilded cage. Her smile lit up the room.

"King Theron, Prince Rainard, please, come and joins us. You are most welcome in our humble home."

"Thank you, your majesty. We accept your hospitality."

They stood next to Galfrid and Jemma, overjoyed at being able to witness the return of the true king and queen.

"We have some business to attend to. Athelina, Devon, Alwin, please step forward," the king called out.

The companions were reunited for this auspicious occasion. Together, they walked to the thrones and knelt down. King Morgan descended the stairs and stopped in front of his daughter.

"From this day forward, you will be known as Princess Athelina. And you, my brave daughter, have honored us with your show of courage." He placed a crown on her dark hair. "Your mother and I owe our life to you and your companions."

She stood, hugged her father and mother. Tears glistened in her eyes with the joy and pride she felt at her accomplishments. "I love you." She moved closer to her mother who stood to one side.

King Morgan took the jeweled sword a servant held and stepped in front of Devon and Alwin.

"As for you, Devon and Alwin, your bravery has earned you the rank of knight. Before all these people, I knight thee." He tapped Devon and Alwin on each shoulder. "Rise, Sir Devon of Wardell. Rise, Sir Alwin of Wardell Forest."

"Thank you, sire," they said in unison

Devon and Alwin bowed before the royal family. Devon went down the stairs and joined his parents. "I always knew you would succeed, my son," Galfrid said.

"Thank you, Father. But I couldn't have done it without my friends. Only in true friendship were we strong enough to defeat evil." He looked at the princess and Alwin and truly understood the meaning of friendship

At the end of the ceremony as the festivities began, Athelina walked purposely toward Devon, stopping from time to time and accepting well wishes from the people of Wardell.

"Princess." He bowed to her.

"Thank you for everything." She kissed his cheek and hugged him tightly. When his arms snaked around her, the crowd cheered. They smiled first at each other and turned toward the cheering crowd.

Wardell was once again whole.

About The Author

Janine Summers lives in Niagara-on-the-Lake, ON, Canada with her husband, two cats, Bonky and Runty, and Lily a German shepherd. Having earned her diploma in Journalism, Janine is currently working on her new novel the first in the Matchstick House Series, Emmy and the Coven of Witches.

Connect With Me Online:

Website: http://janinesummers.com

Twitter: fantasyrtr

Facebook: Facebook profile

Blog: http://janinesummers.com

email: janinesummers1@msn.com

www.ingramcontent.com/pod-product-compliance
Lightning Source LLC
Chambersburg PA
CBHW071308170626
46809CB00001B/373